MEET ME
in the
BLUE

HEMLOCK HARBOR
BOOK ONE

MEET ME
in the
BLUE

HEMLOCK HARBOR
BOOK ONE

A.M. JOHNSON

Editing and Formatting: Elaine York, Allusion Publishing
www.allusionpublishing.com
Proofing: Kathleen Payne, Payne Proofing
Formatting Cover Design: Kate Farlow, Y'all That Graphic
Cover photo/model: Chip Pons

For Kristy

Because you understand, and I love you for it.

"Or if you will, thrusting me beneath your clothing,
Where I may feel the throbs of your heart or rest upon your hip,
Carry me when you go forth over land or sea;
For thus merely touching you is enough, is best,
And thus touching you would I silently sleep
and be carried eternally."
Walt Whitman, "Whoever You Are Holding Me Now in Hand"
from Leaves of Grass

CONTENT WARNING

Grief, death of parent.

PROLOGUE

Luka
The Beginning - 9 years old

BLADES OF GRASS ITCHED at my skin while the salty pine-scented air pinched at my nose. It was too quiet here. Even though we were still in Washington, I missed my city. I didn't care that Mom had said it was dirty and dangerous. I lay in my front yard, hoping for sun and noise as goose bumps ran across my arm. I guess I should have been happy it hadn't rained all week, but the soil was damp enough it seeped into my shirt and jeans anyway. If we were still in Seattle, I'd be with Mika and Alistair riding scooters at Centennial Park, not dying a slow death in my front yard. Could you die from boredom? I exhaled and closed my eyes, resolved to ask Dad about the percentage of people who died of boredom every year. After a few minutes, a cloud decided to block the sun, and I opened my eyes with a quiet gasp. A strange boy stared down at me with giant brown eyes.

"Who are you?" I asked, annoyed at the dumb look on his face. I couldn't tell if he was smiling or about to cry.

1

"Rook," he said, his voice a little shaky. "I live next door."

"What kind of name is Rook?"

He shrugged and rubbed his hands over his shirt as I sat up to get a better look at him. His skin looked soft, the brown color of it almost matched his eyes. I didn't know if thinking a boy's skin looked soft was a normal thing to think, but I didn't care. He was the one staring at me like a weirdo.

"My dad likes chess," he said, but his eyebrows dipped like he wasn't sure what he said was true. "Or maybe the letter R? My brother's name is Reese."

"My little sister's name is Nora." Rook nodded, his curious brows furrowing, like I'd said something important as I stood.

"What's your name?"

"Luka." I scratched at my skin, and he stared at my arms. My skin was pale compared to his and spotted with pink lines and dots of dirt. "I think I'm allergic to Hemlock Harbor."

His smile was sideways as he snorted. "Or maybe the grass. You should ask my daddy, he's a doctor."

"So is mine."

We had a silent standoff until he ran his hand over his neatly clipped hair.

"Guess that's one thing we got in common then." He glanced over his shoulder and rubbed the back of his neck. "So, my mom said I'm not supposed to go into the woods by myself…" He kicked at the ground with the toe of his sneaker, his knobby knees sticking out on his long legs. "You think… well, maybe would you—"

"Sure," I said, too eager. Swallowing, I found my voice again. "I mean if you're inviting me, yeah?"

2

His smile made my stomach do a somersault, and I couldn't understand why. I blamed the strange tofu stuff Mom had made for lunch.

"Yeah, come on… it's kind of spooky and dark, but if you're not scared, I can show you the old fort I found.

"Old fort?"

"Yeah… it's run down, but I like to read in there sometimes, when my mom isn't home. Dad doesn't care if I go into the woods alone." He puffed out his chest and it made me want to stand taller.

"Sounds cool," I managed to say. "I should ask my mom."

"Oh yeah, me too." He pointed a thumb over his shoulder. "Be right back."

I headed into my house, ignoring my little sister as she ran after me. My mom was in the kitchen, mixing what looked like juice in a glass pitcher.

"Thirsty?" she asked, and I shook my head.

"The boy next door asked if I could play. Is that okay?"

"Dr. Whelan's son?" she asked, smiling big enough I felt bad for being mean to her this morning about moving. "That would be great, Luka. I was hoping you two would become friends. He's in your grade. Even has the same birthday as you, kiddo."

"He does?"

Something about that made me feel like I was smiling from the inside out.

"Yup."

"Dr. Whelan is Dad's new boss, right?"

"Partner," she corrected. "The practice belongs to both of them now."

3

My shoulders drooped as I wondered whether or not Rook had been forced by his mom to come over and ask me to play.

"What's the matter?" Mom tapped the spoon on the side of the pitcher and ruffled her hand through my hair. "You look like I canceled Christmas."

"Nothing." Grumbling, I turned to leave. "I better get out there before he leaves without me."

"Have fun," she called, and I slammed the door.

Fun in Hemlock Harbor. Highly unlikely.

Rook stood in my driveway with a worried look on his face. When he saw me though, his eyes brightened. A lightness filled my chest, and I had to look down at the ground to catch my balance. Maybe I should've had a glass of that juice.

"You ready?" he asked, and I nodded trying not to seem too excited.

I walked next to him down the dirt path between our houses, and with him humming under his breath, I didn't feel as nervous anymore.

"Did your mom make you?" I asked. "Make you come over to my house to see if I wanted to play?"

He shoved his hands into the pocket of his shorts. "Not really."

"What's that supposed to mean?"

"I saw you… last week outside by the moving truck. Mom said you were in my grade, and I should go over and say hi but…"

"But?" I stopped and he did the same looking straight toward the trees.

"I don't make friends easily." His throat moved slow as he swallowed. "Get picked on a lot 'cause I'm skinny and read a lot. Mom tries to make me drink this chalky chocolate crap. Said it

4

will help me gain weight. But I don't see why I gotta change. The boys who are mean should have to change."

"I like to read," I said, and he looked at me. "But I'm not as skinny as you." His laugh was loud, and it made me laugh too. A few seconds passed and his smile started to fall. "The boys at school are mean?"

"Sometimes."

"That sucks."

"I don't let it bother me… much. It can be lonely, I guess."

My fingertips tingled like I'd sat on them too long, and I reached for his hand. Rook looked down at our tangled fingers, his lopsided grin appearing again as I said, "Guess we'll both be loners… together."

CHAPTER ONE

Rook

LUKA'S LIGHT BROWN HAIR *was matted to his forehead with sweat as we ran through the trees toward our spot. His laugh more breathless as we neared the small clearing. Stumbling over a branch, he almost fell and swore under his breath. I didn't think a thirteen-year-old should swear as much as he did, but Luka swore all the time. He thought it made him sound older, and maybe it did. But I liked it better when he was just himself.*

"I gotta stop," he said, curling over, resting his hands on his knees. "I won though."

I snorted and wiped the sweat off my forehead with the back of my hand. "If you say so."

Luka barked out a laugh and gave me a crooked grin. "Come on, we're gonna miss it."

"Miss what?" I stared at our old fort, at the surrounding trees, looking for something new.

"The moment when everything turns blue."

6

I scrunched my brows together. "Blue?"

"The blue hour, it's when the sun has almost set..." He stared up at the sky, the pink evening fading into night. "When the sun sits under the horizon, it makes everything look blue. I learned about that in the photography class Mom signed me up for."

"That's cool."

"I think so, too." He smiled up at the sky. "It happens in the morning and at night."

"Does it look the same in the morning?" I asked, watching as the light dimmed around us to a gray blue.

"It's supposed to. We should check it out Saturday."

"I have hockey practice."

"Not that early in the morning."

"Yeah, but Dad will be mad if I'm too tired to run drills."

"Then this will be our blue hour, Rook." His smile spread wide as he turned to look at me. "This will always be our time."

"Hey, Stace." Avoiding her expectant smile, I kept my head down as I grabbed a pint of Rocky Road from the freezer.

I preferred Moose Tracks, but Rett refused to carry it. If he didn't love my father so much, I'd think it was personal.

"I tried to get him to order it, but you know him..." Stacey cringed and narrowed her brown eyes. "He's a stubborn asshole. Rett said..." She lowered her voice to something akin to the man himself and my lips twitched at her attempt to mimic the old bastard. "Rocky Road is a staple."

"I suppose he's right. Can't argue with traditions."

"Isn't the customer always right?" she asked, and I set the pint on the counter.

Chuckling, I shook my head. "I don't think Rett gives a shit."

Stacey bit the corner of her pink-stained lip and looked over my shoulder, grinning like she had some sort of secret. Picking up the ice cream, she shoved it into a brown paper bag. "Well, I give a shit." Her flirty smile and bold eye contact made me wish I'd skipped coming to the pharmacy in the first place. I stared at the bag on the counter instead, feeling my pulse in my fingertips as the seconds ticked by uncomfortable and loud between us. "It's on the house," she said, her confidence fading. "My treat."

"Stace, I—"

"Stop being so nice all the time, Rook. Let a girl buy you a pint of ice cream." I could hear the smile in her voice but kept my eyes down. "I insist."

"Thanks," I said, conceding even though I knew better.

I glanced up and found her big eyes, hopeful, staring back at me. My face heated as her triumphant grin stretched across her face.

"Anytime…" She fiddled with the small stack of flyers next to the register.

My chest ached a little, wishing I could summon some sort of attraction for her. She was sweet and conventionally attractive with a lean, athletic build. She used to be a cheerleader way back when in high school, and I remembered all the guys on my hockey team would talk about her, mostly crude locker room shit. But Stacey was just Stacey to me. Rett's niece. Rett, who'd owned this damn pharmacy longer than I'd been alive. She could hit on me every time I walked through those front doors, which she did without regard for her own feelings, and it wouldn't change the fact I wasn't into her. Or anyone, really. This town was too small and too nosy, at least that's what I'd tell myself when I got home and made dinner for one and ate this ice cream like a sad cat lady. I wasn't sad though, and it was hard for people to understand. Especially my family. *"You're thirty-two, son. The older you get the slimmer the pickings."* And *"I worry about you, worry you're lonely in that big house of yours?"* And *"Stacey... she's a sweet one."* And my personal favorite. *"Son, your mother and I... we want you to know you can tell us anything. We want you to know we love you unconditionally, straight... or gay, we love you and want you to do whatever makes you happy."*

I wished it was as easy as gay or straight. What if being alone was my happily ever after? Would that be so bad?

"I heard Luka's coming back to town," she said, and my heart skipped at the mention of his name, pulling me from my thoughts.

"Yeah?" I swallowed past the twinge in my throat. "I saw Nora at the clinic last week, said he was coming home soon."

"Too bad about their dad. He was a good man."

"Is..." I corrected. "He *is* a good man."

He was still alive, still breathing.

She bit the side of her cheek, her face pale. "I didn't mean... I shouldn't have said—"

"It's okay, Stace." I tried to conjure a smile on her behalf but failed. "Dr. Abrams's prognosis isn't a secret."

I'd known Isaac Abrams for most of my life. He'd joined my dad's practice when I was nine years old and was like a second father to me. I'd grown up with his family, his daughter Nora like a sister, and his son Luka used to be my best friend.

Used to be.

Luka's smile beamed bright behind my eyes, his laugh a distant echo in my ears. It had been five years since I'd seen Luka Abrams. Five years of feeling lost without a compass.

"Is it true?" she asked.

"I'm sorry, what were you saying?"

"Dr. Abrams… he's on hospice now?"

"Yes." I didn't elaborate. A man's life, or end of life, should be his own. Not a juicy piece of small-town gossip.

"Fuck cancer," she said, the frown on her face genuine.

Fuck cancer.

"I should get going." I held up my bag with the ice cream inside before turning to leave. "Thanks, Stace."

"When you see Luka, tell him to stop by. It's been ages since he's graced us with his presence, and I'll never forgive him if he doesn't at least come say hello."

I waved over my shoulder as the damp, frigid February air bit at my cheeks. The wind blew through the open front door and chilled me to the bone. Focusing on zipping up my jacket, I tried not to think about Luka and failed. After I'd spoken to Nora the other day, his name had been on a constant loop in my head, but I thought I had a handle on it. Stace mentioning him again made the realization that he might already be at home, sitting on the couch in the living room, where we used to play *Dungeons & Dragons*, a reality I wasn't sure I was ready to face. After his dad was diagnosed with liver cancer a few years ago, I'd hoped he'd move back then. He didn't. But it wasn't like he hadn't made an effort to keep in touch over the years, keeping tabs on his dad's treatment. But friendship was a funny thing, and like the miles between us, he grew more distant with every missed text, or phone call. Luka used to text or call every day when he and his boyfriend from college had broken up. They'd lived together in Portland, but after they split, instead of coming home to Hemlock Harbor, Luka moved to Los Angeles. His phone calls had always been the highlight of my day, even if he was only calling to vent about the traffic. But eventually, the daily calls turned to monthly updates, and now I was lucky if I got a Happy Birthday or a Merry Christmas. I'd tried to reach out when we all found out about his dad, but it had been clear I was the only one holding on, and after a while, the grip I had on the past hurt more than it was worth. I'd had to let go.

I didn't want to be angry at him for shutting me out, for finding himself, finding the life he wanted far away from here, far from the small-town life he never wanted. But we'd spent almost every day together, every weekend for the better part of my adolescence, and even though we'd gone to separate colleges, we'd maintained our friendship the best we could. I'd gone to the University of Washington in Seattle for both my undergraduate and graduate degrees, which was barely over fifty miles away, and felt homesick every damn day. After graduation he'd chosen to stay in Oregon, and I'd chosen to come home and work as a certified nurse-midwife for our fathers' clinic. I couldn't ever imagine leaving Hemlock Harbor. This place was my home. It was as permanent as the bones under my skin. Our families were intertwined, it was hard to remember a time when I didn't know Luka.

I didn't know him now.

I'd thought we'd be close forever. I'd thought Luka would always be my other half. He knew me better than anyone. I'd spent more hours of my life with Luka than I could count. But something changed, and as much as I wanted to blame his move to Los Angeles, or his dad's cancer, I wondered if it was something I did, or didn't do. I was never as bright as Luka, as audacious. When he walked into a room everyone noticed. The thought of seeing him again, after all these years, had my stomach in knots. I wanted everything to be the same while wanting to hold on to my anger too. But Dr. Abrams was dying, and I didn't think it mattered how I felt about being left behind in Luka's wake.

Once I was in my car, I cranked up the heater and turned onto the main road. The sun had started to set, the overcast sky nothing new, but today the clouds, and their gray fingers, dove into the pines, made everything seem heavier. I glanced at the clock on the car stereo and found myself turning right on Mill Creek Road instead of left toward my house. It took ten minutes, and I was afraid I'd miss it as I parked my car in front of my childhood home. I stepped out onto the wet street, the rain, more of an icy mist, clung to the fabric of my jacket. The lights were off inside my parents' house, but the Abrams's front window was lit with a warm yellow glow. I bypassed their front door and headed down the familiar path between the two houses, walking faster with each passing second, until I was under the shade of the trees. The ice cream on my front seat forgotten and probably starting to melt. Each breath, each beat of my heart, it was like I could feel him there waiting, and as I broke through to the small clearing, I saw him.

A man I didn't recognize stood with his back to me, his eyes on the sky. The tattoos peeking out from under his damp cotton t-shirt were new, his bleach-blond hair was new too. My heart drummed inside my chest, but I was surprised to find it wasn't in anger, but relief. So much relief.

"Meet me in the blue," I said. "I'll always be here."

CHAPTER TWO

Luka

THE FAMILIAR WORDS CUT through the thick fog inside my head, and I wiped at my eyes, at the wet skin of my cheeks. It had always been our thing. This place. This spot. This hour. Where the world and all the doubt inside my head had been the quietest. I didn't turn right away, gathering myself and working a small smile onto my lips. I was a lot of things, a shitty friend, a terrible son, a failed photographer, but I'd be damned if I was ready to admit it to anyone. Especially to him. Especially Rook. He was good and whole, and I was a hot mess express. I never wanted him to look at me the way my parents did sometimes, with sad eyes that wished. Wished for me to get my shit together, wished for me to settle down, wished for me to come home.

Heat emanated from his body as he stood next to me, the smoky smell of burned wood and pine filled my lungs. His scent hadn't changed. Not in five years. Not ever.

"I'm sorry..." he whispered, his voice thick and warm. "About your dad. I haven't had a chance to tell you that... but I am... so sorry."

My throat hurt and my eyes stung and fuck, I hated this. Hated the melancholic tone hugging every one of the syllables. It made it impossible to speak. I nodded, keeping my eyes on the tree line, on the dilapidated fort we used to hide ourselves away in. Skinned knees and pine needles in our hair. Everything had changed. And it was my fault.

"Luka..."

"Thank you," I croaked. "I'm sorry too."

We stood in silence for five minutes or an hour, I didn't know. Time had no space here. It never did. The cold air bit at my tear-stained cheeks as the blue hour faded into night. I collected myself, sucking in the wet clean air, and finally faced him. Soft amber-brown eyes stared back at me, and my breath caught inside my tight chest. He had changed so much. Laugh lines gathered around his eyes as he gave me a sad smile, his broad shoulders wider than ever, and God, had he gotten taller? His jaw was sharp, his face even more handsome with age. It had only been five years. But that wasn't true either. I'd left Hemlock Harbor long before, at only nineteen, and even though I'd visited home every now and then, I'd never truly been present. Those visits, short and to the point, were always happy holidays, and summer breaks with my boyfriend Graham. My *ex-boyfriend*. Those visits I'd been in my head. Grades and portfolios and getting back to my life. A life where I'd tried to stop pining for my best friend. A life I'd tried to make my own, where I played at being successful. I wasn't a doctor like my dad, or a big-time literary agent like my sister, but I was something. I was something more. At least that had been what I'd told myself. And now none of it mattered. All the years had passed, and my dad was dying. I wanted to be mad at my dad for telling me to stay in California after he was diagnosed. I should have moved back to Washington like Nora had, but there was part of me that was grateful too. Grateful he'd believed in me enough to think I could make something of myself.

But my life wasn't mine, I'd made nothing of myself, and Rook had changed.

"What do you have to apologize for?" Rook asked, and I exhaled a long sigh.

Everything.

"You look different," I said instead, and his jaw pulsed.

"You haven't been home in a while." He held my gaze, the shadows dancing along the lines of his nose and cheeks. "People change."

People change. It was an accusation. I couldn't blame him.

"You look good." I summoned the boy I used to be and gave him a playful grin. "Old man."

He chuffed and a real smile spread across his lips. Jesus, he was beautiful. It lit his entire face, any traces of sadness that might have lingered hid away inside two deep dimples. Rook shoved his hands into the pockets of his jacket, his gaze persistent. "You look different too. Bleach blond?" He raised a brow, and I chuckled.

I dipped my chin and toed the wet grass with my sneaker. Self-conscious, I scrubbed a hand through my hair. "Yeah… I dyed it a few weeks ago, not sure how I feel about it."

"I like it."

Surprised, I lifted my head. "Thanks."

We stared at each other. Each of us cataloging all the little things, all the modifications the years had added, ignoring the bigger picture. I didn't know how to begin again. How to make up for ghosting my best friend. How to tell him I was terrified. How to tell him I missed him so damn much. How to tell him I didn't call because it was easier that way, easier for me. Easier to deny how far I'd fallen since I'd moved to California. I'd always been a selfish asshole.

"It's cold," he said and nodded at my t-shirt. "Can't hide out here forever."

I laughed without humor. "Why not?"

"Because…" His smile fell, and he shook his head like maybe he shouldn't say what he wanted to or didn't have an answer at all. But when he spoke, his voice trembled. "Because hiding isn't the answer, Luka. It will only make it all hurt more… in the end."

"He's dying," I said, and the tears I'd been desperately holding back fell anyway.

Rook closed the distance between us, wrapping me up in strong arms and warm woodsmoke and pine, and my body shuddered.

"I know." He hugged me tighter. "I know."

Eventually we made our way inside, after I'd pulled myself together and he grabbed something from his car. Rook had hugged my mom and my sister Nora, and they'd fawned over him like always, offering him coffee and cookies and smiles. At least some things hadn't changed. He'd said, *yes ma'am*, and *thank you* and put a tub of ice cream into our freezer like he lived here too. I sat on the stool at the breakfast bar, watching everything spin around him, and couldn't stop myself from smiling. It was comfortable and familiar and worlds apart from the hospital bed sitting in the other room, where my dad slept and drifted away.

"It's been a while," Nora said as she pulled herself up and onto the edge of the counter. She kicked her feet like she was ten and not a grown woman. She tore off a piece of the cookie she had in her hand and popped it into her mouth. "How are things at the clinic? I think it's so cool you get to deliver babies."

"It's busy." Rook set his coffee mug on the counter and sat next to me. "But it's a good kind of busy."

The heat of his body was a heavy weight. I'd always gravitated toward it. Toward him, and it took every ounce of self-preservation I had not to lean into him. Things were different. Time had passed. Rook wasn't mine to lean into anymore. Even if that hug earlier had been everything I'd needed, I knew it was just Rook being Rook, offering me a stable surface to find my footing.

"Keeping up your practice is always good," my mom said and turned off the coffee pot. "Just remember to take a break every now and then. Isaac worked all the time when he first started his own practice, but it wasn't until we moved here, and he started working with your father, that he learned to take it easy every once in a while. Don't spread yourself too thin. Life is too short." She squeezed Rook's arm, her eyes glassy. "Your mom told me Stacey has been sniffing around again."

Rook's entire body had gone completely rigid, and Nora laughed. "Mom, leave him alone. Stacey is always sniffing around. She's way too obvious."

"Stacey from high school?" I asked, my voice pitching higher than usual.

"She's a nice girl. Smart. Cute as hell." Mom stared at me with shrewd blue eyes. "And available."

"Is that your way of saying she's easy?" I heard myself say and my sister coughed. "I mean, she—"

"Stace is a friend," Rook interrupted, and the tone of his voice was like a reprimand. "You and my mom need to stop gossiping so much." He chuckled and my mom smiled, wiping her hands on a dish towel.

"Can't blame us though. One of these days you're going to have to settle down. And all the single ladies will weep."

"Maybe," he said, almost whispering, his eyes on the mug of coffee in front of him. "I don't know."

Nora stared at me, the conversation we'd had again and again all those years ago crossed between us in an unspoken rush of words inside my head.

He's straight, Nora. He's just a friend. He's not into me like that. I can't keep hoping.

He loves you. He's waiting. He's confused. He's here. He's yours.

"I'm sorry, honey." Mom squeezed his arm again. "I shouldn't meddle."

He gave her his signature soft grin. "I think you and my mom make it your job to meddle."

"Well…" Mom shot me a look. "We can always hope."

She grabbed a bottle of pills and some apple sauce from the fridge before she left the kitchen in a hazy shade of silence. After a few seconds Nora hopped down from the counter, tucking her long brown hair behind her ears.

"I have work to catch up on. It was good to see you, Rook."

"You, too, Nora."

My sister tugged him into a hug, and a pang of jealousy clenched inside my stomach. Not because I thought Rook and my sister would ever be a thing, but because I wanted the right to touch him again. To reach over and hold his hand like we used to sometimes when we were kids. To rest my head on his shoulder and tell him I was lost. To ask him not to leave because I needed him now more than ever.

As Nora pulled away, he stood. "I should get going."

"Right now?" I asked and Rook swallowed.

He picked up his coffee mug, avoiding my eyes. "I have to let my dog out."

"You have a dog?"

"Maribelle," he said, and it sounded like *you would have known about her if you hadn't pushed me away.*

"She's the cutest goldendoodle ever." Nora grinned and took the mug from Rook's hand. "I've got this."

"Thanks."

"I'll walk you out?" I asked and he shrugged.

"Um… sure."

Everything between us was wrong, misshapen. Like a photo out of focus, I didn't recognize the two people inside the frame.

"Don't forget your ice cream." Nora set the cup in the sink and made a beeline for the freezer.

With his bag of ice cream tucked under his arm, we made our way outside onto the front porch. The rain had stopped, but the air was frosted and sharp.

"I missed you," I admitted as he descended the first step. I kept talking when he didn't turn around, finding it less intimidating without his knowing eyes watching me. "After Graham, I didn't know what to do. I moved to L.A. and I thought I could make a go of it. I never meant to… I—"

"You should have come home." His words came out in thick puffs of fog in the cold air.

They hovered in front of him as we both breathed in the truth of what he'd said.

"I had to find my own way."

"Did you find what you were looking for?" He took another step away.

"No… I didn't."

Rook turned, his eyes dark, his face as stoic as ever. "Five years, Luka. What happened?"

"Graham and I… it was too much."

"I know."

"We were together for seven years."

"I know."

"I was lost."

"I know," he said again, his mask slipping as he stepped toward me. "I never liked Graham. He wasn't good for you."

"He was, though, and when he left, I had to prove to myself I didn't need him."

"You never needed him, Luka."

"I did."

He exhaled a gruff breath and shook his head. "I thought when your dad found out he had cancer you'd—"

21

"He told me to stay in California. He said he was fighting it. That he was fine."

"He was... for a while." Rook rubbed his forehead, shadows stealing the light from his eyes as he stared at me. "What happened... with us? Why did you shut me out?"

Because I failed. Because I couldn't admit it. Because I was afraid of disappointing everyone.

Disappointing you.

"I don't know. I just... I fucked up."

"Yeah... okay."

He started toward his car and the space growing between us hurt more than the loss of him over the last five years combined. The hope of fixing our friendship withered away and cut deep.

"Rook," I called out his name, pleading. Undeserving. "I'm... I don't..."

"I'm here, Luka." Without looking at me, he opened his car door. "We'll figure it out."

CHAPTER THREE
Rook

"DO YOU EVER THINK *about dying?" Luka asked, his head in my lap as usual, and I opened my eyes to stare down at him.*

"What do you mean?"

Luka laughed but it didn't sound right. It was heavier somehow. Heavy like the humidity clinging to our skin. The rain poured against the roof of our run-down fort, seeping its way into the cotton of my t-shirt where I rested my back against the wall.

"I don't know," he said, his fingers busy picking at the hem of his hooded jacket. "I wonder what it would be like sometimes. Wonder if it would be easier than living. Like white clouds and rainbows all the fucking time."

I probably shouldn't have smiled, but I did. "Clouds and rainbows?"

He grinned up at me. "And rock giants."

"Aren't you too old to still believe in rock giants?"

He shrugged, the humor in his eyes fading. "I miss those days. It was easier being eleven. Being a teenager sucks."

"Yeah…" Out of habit, I brushed the mop of brown hair from his forehead, and he stared back at me. It felt different. Heavy like the rain. Heavy like his laugh had been. "But there's good stuff too."

He sat up and exhaled an angry breath. "Not for me."

"What's going on?"

He worried his bottom lip between his teeth, casting his eyes to the small puddle of water forming near the edge of my shoe. "Everyone likes you. You and your brother are hockey jocks, you're popular."

"Reese is popular. I'm just me."

"I know." His chest heaved as he inhaled and flopped against the wall, his shoulder brushing mine.

He was taller than he had been last year, like he'd turned fifteen and grew two feet or something. But I still had a few inches on him and had to tilt my head to look at him. I could feel the warmth of his breath on my face.

"I don't think I could survive high school without you," he said, and I saw my reflection in his eyes.

Survive.

"You're freaking me out. Why are you thinking about dying?"

His nose wrinkled. "I'm not. Not really. Not like that. I just wonder sometimes. How it will all play out in the great beyond," he said the last two words in a deeper, more dramatic tone. "If the shit we worry about will even matter in the afterlife."

"Are you going to tell me what's going on with you or not?"

He started to chew his lip again, and I fixated on the movement, wondering what words were choking him up so bad.

"I think…" He blinked and blinked and sighed. Fidgeting, his shoulders sagged. "I think I like guys."

"Like… what? You want to… kiss them?"

"Yeah… I do."

"But not girls?"

"Not girls."

"How do you know?"

"Shit, I don't know I just do. Don't you think about kissing girls? Kissing Zoe?" The little crease between his brow pinched as he scowled.

"I don't think about kissing Zoe."

"No?" He smirked, and I knocked him in the shoulder. "Maybe you'd rather kiss her brother Ron?"

"No…" I said, and I thought maybe it was weird I hadn't thought about kissing anyone before. "I don't really think about kissing people."

"Ever?" His eyes widened.

"Not really. Does that make me a weirdo?"

"I just told you I like guys and you think you're the weird one." He shook his head. "No, Rook, it's not weird."

"You're not weird either," I said, pressing my hip into his. "Did you tell Nora? That you like boys?"

"You're the only one who knows. For now."

"Thank you for telling me."

We weren't kids anymore, playing fantasy games and dreaming of rock giants. We were on the edge of something, and maybe I didn't quite understand everything, but I understood the weight of it. Things were changing.

"You really haven't thought about kissing Zoe?" he asked, and I shook my head.

"I haven't. I know she has a crush on me but…"

"You don't like her?"

Maybe I was wrong, but he almost sounded hopeful.

"She wears too much of that sticky lip stuff," I said, and he laughed.

"Rook…"

"I think kissing is weird, like mouths are weird, right?"

"I think mouths can be nice." His gaze dropped to my lips and a thousand fireflies took flight inside my stomach.

"Maybe…"

I stared back at him, at his mouth, the patchy growth of hair above his lip. He'd started shaving last month. I thought maybe kissing could be okay if you knew someone well enough, knew them like you knew a best friend. Like how they smelled after a shower, or in the rain, and if they liked orange soda better than Coke. I thought sharing something like that would be okay.

I was stuck in a memory as the alarm blared from my bedside table. Luka and me at fifteen, the smell of wet pine, and the salty harbor air blowing through the small fort. The details were still sharp even though it seemed like a lifetime since we'd been that close. I blinked away the fog of sleep. The sound of rain tinkling against my windows threatened to pull me back under, but a quick look at the clock was enough to get me going. I had a scheduled c-section at seven, and a full day at the clinic after that. I didn't have time to dwell in memories, or for the ache in my head. I'd stayed up too late last night, running over everything Luka had said, how different he'd looked, how angry I'd been. I hadn't realized how deep his absence had cut me until I saw him there, in our spot, not quite a stranger but close enough. I was angry. Hurt. But he was here, and he still smelled like rain.

Maribelle scratched at my bedroom door, and I stole another look at the clock again. It was a quarter past five, and if I had any hope of getting to work on time, I had to stop wallowing. Luka was home and I tried to focus on that. Everything else. This knot in my stomach, this simmering something, this itch under my skin could wait. Yeah, I was definitely angry. But he'd missed me too.

"Hey, Belle." I raked my fingers through her curls as she jumped, punching her paws against my chest, and licked my chin. "Want to go outside?" She dropped down, rubbing against my legs like an overgrown cat. "We have to be quick."

I threw on my rain jacket by the back door, flipping on the lights to the kitchen as Maribelle circled me like a shark. Her nails clacked against the wood floors, faster and faster the longer she had to wait on me. I laughed when she whined and decided I'd have to make coffee when we got back from our walk.

"Alright, alright. Let's go."

Maribelle didn't hesitate, taking off toward the dock as soon as I opened the door. The light rain didn't deter her for a second. I reached down and grabbed her rope off the back porch and made my way down the pebbled path, tossing the dog toy as I called her name. She came like a bat out of hell, charging toward me before juking to the left where I'd thrown the rope. She dropped it at my feet, and I threw it again. We did this a few times before she started to sniff around and did her business. I let her be, finding my way out of the canopy of pines and hemlocks surrounding my house. My bare feet were damp, the tiny

27

gray pebbles scratching at the arch of my feet until I found relief on the dock. The water lapped against the jagged rocks of the shoreline, much calmer than the crashing waves and cliffs on the northern shore. As much as I loved to watch the water shape and pull at the earth, it scared me sometimes too. I'd always known I wanted to live close to the ocean. Something about the tides and the moon and how the sun warmed your skin as it bounced off the water. Hemlock Harbor was my home, and now I had a place of my own. I turned to look at my house with its dormer windows lit with a warm yellow light, and the tightness in my chest, that pinch I hadn't been able to get rid of after seeing Luka last night, eased.

I had a life here. All packaged up inside the mossy wooden siding of my home. Years of being on my own, making my way, creating my practice. My life. I was alone, and it wasn't perfect. But I'd chosen it. I was happy enough. Happy despite the fact a piece of me had been missing for a long time. But I thought, or maybe hoped, I'd found it again.

<hr />

"You're late," Morgan snapped as he pushed the clipboard into my hand. "This is new." He flipped his dark brown hair out of his eyes. "Your dad is already in the patient's room, going over everything, just need her to sign these consent forms."

"Shit, he's in there already?"

"For the last fifteen minutes." Morgan's smile widened. "Did you at least do something fun last night... you know, to make his wrath worth it?"

"His wrath?" I raised a brow as I sifted through the paperwork. "That's overdramatic."

"He's on one today."

I lifted my head and stared at the patient's room door. "Shit."

"Yeah, shit… Maybe you should just scrub in, and I'll have him consent the patient without you?"

"It's my patient. He shouldn't have gone in without me, he's—"

"Not her doctor. I know. I know." Morgan waved his hand. "But you know him. He has a schedule to keep."

My father was a good man. A good doctor. The first Black doctor in Hemlock Harbor to have his own practice. He was proud of his accomplishments, and after Luka's dad joined the clinic, he hoped I might join one day too. When I'd decided to become a certified nurse-midwife, he wasn't exactly not pleased. We could still share a practice together, and I had my doctorate. I hadn't gone to medical school like he'd wanted, but I was an advanced practice nurse. Sometimes, though, when I had to have him help with something out of my scope, like a c-section, or I had to consult with him on a high-risk pregnancy, he'd make comments like *if you'd only gone to medical school.* On those days, I'd reminded him he had to consult with Luka's dad all the time, that medicine was a team sport, but he didn't always listen.

"Want me to come with you?" Morgan asked and I shook my head.

"That's okay. Thanks, though."

Dad sat on the edge of my patient's bed, laughing about something, while her partner hid in the corner looking ashen.

"Don't worry, Curtis, you don't have to watch the surgery if you prefer not to." My dad smiled as I shut the door. "Well, look who decided to show up for work today. I thought I might have to deliver this baby all on my own."

I forced a smile. He was joking. I knew he was joking. But it hit me in the gut all the same.

"Hey, Abbey… Curtis… You ready to do this?" I tried my best for a half-hearted chuckle and hoped no one in the room noticed I'd ignored my father entirely.

After a few signatures and a whole lot of questions, my father and I wheeled the patient back to the operating room with her partner in tow. As hoped, the c-section had gone without incident, and despite my earlier tardiness, I'd headed to the office on time. I'd been busy enough that I hadn't had a chance to talk to my father much, and it wasn't until lunch time that I braved my way toward his office and knocked on the door.

"Feel like grabbing a sandwich at the diner?" he asked, pen in hand, scribbling away on the piece of paper in front of him. His eyes never left his work. "And maybe a coffee? You seemed tired this morning."

Exhaling a knowing sigh, I couldn't help but smile at his passive aggression. "I had a late start…" I hedged, and immediately caved when he raised his gaze. His soft brown eyes, the same as mine, assessed me. "You shouldn't have gone into the patient's room before me. She's my patient and—"

"I knew how full your schedule was today." He dropped his pen into a small mug next to his computer. "Forgive me, I was trying to save you some time."

"Dad…"

"What?" He held up his hands. "I was."

"You're a control freak." I smirked when he exhaled and shoved to his feet.

"That simply is not true."

"Okay." I folded my arms across my chest and leaned against the door frame. "Remember that time you reorganized all of my exam rooms because you said the workflow was off, and that one time you—"

"I like things the way I like them. So, sue me." He shrugged and grumbled something under his breath about how when he died, we'd all be lost without him.

I might've laughed at his theatrics.

"Dad…"

"Let's go get a friggin' sandwich."

He rounded his desk, and I held out my arm, gesturing for him to pass me in the doorway. He rolled his eyes. "I'm not a control freak," he mumbled as Charity, our receptionist, met us in the hall.

"Dr. Abrams' son is here, wanting to speak to Rook." She sounded nervous and my stomach dropped.

"Luka?" I asked and felt stupid for it.

Of course, it was Luka.

Her brows pressed together, confirming my stupidity. "Um… yeah."

Luka.

"Well, go see what he wants. Do you think… could it be…"

Dad let the unfinished sentence hang in the air as we all sank into the oppressive silence.

Was he okay?

Had Dr. Abrams passed?

Wouldn't Mrs. Abrams have called my father?

We didn't ask the questions or speak the words, but moved through them to the lobby, and when Luka gave me a quiet smile, I knew he wasn't here about his dad.

He was here for me.

CHAPTER FOUR

Luka

NOT MUCH HAD CHANGED at Harborside Family Practice in the last five years. Charity was still here with her blonde curls and big smiles. The shiplap on the walls was that same washed-out white that had become a Hemlock Harbor staple. The same intricate collection of miniature sailboats, Dr. Whelan's prized possession, sat proud and dust free on the shelf behind the front desk. Even the doctor himself looked the same, like the years hadn't touched him. Dr. Whelan's eyes remained dark and serious as ever, his smile soft like his son's. His son, with his gray slacks and white coat, his name neatly stitched onto the pocket. Rook fit in and stood out. He wasn't that gangly kid anymore, waiting for his dad to finish up for the day, or the boy I'd fallen in love with, studying behind the counter while my dad helped him with math. Rook had changed while everything else had remained stagnant. He had always belonged here. Belonged to this town, to my family. I only wished I could have too.

"Everything okay?" he asked when I couldn't seem to form a simple hello.

"Yeah… I wanted to see…" Rook's father reached out his hand. "Oh… hey, Dr. Whelan." Except when I raised my hand to shake his, he pulled me into a strong hug.

"Enough of that Dr. Whelan bullshit, son. It's Roger, you know that." When he pulled away, he gave me a noogie like I was twelve. "Or did you forget? It has been quite a while since you've been home. Maybe you forgot I'm not as serious as I look."

"I see you haven't forgotten how to lay down the guilt," I teased, and he gripped my shoulders, his lips spreading wide as he laughed.

"And you're still a smart ass. Welcome home, Luka. Hoping you'll stick around long enough for Nat to guilt you into staying this time."

"Tell Mrs. Whelan she doesn't have to guilt me into anything, I think…" Rook shifted on his feet, and I caught his gaze, hoping he could steady me as I said, "I think I might stay. Just finished up an interview at *The Herald*."

"Is that so?" Roger stole a glance at his son.

"You're staying?" Anticipation colored Rook's voice, the warmth of it curled around my spine.

"I mean… yeah… maybe."

"What about Los Angeles?"

I looked at Rook's dad, at his serious fucking eyes, at Charity behind the counter pretending not to listen to our conversation, and wiped away the dampness forming on my forehead. "Um… want to grab lunch? We can talk more, maybe *not* in the middle of the lobby."

Rook's smile was apologetic, almost shy as he looked at his dad. "I was about to grab a sandwich with—"

"Go on, I can meet your mother for lunch. She'll be thrilled. You boys need to catch up." He practically shoved Rook in my direction, and I chuckled at his usual tenacity. Some things truly never changed. "And make sure to give your mom a hug from me and tell your dad I'll see him Sunday."

"I will. Thanks."

"How is he?" Roger swallowed as he leaned down and whispered. Like if his question was too loud, he might not get the answer he wanted. Like the universe would hear his hope and take it all away.

"Today's been a decent day," I lied.

"Good... that's good."

I found it was easier to tell people what they wanted to hear. They wanted something to feel good about, to think their concern had some effect on the shit eating my dad from the inside out. But in reality, the truth was a poorly stacked house of cards, and I had no desire to be the one to knock it all down.

Rook appraised me, like he could tell I wasn't telling the truth, like he knew me even though I wasn't sure I knew myself anymore.

"I'm glad," Roger said. "He deserves some good days."

"He does."

Rook shrugged out of his lab coat and swapped it out for his scarf and jacket from the nearby coat rack. "I'll be back by one."

Outside the wind whipped through my hair and nipped at my nose. The cold leaking through every seam of the jacket I'd gotten last winter on Melrose, reminding me I wasn't in the city anymore. I'd returned to this place where the fog hugged the tops of the trees and hovered above the marina while the sun played hide and seek behind the cloud bank. It was otherworldly, the colors steeped in grays and blues and deep greens. A place where, regardless of the cold, the seagulls always squawked, swooping, and flying overhead. I was in a postcard, a picture I hadn't ever been able to capture on my own. Except today was different. The town square was almost vacant, unlike the summer when people milled about the cobblestone sidewalks, popping into and out of the shops. It was quiet enough I could hear the waves, hear the rustling of the nearby trees as Rook and I headed south. Quiet enough I could hear the distance my absence had created between us.

"The Early Bird won't be open," Rook said, and I was glad it wasn't quiet enough for him to hear my heart trip over itself.

The Early Bird Diner had always been our place. When we were in high school, we'd sometimes skip first period and eat our weight in pumpkin pancakes. It didn't matter what time of year it was, they were always on the menu. But in the fall, people came from all over to try them and to take pictures of the nearby foliage, the fiery reds and oranges, the bright golds against the backdrop of evergreen. The larches, maples, and aspens were more of a tourist trap than the cute seaside town itself.

"They close at eleven… I remember," I said, smiling up at him. "What about Two Trees? Are they still around?"

He finally looked at me again, the man I'd always known blossomed with tiny laugh lines around his eyes. "Yeah… Tricia's niece is running the place now."

"Where did Trish go?"

"Florida, she said her bones hurt too much in the winter."

We both laughed and I wondered if he had the same picture in his head as I had in mine. Tricia with her wild gray hair and that perpetual streak of red lipstick on her teeth.

"Her niece is sweet, moved here last summer."

I couldn't help but notice the way his smile grew at the mention of her.

"Sweet, huh?"

"What? God, not like that. You're just as bad as my parents. I don't want to sleep with every girl I know."

"Only some of them." I laughed when he shot me his familiar fuck-off glare, his lips pinching into a strict line.

If I hadn't known him for most of my life, I might've actually thought he was pissed.

"None of them." He pulled his scarf tighter around his neck and shoved his hands into his jacket pockets. "And anyway, Harriett is married."

"But if she wasn't…"

I didn't know why I kept pushing. I didn't have a right to know his life. I'd given that up when I stopped calling, stopped being his best friend. Stopped being a friend at all.

He came to a sudden stop, and I accidentally clipped his shoulder. The skin on the back of my neck prickled from the touch.

"You don't get to do this," he said. "You don't get to come back and act like everything is fine. Like nothing has changed."

"Shit, I'm sorry."

"And stop apologizing," he grumbled and started to walk again. His big stride faster than before. "You only have to say it once, otherwise sorry becomes just another word, and the entire point of it is lost."

"Okay."

Rook kept to himself for the rest of our short walk. Nodding at a few people as they passed, I wanted to reach out and take his hand in mine like we used to do. His touch had always centered me, and I thought mine had done the same for him. But being near him now, his proximity, it made me dizzy, made my heart race with regret, and I didn't know how to find a way to make everything stop spinning. It made me feel sick. I fucking hated it. Hated that it was all my fault.

"Hey, Rook." A pint-sized ball of sunshine beamed up at him as we walked into Two Trees Tavern. She couldn't be more than five-feet tall, but her energy made up for her lack of height. Her brunette ponytail swung from side to side as she bent over to grab two sets of silverware rolled up in napkins from a bucket next to the hostess stand. The V-neck shirt she wore plunged low enough to expose her ample cleavage, and if it wasn't for the giant rock on her left finger, I might've hated her on sight. "Who's this cutie?"

"This is Luka, Dr. Abrams' son." The formality of his tone cut through me like a knife.

It wasn't a *hey, Harriett, this is my friend, Luka*. It was cold and to the point, and I guessed I deserved it. I wanted the smile he'd given this stranger, this woman who'd just moved to town last summer. I wanted his high praise. I wanted to be sweet too. All of these things were reminders, little sticky notes, whispering, *this is why you left, this is why you stayed away*. When I had Graham, it wasn't this hard. Everything didn't sting as much. All the things I could never have had become things I might've never needed. But here. Now. I realized I'd always needed Rook.

"Oh," she said, her sparkle dimming around the edges. "I'm so sorry about your dad. I can't imagine—"

"Thanks," I snapped even though she didn't deserve it. "But he's not dead yet."

"Luka," Rook sighed and shook his head. "She didn't…"

"Oh God, I'm sorry," she said. "If that sounded like… I didn't mean it like…"

"No… I'm sorry," I said as Rook's disappointment filtered through me, making it hard to breathe. "I shouldn't have spoken to you like that. It's been hard… with everything. But thank you… for thinking of him."

"Of course," she said, and guilt settled inside my stomach for stealing a bit of her shine.

I wasn't allowed to be jealous of pretty girls, of the people in Rook's life. I'd made the choice to stay away. I was the one who put that empty look on his face. The look that asked me, *who are you?*

Harriett gave us both a quick smile before leading us to a table by the front window. From here we could see the entire marina, the small boardwalk that led north to the Edgewater Inn. The ever-present sea mist swirled around the rocking boats, the vacant vessels left behind for the winter. The dreary gray ocean water slapped against their hulls and spilled over portions of the dock. I stared, wishing I would have brought my camera, wondering if I'd be able to capture the loneliness of it all.

Rook kept his eyes on the menu in front of him as he spoke. "The clam chowder here is pretty good."

"Oh… good to know." God, we were awkward. The remnants of our friendship lost inside the small talk. "Rook, I—"

"I swear to God, if you say sorry again I'm leaving." He set his menu down, his glare piercing straight through me. "I don't know how to do this with you. I want everything to be okay, but I'm angry. And your dad—"

"My dad being sick doesn't give me a pass. It didn't when we found out, and it still doesn't now. I get it. I stayed away. I messed everything up."

He didn't say anything.

I chewed the corner of my lip as he stewed in his thoughts. Rook was the strong and silent, still waters run deep kind of guy. I had to wait him out. Once, when we were thirteen, he'd gone a whole week without speaking to me. I'd started hanging out with some of the troublemakers at our middle school, trying to get in good with the cool kids. Because even then, I'd known, known that I was different than Rook, than most of the boys in my class, and I'd thought if I'd been able to hang with the right crowd, me liking boys wouldn't matter. I hadn't come out to Rook yet, or anyone, and he didn't understand why I'd want to be around the guys who had bullied us the entirety of our sixth-grade year. I'd told him it was the whole, keep your enemies close thing, but he hadn't bought it. It had only taken a couple of days for me to find out hanging with those guys had been a bad idea. Eventually, Rook had forgiven me, and we'd spent that weekend camped out in our fort, planning our next big D&D campaign.

"I need time," he said, and I forced myself to hold his gaze. "I feel like a jerk for saying that because of everything with—"

"My dad."

"Yeah." He licked his lips, and I looked away, picking at the edge of the menu.

"I needed you too much. After Graham left, after I decided to go to Los Angeles. Every time I called you, it got harder and harder to hang up. And then Dad got sick, and I needed you… fuck… more than I should. I should have come home then… I know that, but Dad wanted me to stay, and I used that as an excuse. I had to find my own way. Shit, I'd never been on my own before. Not really. I had to try. I had to stop depending on everyone else. I know that sounds like a shit ass cliché excuse, but it's the truth, Rook. I never fit in here. And—"

"You did. You just didn't want to."

"That's fucking bullshit. You know I didn't." I'd spoken louder than I should have, and the room took notice. Some of the patrons stared at us and I lowered my voice. "After I graduated, I had this great job. I had this great guy and I fit. Portland felt like home, and I finally fucking fit. This town has always been too small, it's stifling. Everyone's always in my business, always asking me why I didn't become a doctor, and all the expectation and disappointment because I'm not my dad. I would have drowned if I came back here then. I wasn't ready."

"And you're ready now?"

"My dad…"

Rook exhaled, like he'd been holding his breath for five years, and I noticed the dark circles under his eyes.

"Luka…"

"I wasn't ready then, and I'm not sure I'm ready now. But I want to be here. I'm a selfish asshole. I shut everyone out and wasted so much time."

He reached across the table and covered my hand with his. I hated how my fingers trembled.

"He's my family too… you're my family, Luka."

Family.

Why couldn't that be enough?

"I know." My throat burned. "I missed everyone and I was scared. I just… I couldn't come back, I couldn't…"

"Couldn't what?" he asked, and he sounded bone tired.

As much as I was terrified to say it, I had to tell him the truth.

"I failed. At everything and I couldn't come back here and prove everyone right."

His jaw flexed, and a flash of something crossed his eyes. More of his anger, maybe? But definitely not forgiveness. He moved his hand, taking the steadying heat of his touch with him. "You're right about one thing," he said, his grip tight around his menu. "You are a selfish asshole."

CHAPTER FIVE

Rook

"I FEEL STUPID," HE *said, tugging on the hem of my hockey jersey. I didn't know why, but I kind of liked having him wear my number. Pride swelled inside my chest as his fingers traced the logo on the front. "I hate hockey."*

"I thought you said hockey players were hot?" I stole another glance at my best friend and hid my smile as I zipped up my gear bag. "And it's the last game of the season, we need all the fan support we can get."

"Fan support?" Luka turned away from the mirror and glared at me. "I'm not one of your groupies."

Chuckling, I nodded as I took in his appearance one last time. My spare jersey, the one I usually wore at away games, swallowed him whole, hanging partly off one shoulder and covering the majority of his torn skinny jeans. I loved it.

"No… you're my best friend. And I need you there."

His annoyed grimace crumbled, giving way to a sheepish smile that made my stomach warm. "Yeah… alright. But for the record,

I hate jocks and all jock bullshit, and if any one of your dude bro buddies talks shit to me, I'll—"

"No one will talk shit to you." I adjusted the collar of the jersey and he bristled. "Not anymore… I'm sorry I didn't know about… everything. But it stopped, right?"

"You didn't have to go all aggro on your teammates. I can take care of myself." Clearing his throat, he said, "I'm used to everyone talking shit, being the only out kid in school… it sucks, but it is what it is."

"That's stupid. No one should care. And if they start their shit again, you better tell me… no hiding this time." I dragged him into a hug. His skin was warm and soft, his hairline tickling my fingertips where they rested on his neck. "I'm sorry they hurt you."

Luka didn't say anything at first. He was quiet, his arms tight around my waist, his face buried in the fabric of my hoodie. I closed my eyes, trying to wrest away the images of him bruised with a busted lip and tear-stained cheeks. It had been weeks since the assholes attacked him in the bathroom at school, weeks since they'd been expelled, weeks since the bruising had faded. But I had a feeling Luka hadn't healed well at all.

"The guys on my team," I said, and squeezed him harder. "They're not like those assholes."

"They sure as fuck were friends with them."

"Not anymore."

Luka pulled away. "Because you lost your shit and—"

"Yeah, and because they're friends with me too. They didn't know how bad it was… how shitty those guys had been to you." I rested my hands on the sides of his neck, the bounding thud of his pulse like a drum against my skin. "Shit… Luka… I didn't even know. No more hiding," I said again, and he swallowed.

"No more hiding."

44

Luka hadn't stopped hiding.

Portland. Graham. Los Angeles. He'd disappeared, hid in-side his work, inside a dead-end relationship, inside a city where everyone hides. But instead of bullies, this time, he'd been hiding from himself.

"God, tell me how you really feel," he said, and I couldn't help but smile. Angry as I was, I missed him too. "I'm selfish and I'm an asshole and…"

"And…" I shook my head, my short-lived smile failing. "And maybe you should do something about it. Instead of mak-ing the same mistakes over and over again."

"Maybe." Luka picked at a rough spot on the table.

I could hear him thinking and I let him. I let the silence be-come substantial and foreign. It was exhausting. The quiet wore down my resolve, my resentment. This wasn't us. This couldn't be us.

"Do you need more time to decide?" Harriett asked as she approached the table, pulling out a pad and pen from her apron.

Did I need more time to decide?

Yes.

This wasn't us.

This was something new.

And I needed to decide how I was supposed to muck my way through it.

"Um…" Luka picked up his menu, giving it a cursory glance before handing it to Harriett. "I'll have the chowder and an orange soda if you have it."

I bit back my smile, a crashing wave of nostalgia making my anger seem juvenile.

"What about you, Rook? Want your usual?"

I stared at my friend. My best friend. This stranger I wanted to know. "Nah… I think I'll have what he's having. But water instead of soda."

"You got it." She scribbled our orders onto the small pad in her hand and took my menu before walking toward the kitchen.

"Orange soda?" I asked and Luka raised a brow.

"What? It's refreshing."

I allowed myself to smile and leaned back in the booth. "I guess some things haven't changed. It's nice."

"Rook… I still like the same things, maybe I've added to the list over the years, but I'm still me."

"Tell me something I don't know, something you've added to the list."

Part of me didn't want to know. Part of me wanted to keep my memory of Luka in a box I could neatly store inside our childhood fort.

"I'm not afraid of food trucks anymore."

A laugh burst past my resolve and God, the smile on his face. It nearly took my breath away. It was every bit of, *I'm still me* and *we're still us* and as I caught my breath, he laughed too.

"How did that happen?"

"It's an L.A. thing. I fell in love with street tacos. I think I gained like fifteen pounds in the first few months I was there."

"And you didn't get E. coli?" I asked, adding every ounce of sarcasm I could muster.

"Miraculously, I didn't." He grinned, laughing under his breath. "I'm not as picky as I used to be. It's liberating."

"I bet."

Harriett brought our drinks to the table then, and as she set them down, I caught Luka staring at me. When she walked away again, he said, "You can have as much time as you need, Rook, but I promise, I'm not going anywhere. I'm here, and I want my friend back."

I wanted more than anything to believe him.

My last appointment of the day went longer than it should have, and by the time I'd gotten home it was after seven. The guys were supposed to come over tonight for our monthly card game, but after lunch with Luka and getting hardly any sleep last night, I almost wanted to cancel. I opened the back door to let Maribelle outside, watching her from the porch as she barked at a squirrel.

"Leave it be, Belle."

She snapped her teeth at me in a silent bark and headed into the trees to pee. Leaning against the railing, I exhaled. All the things Luka had talked about at lunch spun inside my head like a rat on a wheel. He had changed. He was quieter than I remembered, nervous, like he was afraid he'd say something wrong, as if he was holding on to something, and if he let go of whatever it was haunting him, he'd unravel. I didn't think that would have been such a bad thing, watching him let go of whatever it was wedging itself between us. Maybe then I might've believed him when he'd said he wanted to stay. After a few minutes, Maribelle made her way back to the porch and I ran my hand through the thick thatch of curls on the top of her head. She wagged her tail as we headed inside, and for the moment, the loneliness creeping its way inside me won.

I decided not to bail on my friends after all and cleaned up before I ordered a pizza, finally going through the growing pile of mail I'd been avoiding all week. I took a quick shower and threw on a pair of sweats and a t-shirt. I debated whether or not I should call Luka and invite him over, too, but he needed to spend time with his dad. And I'd meant it when I'd said I need-ed my space. My life wasn't complicated. I worked. I had a few friends. I lived. Luka was complicated. His absence the last five years had created an emptiness I was used to ignoring, but now it ached. It ached so much I couldn't take it. I flipped on the radio, needing something to quell the silence, and sighed in relief when the doorbell rang.

"Hey," I said, giving my friend Ron a smile. "Come on in."

"Why am I always the first one here?" he asked, laughing as he bent down and scratched the dog behind her ear.

"I always equated your punctuality with you being an ex-Marine," I offered and shut the door behind us.

"Ah… the whole, 'You can take the boy out of the Corps, but you can't take the Corps out of the boy.'"

"It makes sense," I said, and he laughed.

Rubbing his palm over his short and tightly trimmed dark brown hair, he gave me a shy smile. "Yeah. Maybe next month I'll show up late. Shock everyone."

"Uh-oh… don't get too wild."

He leaned against the kitchen counter, and I grabbed us both a beer from the refrigerator. "The pizza will be here soon."

"Perks of being on time. Hot food."

"Spoken like a true man," I said and handed him his drink.

He held up his bottle and lightly knocked it against mine. "Oorah."

Ron took a sip of his beer as he pulled out a stool on the other side of the kitchen island.

"So… Carter mentioned he saw you and Luka walking in town today."

"We went to Two Trees for lunch," I said, and he nodded, a spark of a smile hiding behind his bottle of beer as he took another swig. "What?"

"How's that going? You already forgive him for being a dick?"

"He's not a dick, he…" I groaned. "I'm not sticking up for him."

"Uh-huh."

"I'm not. I told him… he knows how I feel." I rested my hip against the side of the island. "I don't hate him. It just hurts that he—"

"Ghosted everyone."

"I need time and he knows that."

"I bet you wanted to invite him tonight." When I flinched, he laughed. "Oh my God, such a pushover."

"Says the guy who dropped everything in San Luca and came running back to help Carter set up his new business."

"Ouch." He smiled at me. "Way to hit a guy where it hurts."

"I'm not trying to be mean. I'm being honest. Why did you come back?" I asked, no derision in my tone. "Are you still—"

"In love with my best friend?" he whispered, his blue eyes fixed on something behind me, something I couldn't see, something that was just his. "No… not anymore. I let that wound heal a long time ago. I needed… I was at a dead end in California. Working with Carter is a good opportunity."

"It is." It wasn't the full truth, but I didn't think it was right to use his pain as a distraction for my own. "Will and Travis should be here soon," I said, changing the subject.

"Is that new guy Ryan coming again?" he asked, and I grinned.

"Why? Do you like him?"

"He's straight. And divorced. That's a whole lot of nope." Chuckling, he said, "He's hot, though."

"Objectively, he's attractive."

"Objectively, because you're straight?"

"Because he's my friend. And back to the point… no, Ry's not coming tonight. He's in Oakville visiting his mom."

He hummed and set his beer on the countertop. "I wonder about you sometimes."

"You and me both." I dropped my eyes and peeled the label off my beer into tiny little strips, wishing the pizza would show up and save me from this recurring conversation. "It's not so black and white for me, you know that."

"Do I? You've never dated a guy before, never showed interest in—"

"I haven't dated very many women either." I shrugged. "Why does it matter?"

"It doesn't." When I didn't respond, I heard the stool scrape across the wood floor, felt the brush of a warm hand on my shoulder. "Rook. I didn't mean to… fuck… I don't know what I'm saying. I'm sorry, man. I shouldn't stick my nose in your business. I just care about you."

"Thank you… For caring about me. But I promise, my sexuality is as confusing for me as it is for you." I raised my head and my old friend stared back at me, the worry in his eyes endearing. "I'm not straight." The three words snapped the chains to the concrete blocks holding my feet to the ground. "I've never said that out loud before."

"Not even to Luka?" he asked, squeezing my shoulder. "Shit… I feel special." I shoved him in his chest, and he grinned. "I'm serious."

"You didn't sound serious."

"I mean… Like I said, I've always wondered." He plopped back down on to his stool. "Even back when my sister wanted to date you. I told her she was barking up the wrong tree, but then you dated that girl after Luka came out… shit, what was her name, Nikki? Nicole—"

"Nicolette."

"*Yes.*" He pointed at me, his face wide open with a huge smile. "Nicolette. Shit… that feels like forever ago."

"It was."

"We're old."

A comfortable silence fell between us, and I finished off the last sip of my beer before I found the courage to speak again. "What if I'm meant to be alone?"

"I don't think so, half your friends are single and gay… I mean, if neither one of us is hitched by the time we're forty, I'll marry you."

"I'm not gay."

"*Okay,*" he said, stretching the word into two long, confused syllables.

"How you feel about Carter, I—"

"Felt. I'm not in love with him anymore."

"Sure." I smiled when he flipped me off. "I've never felt like that about anyone. Well… except…"

He raised his brows, something dawning in his bright blue eyes. "Except for Luka."

"But it's different because I… I don't—"

"You don't want to fuck him?"

"Jesus, Ron."

"What?" He shrugged. "I'm right, though. Maybe you're demi or ace, who knows. Christ, there're so many labels now. Want to know what I think?"

I turned and grabbed two more beers out of the fridge, terrified of what he was about to say. Terrified he was right. Terrified the hole in my chest would never be filled, because I didn't think Luka could ever love me the way I needed him to.

"Fuck the labels. There are all types of love, Rook."

My throat tightened as I faced him again, the cold glass of the beer bottles stinging my hands as I gripped them with all my might.

"You love Luka. You love him like I loved Carter, and having, or not having sex with someone doesn't define that. Not for me and not for you."

Behind the rush of white noise inside my head I heard the doorbell ring.

Ron clapped me on the shoulder again. I hadn't even realized he'd moved from the stool. "Let yourself be happy, whatever that means for *you*."

I thought of Luka. Of all the years. The path between our houses. The blue hour. The fort. Rock giants and skinned knees.

I thought of him, and maybe he couldn't love me the way I needed him to, but he did, *love* me. And all the pain inside me intensified, crested like an ocean wave in a storm, but from up here I could see everything, and I decided happiness was forgiveness.

CHAPTER SIX

Luka

THE HOUSE WAS QUIET except for the sound of rain outside and the soft crackle and pops of the wood as it burned inside the fireplace. Nora was in the kitchen with my mom whispering about some recipe they were thinking of making tonight, while I sat in the living room watching my dad sleep. The mechanical bed hospice had provided was out of place among the childhood pictures hanging on the wall, and the giant sectional sofa that was worn with family and years of a life well lived. Shadows crept across the floor, the sun had set a few hours ago, but the disappointment in my chest lingered. I'd thought lunch with Rook had gone well today, and I hadn't been able to stop myself from hoping he'd meet me at our spot tonight. I hadn't asked him to come. But then again, I hadn't ever had to ask before. Rook used to know when I needed him. He didn't anymore.

"Why the sad face?" My dad reached out and tapped my knee. He looked small. His frail frame was lost under a quilt my

54

mother had made him last Christmas. She'd sent me one, too, with a note that said something about a little piece of home. At the time I'd thought it was her usual passive aggression, now I wished I would have thanked her more for all that she had done for me. For my dad. "Everything okay?"

"Yeah…" I rubbed the back of my neck, not meeting his eyes. I shook my head, my forced smile faltering. "No… Dad… everything is sort of fucked."

His chuckle caught me off guard. "Son."

"How can you laugh? You're—"

"Dying."

"Sick."

"I'm dying, Luka. Let's call it what it is. I have been. For a while. It's just closer now." He squeezed my knee. It barely felt like anything. No grip. No strength. "I'm sorry."

"What? Why are you sorry? I… I should have come home when you were diagnosed. Like Nora did. I should have—"

"Nora was lucky, she has a career that moves with her. You… you were still finding your way." He coughed and I felt it inside my own lungs. "I was fighting this… I had a handle on it. But—"

"The treatment stopped working."

He exhaled and wiped his forehead. Staring at the sweat on the tips of his fingers, he said, "We tried everything. And I feel good about that. Stage four liver cancer, kid. I got more years than most."

"I wasted time. I should have come home."

"Maybe. Maybe not. I got to visit you in Los Angeles." Dad attempted to waggle his brows, a lopsided smirk on his lips. "Got to see the Hollywood sign. Got to see you in your element."

"It's not enough."

"It has to be, Luka. This is what we have. And maybe I shouldn't have told you to stay. I hid a lot from you. I guess I hoped it would get better."

"Nora knew. I should've known too. I'm sorry." I stood and sat on the edge of his bed, running my fingers through his hair. He closed his eyes. "I should've been a better son."

He grabbed my wrist, his fingers like thin reeds as they shook. "Stop feeling sorry for yourself. I love you, Luka. I love how passionate you are, how even though you weren't here, you were. All the photos you sent, every time I'd hear the joy in your voice about something you were working on… it helped. It was better than the treatment. You and Nora are different. She hovers like a helicopter. It's her way. It makes her feel necessary. But you… you're like the sun, I can feel you from millions of miles away." He let go of my wrists and I threaded our hands together. My lashes were wet, my eyes stinging as he continued. "I just want you to be happy. I want you to be you, and I'm sorry if I ever pressured you to be something you're not."

"You didn't," I said, trying like hell to speak through the thickness in my throat. I wasn't being completely honest, but it didn't matter. He wanted me to be happy, and back then he thought he knew what was best for me. "Okay… maybe you did, just a little." We laughed and I wiped at my eyes with my free hand. "But I figure it's a parent thing, right?"

"I'm proud of you," he said after he caught his breath. "I always have been. My only wish is that you could be proud of yourself too."

I breathed through the growing discomfort in my chest. There was no way I could grant that wish. He didn't know how much I struggled in California, that most of the photography jobs I'd had barely paid the rent, and that I'd had to work at two restaurants to get by. He didn't know I'd messed up everything with Rook. I was a fuck up on all accounts, except for one. I loved him too much to tell him the truth.

"I'm proud, Dad." He sighed and I gently squeezed his hand. "What? I am. I promise. I interviewed today for a job at the paper. If I get it, I'll get to work with one of their top journalists." For a town this small, *The Harbor Herald* was as prestigious as it gets. I dug deep and gave him a smile. "It would be an amazing start."

"That's good, son..." He yawned, his eyes fluttering shut. "That's really good."

I stood, hesitating, watching him breathe in and out, in and out before I let go of his hand and bent over to kiss his clammy forehead. "Love you."

Mom and Nora were working on dinner when I walked into the kitchen. "Can I help?"

"I think we have it handled." Mom kissed my cheek and Nora snorted.

"That's code for, get the hell out before you burn something."

"I do not burn... everything. Only some things."

Nora grinned at me over her shoulder as she sautéed onions in a pan. "Oh, the lies we tell..."

"Don't you have an apartment in Seattle you have to get home to?" I picked up a grape tomato from the large salad bowl on the counter and popped it into my mouth, chuckling when she scowled at me. "I'm kidding. I love having you here, making fun of me. It's my favorite."

"Stop it, you two." Mom pointed a wooden spoon in my direction. "And you. What's going on with Rook? Natalie told me today you two had lunch, and he came back to the office upset. What did you do?"

"Why is it something I did? Maybe he had… indigestion?" I shrugged, eating another tomato before she smacked my hand.

"Luka…" My mom exhaled and grabbed the salad bowl, sticking it into the refrigerator. "Something is not right between you two. I noticed it the other day. I'm surprised he's not here, trying to steal tomatoes too. You were inseparable. Last time I checked, things were good. At least that's what you've told me whenever I called."

"Life, Mom. It happens."

Nora coughed muttering something under her breath about stubborn idiots.

"Life happens?" Mom sounded like she wanted to hit me. I cringed when she turned in my direction again. She poked me in the chest. "You and that boy are soulmates. Whatever's broken, fix it. You only get so many chances in life." She stared out toward the living room, her throat bobbing. "I've known you both since you were little boys with Kool-Aid-stained lips and grass stains on your knees. He loves you."

"That's what I've been saying for years," Nora said, throwing her hands into the air. "Thank you."

Taking a steadying breath, I sat down on the barstool. "Rook is straight and has always been straight, that's not going to change. We're friends." Or we used to be.

"And I don't care about whatever sexuality is what. Sometimes love is just love." Mom nodded like she'd said the most profound thing ever. Nora covered her smile with her hand.

"Did you get that from the queer section at the Hallmark store?" I tapped my lip. "Wait, is there a queer section?"

She narrowed her eyes, that wooden spoon in her hand again. This time she actually hit me. Once on the shoulder and then again on my ass. "Ouch, what the fu—"

"*Luka.*" She hit me again and Nora cracked up.

Jesus, was it too cold to sleep in the fort? Was I too old? Would it even hold my weight anymore?

"I'm surprised he didn't invite you to his fancy nerd party." Nora dumped a bowl of mushrooms into the pan, the sound of the butter sizzling made my stomach rumble. "He hosts it once a month."

"Nerd party?" I asked, and she lowered the heat on the stove before turning a knowing smile in my direction.

"They get together and play magic cards or something."

"*Magic the Gathering?*"

"That." She pointed at me. "That's what it's called."

"How do you know—"

"I was at the bar last month with Travis' sister. She told me. It's Rook, Travis, Will, Ron, and this new guy, Ryan, aka Ry. He moved here recently. They get together and revert to their teenage years and talk about how sad their lives are. I'm sure it's a blast." Nora flashed her perfect white teeth as she laughed. "Text him, I bet they could use one more sad sap."

"You're an asshole."

"Don't swear," Mom said as she massaged her temples. "It gives me a headache."

Nora kissed my cheek, and whispered, "You're welcome."

All the guys from school were at Rook's playing our card game? None of those guys were into that shit. Were they? It had always been our thing. Me and Rook. Irritation, or maybe jealousy, had my heart tripping over itself as I pulled my cell phone from my pocket.

Me: It was good to see you today.

I stared and stared at the screen. My mom and Nora aggressively quiet as they made themselves busy pretending not to watch me.

My phone buzzed and I almost dropped it.

Rook: Yeah.

My stomach lurched at the one-word reply. How did I respond to that? Did I respond at all? I was about to say fuck it and invite myself over when another text came through.

Rook: Feel like playing Magic? A few of the guys are here, we could use someone who knows their way around a red deck.

Shit.

A ten-ton block lifted off my shoulders.

Me: Right now?

Rook: Are you busy?

I raised my head. Nora and Mom studiously working on dinner.

"Would you guys hate me if I   "

"Go. Have fun." My mom waved me off.

Nora's smile was victorious. "Tell Rook I said hi."

Me: No.

Rook: Then come over. We have pizza.

Me: I'll be there in fifteen.

I pulled up the long, tree-lined driveway toward Rook's place, the gravel crunching under my tires. The house didn't look the same as the pictures he'd sent me when he'd thought about buying it. The moon spread shadows over the property, giving it an eerie feeling. Or maybe that was my nerves coming out to play. How shit of a person was I that I had to ask my mom for my best friend's address? I should have had it in my contacts list on my phone. I should have been brave enough to visit ages ago. But I was a broken record, and I couldn't fix the mistakes I'd made. I could only try and do better.

Warm light spilled from the front windows, and from one of the dormers on the second floor as I shut the door behind me. I could hear the ocean, smell the salt in the air. Wet pine needles were scattered along the walkway toward the front door, laughter from inside bled through the siding of the house, and that unnerving feeling faded. This place felt like Rook. I took a long breath and rang the bell.

"You made it." Rook gave me a half-smile, leaning against the door frame, his dimples hardly noticeable. "I didn't think you'd remember the address."

I dropped my gaze to my feet, ran a hand through my hair. I'd never been able to lie to him. "My mom gave me the address."

"Of course she did," he said, but it hadn't sounded rude, or like he was angry. Just a statement of truth. "Come on in."

The guys were laughing about something, and we followed the sound of it through the entryway. I fell behind, trying to absorb everything, every detail of the man I'd once known better than myself. The space was open and welcoming. The dark stone of the fireplace rose all the way to the top of the vaulted ceiling, and right above the mantel, the Vancouver hockey game played on a huge, wide-screen television. The sound was muted, but I smiled when the camera focused on Rook's brother Reese as he took the ice. Rook's dog jumped down from the large, gray, overstuffed sectional that was the centerpiece of the room, and nudged her wet nose into my hand, snuffling against my palm.

"This is Maribelle," Rook said, the deep rumble of his voice vibrated around my spine. "She can be kind of needy."

"I don't mind." I bent down to pet her, and she licked my face.

Chuckling, I wiped the slobber from my cheek.

"Travis and Will are here, Ron too." He nodded. "They're in the kitchen."

"When did they get into Magic?" I asked, the question more accusatory than I'd meant it to sound.

"This summer." He eyed me, the corner of his lip twitching as he asked, "Why does it matter?"

"They used to make fun of us for playing shit like this," I said and caught a glimpse of Ron in the kitchen. "Well… Will and Travis made fun of me."

"Hey, they bullied the hell out of me in grade school."

"Then you joined the hockey team and—"

"They're good guys. You've never given them a chance." Rook shoved his hand into his pocket. "They're your friends too."

"By association." My jaw clenched, but then Maribelle licked my fingers and I exhaled. "I never understood why you trusted them… after how they treated us in elementary school."

"They were kids," he said, and his shoulders stiffened. "And people change. Some for the better."

And some for the worse.

The five words were left unspoken, but they hit their intended target just the same.

I shouldn't have come here.

"I—"

Rook gripped my shoulder. The contact was sudden, and the heat of his skin soaked through the fabric of my hoodie. Or maybe I'd imagined it, wanted it. Needed it more than I'd needed anything in a long time. "I'm glad you're here." A soft, hesitant smile lit his eyes. "Come on, before those idiots eat all the pizza."

The guys were huddled around the kitchen island. Like the rest of the house, the kitchen was colored in steel and stone and driftwood grays. It was open with a tall ceiling and more cabinets than a single guy would ever need. Ron was the first to acknowledge me, lifting his chin in a silent hello. He held out his hand, and I shook it.

Pulling me into a side hug, he said, "Welcome back."

"Thanks."

My cheeks heated as everyone stared in my direction. I was out of place in a house where I should have felt like I belonged, and I had no one to blame except myself. "Travis, Will. It's good to see you."

"Yeah, man." Travis stole a glance at Rook. "What's it been? Four, five years?"

"It's been too long," I said. I only had eyes for Rook. I didn't owe these guys anything. I was here for my best friend. "I have a lot of catching up to do."

"Sorry about your dad," Will said, and it hit me how much I'd started to hate the word sorry.

I was sick of it, sick of everyone's obligatory sympathy. Like Rook had said, the word lost its meaning after a while.

"Yeah… thanks." I brushed my hair from my forehead, chewing my bottom lip as I searched for something more to say.

I had nothing.

Everyone looked the same, and yet they didn't. Travis had the same cunning brown eyes, same jock build, but his blond hair had started to thin on top. And Will was the same, too, except his laugh lines were deeper around his blue eyes. Ron gave me a sad smile, running his hand over his buzz cut. Out of all the guys, he'd changed the least. He still looked like a dutiful soldier, built like a brick house, except his stomach had gotten softer over the years. Looking at them was like staring at a high school reunion photo. I searched their faces, but there was only one person I cared about, only one person I wanted to know again.

Rook.

With his nervous laugh as the silence in the kitchen deepened, and his amber eyes that reminded me, no matter what, I'd always belong to him.

CHAPTER SEVEN

Rook

THE STARS WERE ENDLESS. *I wondered how long it would take to count all of them. The treetops reached and reached, but I didn't think they'd ever truly touch them. A mild breeze moved the blades of grass under my arms. It tickled too much, and goose bumps prickled all the way down to my wrists. It was warm for late September, one last chance to camp, one last time to count the stars.*

"How many have you found?" I asked and Luka groaned.

"I lost count at fifty-three." He rolled his head to the side. "You?"

"Seventy-two."

His blue eyes looked almost silver in the dark, like one of those cool looking elves from the video game he got a few weeks ago. He reached out and brushed his pinky over mine. I didn't mind it, even though most people thought it was weird how we both liked to hold hands sometimes. We'd stopped doing it at school. The kids were mean and called us names. Mom told me it was okay to hold hands with my best friend, but that maybe we should keep it between us. I didn't understand why the kids cared so much. It didn't hurt anyone. But Mom had said fifth graders were assholes. It was the first time she'd ever used a swear word like that in front of me. I'd heard her swear before, but it was usually by accident.

"Should we try again?" Luka hooked his finger around mine and scooted close enough our arms were pressed together.

"I don't think we'll be able to count them all tonight."

He enclosed my entire hand with his and turned his face toward the sky. "Even if it takes our whole lives, we'll count them, Rook. I know we will."

Luka hadn't said much over the course of the night. The guys had tried to ask him about California while we'd eaten pizza, but all they'd gotten in return were vague pleasantries. He'd mentioned working as a waiter and how it had been hard to sell his photography because there were already too many artists. He'd said things like, *I loved the culture and the clubs, and the beaches were different.* But he hadn't given too much away. For the majority of the game, Luka had sat in silence, his mind somewhere else, his tired eyes, every now and then, found mine. I'd had to remind him it was his turn to play a few times. And after he'd lost all his hit points, he grabbed a beer from the fridge, and sat behind the table on a barstool like an outsider looking in.

I hated it.

"You might as well give up, it's almost ten and you have less than five HP left on your commander." Ron smirked when Will scowled. "What's it going to be?"

"It's almost ten?" Travis snorted. "We're not that old."

"Some of us have work in the morning," Ron said, grinning even wider when Travis narrowed his eyes.

"Just because I work from home—"

"In your underwear." Will laughed and Travis punched him in the shoulder.

I couldn't help but laugh too. Luka's face paled as he inhaled a shaky breath.

"Are you okay?" I asked and he bit his lip as he nodded.

"Yeah… just tired." He forced a smile. "You guys are pretty hardcore players, huh?"

"Who knew?" Will set down his cards. "I've always been competitive though. Apparently, that's not just for hockey."

Luka raised his brows, his tone sardonic as hell. "Apparent-ly."

Will being Will, he didn't notice, but I shot Luka a look and he shrugged.

"What's the plan, Will?" Ron asked again and Will looked around the table, strategizing in vain.

"Fuck."

"Do you fold?"

"Wrong game, asshole."

Ron chuckled.

Will checked his watch again and nodded. "Shit, we better get going."

"Why is it that we never finish an actual game?" Travis stood and stretched his arms over his head. "Isn't it the point to be the last man standing? We never have a winner. I feel like we're doing this wrong."

"Next month, we should play on a Saturday and maybe we'll actually finish this time." Will gathered his deck as he stood too.

"Well, I had the most hit points left so I'm the winner."

"Fuck off, Ron."

Ron threw Travis a kiss. "Always the sore loser."

Luka stood, tangling his fingers together while he watched us clean up the game. His red deck was neatly piled on the kitchen island next to his car keys. It was his deck from when we were kids. I'd kept it for him all this time.

"Stay a minute," I asked him as the guys started for the front door. "If you can."

"Yeah… okay."

Ron gave Luka another hug, while the other guys gave him a nod as they left the kitchen. On my way to say goodbye to my friends, I thought I heard Luka ask Belle if she wanted to go outside.

"Next month I'm winning this shit," Travis said as he pulled me into a hug, smacking my back, like some men did, hard enough I almost coughed. "Talk soon, man. Come on, Will, or I'll make you walk. Lord knows you could use the exercise."

"What a dick," Will said, laughing as he waved at me. "See you later. Thanks for having us."

Ron lingered, looking over my shoulder through the open door. Once the engine on Travis's truck rumbled, he said, "Luka is different now."

"I know."

"He's hurting. Go easy on him, even though he doesn't deserve it." Ron rested his hand on the back of my neck and pulled me in for another one of his big hugs. "Don't forget what I said. We all love in our own way, and that man loves the fuck out of you." I didn't move, needing to breathe, needing to take a few minutes to gather my thoughts. "It's going to be okay."

"I'm nervous," I admitted as I pulled away. "I want to stay mad at him, but I also want things to be like they were."

"You'll figure it out." He bumped his fist lightly into the center of my chest. "Call me this weekend. Maybe we can go fishing."

"Sounds good."

I waited till he was pulling out of the driveway before I went back inside. The house was empty, but the back door was cracked open. Luka was in the middle of the yard, eyes to the sky. A tan, fluffy smear of color ran through the woods toward the dock, barking happy little barks, most likely chasing another poor small animal.

"How many did you find?" I whispered, staring up at the stars as I stood next to Luka.

"Only twenty so far."

I pressed my lips together, fighting myself, fighting the words I wanted to say. We were kids again, counting stars, and like he could read my mind, he reached out and looped his pinky with mine.

"I'm glad you have the guys," he said, and I turned my head and faced him. He didn't look back, his throat bobbing as he spoke. "I didn't have friends in California. I went out to the clubs sometimes with some of the waiters I worked with when I needed to get out of my head. But I didn't have friends. I'm glad you weren't alone."

69

"I wasn't alone. But I was lonely." That got his attention. We stared at each other, his silver-blue eyes sparkling under the low light of the moon. "I'm lonely, Luka. I think I've been lonely for a long time."

"You and Ron seem... close."

"He's been a good friend."

Luka tried to move his hand, but I held on tighter, lacing my fingers through his. Palm to palm, he lowered his eyes, staring at the connection. I always liked the way his pale skin looked against the darker shade of my own.

"That wasn't... I didn't mean it like you think I did."

"You can read minds now?" he asked, raising his head, he held my gaze.

I could feel his pulse through the pad of my thumb. Its rapid beat matched mine.

"Ron is a good friend. Not a better friend than you. Just a friend. He understands me... understands what I've been going through."

"I used to understand you too."

"I know. And I want that again..."

"But you need time." He briefly tightened his grip on my hand and looked up at the sky. I followed his gaze. "I understand that... See," he said, and I could hear the smile in his voice. "I'm already starting to understand you better." I bumped my shoulder into his, and instead of pulling away, he pressed in closer. "I want you to stay mad at me."

"Why?"

"Because I deserve it."

"It hurts too much... being mad. I want to move on. You're here, Luka. And it feels right." I could sense him watching me, but I stared at the moon. "Ron and I are close, and Will and Travis are fun, but it hasn't always been like that. I bought this house when you moved to L.A. and I don't know what I thought, but sometimes it feels too big, and having them here helps."

"Did you think you'd be married by now? Maybe some kids?" he asked, and it sounded strained. "I thought you would be."

"I don't know… Kids would be nice." Belle barked, once and then again, her tail wagging like crazy as she hopped around the dock. I focused on her as I struggled on whether or not I was ready to tell him the truth. "I'm not built like everyone else, I guess."

"What do you mean?"

The heat of his body was a solid weight, it made me feel safe, and he smelled like him, like rain, and maybe I wasn't ready to forgive him, but I needed to start somewhere.

"I'm not sure how to explain it. I tried to tell Ron and he said maybe I was—"

"Ron?" His eyes widened. "Are you in lov—"

"Luka." I chuckled. "Give me a second."

"Sorry." He shook his head. "I mean… shit, I hate that word. Talk to me, Rook. I'm here, for whatever you want to say."

He didn't seem like he was ready to hear anything. His palm had gotten sweaty, his pulse threaded. I started to second guess myself, but I didn't want him to misunderstand me, misunderstand this giant thing building inside me that I had no idea what to do with.

"I've dated women, had sex with a couple of them, and it never felt right. I did it because I thought I had to."

"Have you had sex with men?" Even though he'd attempted to hide it, I heard how his voice trembled.

His hand held on to mine for dear life.

"No… but that's the thing… I've never wanted to have sex with anyone. And Ron said maybe I was asexual or demisexual and I had to look up what demi was, and that felt more like me, but I have no idea. Sometimes I want things, but I've never cared…" *I've never cared about anyone like I care about you.* "I feel like I'm not making sense."

"Hey." Luka lifted my chin. Two points of heat against my skin, and for the first time in my whole life, I actually had the urge to kiss someone. I was angry at him for leaving. For making me love him. For looking at me like he knew me. "You're making sense." He dropped his fingers from my chin, his smile sort of lopsided. "Asexuality is a spectrum on its own. It can be complicated. Feelings are tricky no matter your sexuality." Luka kept his eyes on mine, but his lips fell into a flat line. "But if you love Ron, and he can't accept who you are, then he isn't worth—"

"I don't love Ron." I laughed and tugged on his hand. "We were just talking, like *friends* do, and I told him. I've been confused for… it seems like forever. It was nice to tell someone."

"Oh."

"He's in love with Carter, though he won't admit it."

"Still?"

"Yeah."

"I guess sometimes it's hard to let go… when you've loved someone your whole life… Even when it hurts you over and over again."

I wanted to ask him how he knew that. If he loved me like I loved him. If he was hurting too. But I let go of his hand, my confusion and fear winning in the end. I called out to Belle, and she ran back toward the house.

"Thank you," he said, and I curled my hand into a fist, trying to hold on to the feel of his touch.

"For what?" Maribelle pushed against my leg, panting as she nipped at the hem of my sweats.

"For trusting me with everything. As hard as it was to come out when I did, I was never confused. I knew I liked men. But it's not always that easy, and I know I'm on your shit list, but I'm here if you need to talk, or if you have questions. Or—"

"Thanks," I said, and without thinking about it too much I pulled him into a hug.

Wrapping him in my arms, he melted into me. My fingers curled into the cotton of his hoodie as he tucked his nose against my neck. He rested his palms along my spine, and I perched my chin on his shoulder. It was like he'd never left, and there were a million-and-one stars to count, and the tip of his nose was cold. The scruff on his chin was new, but I liked it. We couldn't stay like this, or I'd have to tell him, have to be ready to forgive and forget, and I had too many small cuts that were barely healing. I pulled back and a tear fell down his face. I wiped it away with my thumb and he shivered.

"Rook..." He chuffed out a wet laugh. But there was no humor in it. "Shit." He rested his forehead to my shoulder, holding on to the sleeves of my t-shirt. "My dad..."

Everything could wait.

The years he'd so carelessly thrown away.

My confusion.

My best friend. The man I loved so much it hurt. Was breaking.

"I know… Luka. God, I know."

CHAPTER EIGHT

Luka

SLEEP HAD ELUDED ME last night as I tossed and turned, thinking too much about my dad and the time I'd lost and Rook and his sexuality. As much as Rook hadn't changed, he was different too. He'd always been reserved with an underlying confidence that could light up an entire room. And last night I saw glimmers of it in the way he held himself and in the way he joked around with his friends, but his smile was quieter somehow. Like he held a million secrets, and he was afraid to smile too wide or they'd come spilling out. I'd do anything to know him, to know what he was too afraid to say. I exhaled, leaning back in my seat, and stared at the front door to *The Herald.* I needed to focus. I'd gotten a call earlier this morning from the editor-in-chief, asking me to come in for a meeting around ten. I was unsure about a lot of things. How much time I had left with my dad? If I would ever become the man he thought I could be? If Rook would ever fully forgive me? But this job. This was the one thing I was sure of. If I could get this, carve a path for myself here, in this town, maybe staying could be permanent. I checked my reflection in the rearview mirror one last time, zeroing in on the thin skin under my eyes. Dark and hollow.

Perfect.

I pulled my keys from the ignition with more force than necessary and grabbed my portfolio from the passenger side seat. I had to practically manhandle the door to the ancient, or as my dad called it, vintage Volkswagen Bug, to get it open. The heavy thing swung open with a loud creak, drawing a few stares from passing foot traffic. With a sheepish wave, my dignity blew away on the crisp breeze. But I had to admit, I loved that my father had held on to this rust bucket as long as he had. He'd purchased the car when he was in college, and I inherited it when I turned sixteen. I remembered hating it at first, but after I'd gotten my first blowjob in the back seat from some closet case I'd met at one of Rook's hockey games, I'd learned to love the freedom it afforded me. When I'd decided to move to California, I'd left it here and thought for sure he'd sell it. I ran my fingertips along the cold metal hood as I stepped onto the sidewalk. I was happy he didn't. It was a trivial thing, but it was a piece of us, and something tangible I might be able to hold on to long after…

"Luka?"

I raised my head and smiled at the pudgy-looking man standing on the front steps of the building I'd been staring at earlier.

"I thought that was you," he said, the thick salt-and-pepper mustache above his lip came alive as he spoke and waved for me to come inside. "I saw you standing out here from my window and figured I'd rescue you from your anxiety."

"Mr. Burgess?" I asked, his voice familiar from the conversation we'd had on the phone this morning.

When I'd interviewed the other day, it was with his assistant.

"The one and only. Come in, come in, I'm freezing my balls off."

I blurted out a laugh and headed up the stairs. I guess I didn't have to worry about being overly professional.

He clapped his hands together and I followed him through the small lobby.

"Weather is a lot different up here, eh? Not like California?" he asked as he hit the call button for the elevator.

"Very different," I said and gave him a polite smile as we both stepped inside.

The building was only two stories, but the ride up took forever. I could feel him staring at me.

"I'm sorry to hear about your dad, we all thought... well, we all thought he'd beat it."

That word again. I swallowed it down and nodded. This was how people rectified things. How they thought they could contribute. Pleasant words and condolences. I couldn't hate them for it, even if it made the anger in me swell. My dad deserved so much more than *I'm sorry*.

"We're lucky," I said but didn't believe it. "He's had more time than we could have hoped for." Time I'd squandered away. "But thank you. I'll tell him you've been thinking about him."

"And your mom."

"Of course."

After a few more long, awkward seconds, the doors opened. The respite was short lived, and once I was sitting across from him in his office, all my nervous energy came rushing back. I hadn't stressed about a job like this since I'd interviewed for the magazine I used to work for in Portland.

Setting my portfolio on the desk in front of me, I cracked it open with trembling fingers. "This is only some of my work, I have a digital file I emailed you this morning and—"

"Luka…" He smiled and my gaze fixed on his mustache. Shit. He was going to tell me no. I recognized that placating tone. I'd heard it enough in Los Angeles. "Your work is… impeccable."

But…

I waited for the inevitable, *you're not what we're looking for*, my knee bouncing incessantly without my permission.

"And I particularly love the work you've done outdoors. You really capture it. I can smell the pine of the trees, the fog over the city."

"Uh… thank you, I—"

"*The Harbor Herald* is the oldest publication in Hemlock Harbor," he continued like I hadn't spoken at all. He puffed out his chest and knocked his fist against the desktop. "Those people in Seattle think they have it all. They think they're so hip… well…" he grumbled, running a palm down his sweater vest. "We don't need that at *The Herald.* Tradition has never let us down, and I think you—"

"Mr. Burgess," I interjected with my widest smile. "If you could give me a chance… I have no desire to come in here and shake things up. I can do traditional. I love tradition." I tapped my finger against the side of my portfolio. "If you flip to page five, you'll see some of the photos I've taken of the town. I want to work with Zach because I love the way he captures small-town life in his articles. I'm not going to lie and say I knew anything about him before last week, but after researching, reading his columns... I want to be part of that, part of this town's history too."

In my own way.

My dad had his life, his legacy, and I wanted one of my own. Something we could both be proud of. Something I could give him before he died.

Mr. Burgess didn't speak, flipping through my portfolio a page at a time.

"Zach Waskin's column is known for its homage to small-town Americana, but what if we highlighted the locals more, not just the surrounding landscapes and shops. What if I worked with him, and each week he wrote a feature about one of the locals, telling the history of the town *and* its people. He'll write it like no one else can and I'll capture it forever on film."

I sat up straight as he raised his cloudy gray eyes and scratched at his mustache. "I like it."

"Yeah?"

"I think it's a damn good idea."

"Really?" I didn't even try to cover the squeak in my voice. "That's... I—"

"And I think we should start with your dad." He nodded his head, his focus on my pictures, nonchalant like he hadn't just given me the fucking moon.

"My dad?"

"Yes." Closing the portfolio, he said, "Everyone adores your father, and this would be a great way to introduce this idea to the town. They love Zach's contributions to the paper, they look forward to all his insights and tidbits of history about this county and our modest city, but this… this is something more."

Honoring my father this way, I didn't think it would make me a better son, or take back all the time I'd wasted, but it would give me something that was just ours. A way to show how much he'd impacted my life, how much he'd done for everyone.

"More… not hip," I said, and he chuckled.

"Exactly."

"When do we start?"

"Today… if you can?" he asked, and I had to pinch myself to make sure I was awake.

"I'm definitely available."

"Great." He shoved himself to his feet, inhaling a lumbering breath. "I'll show you to your office."

"My office?"

"Yes." He furrowed his thick brows and laughed. "Your own office, it's small, more like a closet, don't get too excited."

Too late.

I thought if it had been possible, I might've actually fucking burst at the seams with excitement. After Mr. Burgess had shown me my office, which was, in fact, as small as a closet, he'd introduced me to the staff. Everyone was welcoming, even Zach, whom I'd been most worried about meeting. Journalists had their own way of doing things, and I didn't want to step on anyone's toes.

"Would your dad want to be interviewed?" he asked when Mr. Burgess finished pitching him the idea.

"It depends on how he's feeling." I pushed the mop of hair from my forehead and took a deep breath, looking to Mr. Burgess for support.

"Well, yes. Only if he agrees," he said.

"I was hoping we could focus on his work, talk to Dr. Whelan, some of my dad's patients, stuff like that. And I'll grab some older photos of him from my mom, and take a few of him now, if he's up for it."

Zach frowned as he flipped through my portfolio on his desk. "Not to be a dick... I mean no offense. But isn't that a little macabre?"

"No offense taken," I said, though I started to think I might've put Zach in the nice column too quickly. "I can assure you any pictures I take of him will be shot with a respectful lens. He's my father, the man who raised me with love and strength. I want to show that, show his strength even in his darker days."

"Then it's settled, let's have it ready for next Friday, okay, boys?" Mr. Burgess cuffed Zach on the shoulder and stalked off.

"That man is insufferable." Zach shook his head and gave me a grim smile. "Welcome to *The Harbor Herald.*"

"Next Friday seems fast."

"Tell me about it." Zach nodded toward the office across the hall where a couple of interns were hovered over a laptop. "Let's brainstorm."

It was almost three by the time I left. The sun was out in rare form. The scent of fresh baked bread drifted along the walkway from the bakery up the street, and I followed the smell instead of heading to my car. A few people waved at me, their curious eyes lingering longer than what was considered polite. But it didn't faze me, it was just part of the so-called charm of this town. It was one of those things I used to hate about Hemlock Harbor but was juvenile to me now. I was too tired to care what these people thought they knew about me. There was only one person here, besides my own family, who mattered to me, and I hoped after last night we were on our way back to one another.

Eventually, I found my way to Dot's bakery, which was only a few doors down from The Cozy Wolf, the same bookstore Rook and I used to haunt when we were kids. I grabbed a fresh loaf of bread and couldn't resist buying a few chocolate croissants for my mom. I considered popping into the bookstore but didn't want the pastries to get cold. I was almost to my car when I spotted Ron crossing the street.

He waved, breaking into a slow jog when he noticed me. "Hey, wait up." Ron moved easily despite his large frame, his long legs sheathed in dark denim. As he neared, I was able to make out the blocky logo on his blue polo. North Shore Security. "I see you stopped at Dot's." He patted his belly and laughed. "That place is lethal."

"I followed the scent of carbs and gained twenty pounds by the time I walked in."

"I was on my way there, actually. Dot called and said her security cameras were acting up." He smiled, glancing at the front door to *The Herald*. "Are you in town to see Rook?"

"No. I… I had a second interview with the paper." I tried not to be annoyed with his not-so-subtle dig for information and held up my hands in a silent ta-da. "Looks like I got the job."

"No way, that's amazing, man." He pushed his hands into his pockets, the muscles in his biceps flexing. God, was he always that cut? Something akin to jealousy nestled itself inside my stomach, and the scent of the bread soured in the air. Rook had said they were close, only friends, but I couldn't shake the feeling of loss whenever I looked at Ron. He'd had time with Rook, time I should have been there for my best friend. "Listen, if you have a minute, I wanted to talk to you about—"

"Holy shit, is that Luka Abrams?"

Carter Williams flashed his brilliant smile in my direction as he crossed the street. I almost didn't recognize him under his long brown beard. The thing was impressive, about four inches long but well groomed. His hair was short like Ron's, cut into the military style they both had never grown out of even though they'd been out of the Corps for years. He wore the same polo shirt with the same North Shore Security logo as Ron, but instead of jeans, he had on a pair of khakis.

"Carter?"

"Alive and in the flesh." He reached out his hand, and as soon as I took it, he pulled me into a full side bro hug. "You look skinnier than I remember."

"You have a dead animal on your face."

He chuckled as he pulled away, rubbing his beard through his fist. "Ah… this thing." He elbowed Ron in the ribs. "This fucker said I couldn't grow a beard if I tried. Looks like he was wrong."

"For the record, I can grow a better beard than you. But why would I want to cover up all this sexy? You know you love it." Ron laughed, but I saw the imperceptible dip in his smile when Carter rolled his eyes.

He was definitely still in love with his best friend.

I hated how relieved that made me feel because Carter was as straight as it gets.

"It's good to see you. You plan on sticking around for a while this time?" Carter asked and Ron shot him a look. "What?

83

I can't ask an honest question?"

"It's fine and well deserved… Yeah. I'm here for good, I think. Just started at The Herald." I held up the bag in my hand. "Hit up Dot's bakery. I mean, I'm basically a local again."

Carter hummed, something serious crossing his expression. "I'm sorry about—"

"It's okay. I know… and thank you, it's just… God, I don't think I can handle one more person saying how sorry they are. You know what I mean?"

"I do," he said, reaching out to settle his hand on my shoulder. "But maybe I'm sorry is just another way people can let you know they're here for you, if you need it."

"Thanks," I said, feeling like an asshole. "It's hard remembering that sometimes. That I'm not alone."

"You're home, Luka." Ron squeezed my other shoulder, and I had to blink away the sudden sting in the corner of my eyes. "You're not alone anymore."

I croaked as they sandwiched me into a giant bear hug. "Fuck, Carter, when did you get so touchy feely? You used to threaten to flush me down the toilet if I looked at you the wrong way in high school."

"I was a dick. Chalk it up to growing pains," he said, shrugging as he squeezed me tighter.

I didn't think it was possible to laugh and cry at the same time. But there I was, in the middle of the sidewalk, falling apart, with an arm full of pastries and ex-Marines.

CHAPTER NINE

Rook

"I'M GOING TO TELL *them tonight, at dinner. Tell them I'm gay." Luka blew his hair out of his eyes and flopped backward onto his pillows. The latest edition of* Amateur Photographer *he'd been flipping through earlier spilled to the floor with a quiet thump. "I think I'm ready."*

"Oh?" He rested his sock-covered foot in my lap, and I tugged on his toe. "Are you scared?"

"I should be." He shrugged, staring at me as I pressed my thumb into the arch of his foot, worry and something I couldn't decipher narrowed his eyes. His voice had an edge to it, rough and deeper than usual when he said, "I can't change who I am. This isn't a choice. And I think… I hope they know that."

The footboard post dug against my spine as I tried to think of something supportive to say. This was big. And I didn't think his family would care, but I guess you never knew how people truly felt about the way the world worked sometimes.

"Your parents are chill. I don't think you have to worry." I squeezed his ankle. "And if they're assholes about it, you can come live with me. I swear, my parents love you more than their own sons sometimes."

"Shut up," he said, and his quiet laugh made me laugh too. "They do not."

"My mom told you the other day you were her favorite son. Remember?"

"That's because Reese got caught making out with that girl in his room."

It was more than making out, but I'd promised Reese I wouldn't say anything to anyone. It wasn't my story to tell anyway.

"If you want… I'll stay. They can't get too mad if I'm here, right?"

The corners of Luka's mouth tipped as he nodded. "Shit. Yeah… okay. Thanks."

"I've got your back, Luka. Always."

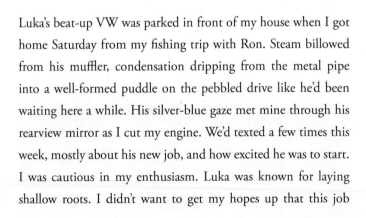

Luka's beat-up VW was parked in front of my house when I got home Saturday from my fishing trip with Ron. Steam billowed from his muffler, condensation dripping from the metal pipe into a well-formed puddle on the pebbled drive like he'd been waiting here a while. His silver-blue gaze met mine through his rearview mirror as I cut my engine. We'd texted a few times this week, mostly about his new job, and how excited he was to start. I was cautious in my enthusiasm. Luka was known for laying shallow roots. I didn't want to get my hopes up that this job meant anything permanent. With a weary smile and a stomach full of butterflies, I got out of the car. He did the same, giving me a small wave as the door to the Bug slammed shut.

"I can't believe that thing still runs," I said and contemplated giving him a hug. Five years ago, it would have been second nature. I pushed my hands into my pockets. "What's up, everything okay?"

Luka lightly kicked a stray pebble, running his hand through his bleach-blond hair. My fingers itched to feel the strands, to know if they were as coarse as they looked. His shirt collar was stretched out, revealing a tattoo. His collarbone was sharp beneath his pale skin, the scribbled ink almost indecipherable.

Meet me in the blue.

The words were ours. I wanted to reach out and touch them, but his fingertips traced the delicate sentence and I realized he'd caught me staring.

"I got it when I moved to California," he said, softly enough I wasn't sure if he was reminding himself or talking to me. Luka adjusted the shirt, pulling his jacket closed as he shivered. His eyes never left mine. "I got a few others too. But this one is my favorite. A reminder of home."

He didn't have to tell me why it was his favorite. It was ours. It was special. I'd never wanted a tattoo before. I didn't need reminders. I lived it every day. Every time the sun set and he wasn't here. *Meet me in the blue.* I remembered because it was etched into my bones just as much as my marrow. Luka had always been a part of me.

"I like it," I said, and his cheeks tinged with pink.

"I didn't mean to ambush you, I tried to call." He bit his bottom lip. "But it went straight to voicemail."

87

"Phone died out on the water," I said. "Left my car charger on the kitchen counter."

"You always forget your charger."

We both laughed, and the bright sound released the tension in my shoulders. "Want to come inside?"

"Yeah, sure."

I figured if something had happened with his dad, he would have told me right away. I wasn't in a hurry to dissect why he was here. It was nice to think he was here without an agenda, here to see me.

Maribelle was beside herself when we walked in. She didn't know who to jump on first, and decided Luka was the easier target. He almost tripped over her a few times as we pushed our way through the house.

"Belle, get down, girl." I grabbed her by the collar when she nearly pushed Luka over the kitchen table. "Sorry, I'll let her out."

"It's okay, she's just excited," he cooed. "Right, girl?"

Watching Luka wrestle with Maribelle loosened the remaining tightness in my chest.

"Feel like going for a walk?"

He scrubbed the top of her head, all smiles, and big eyes. "Sounds good."

We'd made it down to the dock, Maribelle trotting ahead of us with a stick in her mouth, before either of us spoke again. He was the one to break the silence. "This is gorgeous."

The sun was slung low in the sky, painting the clouds in deep oranges and pinks. The tree line a dark shadow hovering above us. The water was choppy, lapping against the shore, and for a second it was all unreal. Like at any minute I would wake up and Luka would disappear, leaving only the sound of rain in his wake.

"Why are you here?" I asked and regretted it immediately when he winced. "I didn't mean for that to sound as harsh as it did."

He chuffed and bumped his shoulder into mine. "I know." His Adam's apple bobbed as he bent over and retrieved the stick from Maribelle's mouth. He tossed it hard, and we both watched as she chased after it. "I wanted to ask if you wanted to come to Sunday dinner tomorrow."

"Your mom asked me already."

"She did?" He shook his head, smiling a smile that was only his. Half-crooked, all teeth without any reservation. It was beautiful. "She didn't mention it to me."

"My parents are coming too."

"That I knew."

"You really drove all the way over here to ask me to Sunday dinner? Luka?" I stopped walking and he paused, exhaling a long breath.

He knelt down, picked up another stick, and threw it. Maribelle dropped the one in her mouth and chased after it, her feet splashing in the water when she got too close to the shoreline.

"I wanted to see you," he said as he stood again. He turned to look at me, his nose crinkled. "Is that okay?"

No agenda.

Just me.

"Yeah, Luka. It's okay."

"I know you're working through things, and I want you to know I'm here. You have more than Ron in your corner."

I didn't miss the way his voice sharpened when he mentioned Ron.

I grinned.

"Uh-oh… Be careful. That sounded a lot like jealousy."

"Because it is," he said, his cheeks a deep shade of red. "I'm so fucking jealous I could scream. But I can't be and that makes it worse, and… Oh my God, why are you laughing at me?"

"You're ridiculous."

"I know. It sucks."

I draped my arm over his shoulder, and like a million times before, he leaned into my side. With his hair against my neck, I was able to feel the texture. It felt the same as it always had, and it made me smile even wider.

"You sound like a whiny teenager."

"Way to rub it in."

"I've always been real with you."

He was quiet as we both stared out toward the horizon. "Be real with me," he whispered, like the words had trapped themselves inside his throat. "Are we… okay?"

It wasn't that simple. But it could be.

It wasn't about best friends and hurt hearts. Not anymore. Luka meant more to me than that, and maybe it took me forever to figure it out, but what we had was bigger than I ever knew, and it took me losing him to acknowledge I never wanted to let him go again.

I turned, any trepidation I had seemed foolish to me now, and pressed my nose to his temple. He snuck his arm around my lower back. We were kids again, watching the sun dip below the horizon. "We will be."

The Abrams's house was all laughter and light when I arrived the next day. My parents had already been here for the past hour and were in the kitchen with Luka's mom. Nora was snuggled next to her dad on the couch, and I was surprised to see him up and awake. Last night, Luka had stayed for dinner and had caught me up on his dad's condition, both of us silently agreeing the last five years could wait. We skirted around the issues we should have been working through, focusing on his dad, and reminiscing about the old days over beer and tacos. And being here now, all the warm chatter, and the smell of garlic and butter in the air, I could pretend like nothing had changed. That his dad, at any minute, would start bitching about the game not being on, while Nora teased her brother, calling him a remote hog. The private scene in my head played out as I leaned in the doorway to the living room. Luka hadn't noticed me yet, and I took the rare few seconds to admire him. His hair was damp, flopping over his forehead. A five o' clock shadow dusted across his jawline, carving it out in stark angles. It wasn't necessarily attraction that warmed my stomach, but more the familiarity of him. The stead-fast lines of him I could trace with my eyes closed, the sound of his voice as grounding as it had always been. My heart spread out inside my chest, stretching far enough it almost hurt to breathe as Luka laughed. He tilted his head and found me watching, giving me a nod, I pushed away from the wall.

"Hey," he said, and his sister waved.

"Like old times." Nora gave her brother a pointed look.

"Rook?" His dad's voice was too thin. "It's good to see you, son."

91

"You, too, Dr. Abrams."

"Rook… come on. Before I die, just once will you call me Isaac." He was joking and I tried to smile.

"Isaac."

He yawned and sank deeper into the sofa. "I like the way that sounds."

My throat pinched as I blinked back the moisture fighting its way to the surface. Luka looked up at me, his eyes glassy, while Nora curled her fingers in the fabric of her father's hoodie.

"Me too," I said, and Luka stood.

"Should we see if they need help in the kitchen?"

"I should say hello to your mom."

Isaac's eyes closed as Luka and I made our way to the kitchen.

"Fuck," I whispered, and the word was strained, wet with the tears I couldn't hold on to any longer.

Luka took my hand, pulling me into the hall, and I wiped my cheek with the other. "Are you going to be okay?"

"I have no idea how you're okay."

"I'm not."

"Luka." I reached out and took his other hand in mine, slotting my fingers next to his. "What can I do?"

"Nothing. This is what it is. I'm used to seeing him like this. Today is a good day. I'll take what I can get."

I didn't want to know what a bad day looked like. I hated myself for not coming around more, hated that I stayed away to protect myself from the memory of Luka. A few more tears spilled down my cheeks, and Luka's breath hitched. I let go of his hands, letting him wrap his arms around me. We stood like that, in the foyer, our limbs tangled, chest to chest, for what felt like forever. No matter how mad I thought I should be, Luka was broken. And I wanted to hold all his pieces together, and I wanted him to hold mine. Leaning back, I cupped his face in my hands, my thumbs wiping the moisture from his cheeks. His eyes were red rimmed, and I imagined mine looked the same. The flat palm of his hand rested against my chest. We searched each other's expression, a quiet sort of armistice between us, breathing itself into our lungs, filling all those regretful spaces inside us with something more. *Are we okay? We will be.* We had to be. I wanted him back. I wanted to be done. Death had a way of making anger feel petty. What was five years of misunderstanding to a lifetime ready to be buried?

"I'm so fucking sorry," he whispered. "I *hate* that goddamn word, but I mean it, Rook. I fucking mean it more than anything I've ever said in my stupid life."

My heart thudded and tripped as I wiped a stray tear from his trembling bottom lip. I couldn't hang on to the past, not when everything was so suddenly fragile. Maybe it was all the years before, or the shell of the man sleeping on the couch in the living room, but I couldn't find the spite or the will to hold onto a grudge. I'd always loved Luka, no matter how or why. Forgiving him was easy. But in a week or a month or an hour, Luka's life would be irreversibly altered, and if I left him alone in that terrible void to fend for himself, I'd never be able to forgive myself.

"It's done," I said, and he tried to argue, shaking his head. I held his face, wiping the rest of the dampness from his skin. "No more apologies. No more anger. I know you, Luka. You did what you did, and we can't change it. But it's done, and we'll deal with it."

"We will?" The hand against my chest twisted, clutching my sweater.

I lowered my hands to his hips, and he held his breath. "I want to understand why you pushed me away. I want to know why you thought you didn't need me."

"I need you, Rook." His voice was low and desperate, like if he didn't get the words out fast enough, they'd disappear. "That's part of why…" He swore under his breath, dropping his gaze. "I always need you… Shit… Rook, I lo… I…"

"Everything okay over here?" Eliza stared at her son, then at me, and then at my hands where I had them on his hips. I stepped away.

Luka wiped at his eyes with the back of his hand, and I swiped a few from my own cheeks. "Yeah," he said. "Just… catching up."

"Ah-ha." She nodded, a doubtful quirk in her brows. "Well, when you two are done kissing and making up, we could use some help in the kitchen."

"Mom," Luka groaned. "That's not—"

"Not my business," she said and held up both of her hands, a wry grin forming on her lips. "It's nice to see you again, Rook."

"You, too, Mrs.…" I stuttered as she shot me a glare. "Eliza."

"That's better," she said and turned and walked away with a wave over her shoulder.

"Jesus Christ, that woman has an uncanny ability to make me feel eleven years old."

"She's always been that way. It's a mom thing," I said, Luka's words still ringing in my ears. *I always need you.* "Hey, what were you going to say? Before she interrupted."

"Um." He looked away into the living room. "I… I feel like you're letting me off easy."

"I am. It's exhausting, fighting, being angry. I'd rather work things out as we go than have this… cloud hanging over us. I don't want to ignore it, Luka, but I don't want to give it too much power either." I reached for the collar of his t-shirt and moved it aside, my fingers tingling as I trailed them over the tattoo. "I need you too," I said the four words in a shaky whisper. "You're my best friend… I love you too much to throw that away."

"I love you too," he said, but it wasn't like that. Like *I love you*. Those three words for him meant growing up together, camping, s'more sticky fingers, Magic the Gathering, and awkward teenage angst. They meant forgive me and I'm sorry and I missed you. We were years together and years apart, and somewhere along the way, in the loss I'd felt in his absence, the lines had blurred for me, and I wished like hell they had for him too.

CHAPTER TEN

Luka

THE SENSATION OF ROOK'S fingerprints against my skin lingered throughout dinner. I'd catch myself, touching my collarbone, and drop my hand before he could notice. Everyone sat at the table, including my dad. Polite conversation hummed around us, laughter, and smiles, and we were years in the past, like the old days. My dad looked different, but it was easy to see the man he was underneath the fragility of his skin. I'd spoken to him about the interview, and he was more than happy to participate. A full-page piece in a newspaper would never capture all that this man meant to his family, to this town, to me. But it was something he deserved. Better than the single-column obituary we'd eventually have to write. I set my fork on my plate and reached under the table for his hand. His skin was cold, but his smile was warm.

"What's this for?" he asked, and I shrugged.

"I'm glad you're having a good day." The table of people graciously ignored us. "Do you mind if I take a few pictures?"

"Not at all."

I let go of his hand and wiped my mouth with my napkin, no longer hungry. "I'm going to grab my camera," I said out loud to no one in particular. "I'd like to get a few shots for the article if that's alright with everyone?"

After a chorus of *sures* and *how special* and *yes, please*, I stood and headed upstairs to grab my bag. I didn't have to turn around when my bedroom door creaked open to know Rook had followed me. Something between us had shifted today. The practical part of my brain told me Rook was the way he was, and forgiveness and friendship meant more to him than anything. He had always been sensible and understanding, and the way he looked at me today didn't mean anything more than a friend needing to throw down a white flag. But he'd never looked at me like that before, like his heart could finally, *finally*, hear mine. My stupid needy heart was a bramble of hope and years of yearning. The tight skin against my collarbone tingled again like the ink underneath had come alive with his touch.

"This place looks like it did when we were kids," he said with a soft laugh, and I looked around at all of the framed pictures I'd hung on the wall in a neat pattern I'd found on some design website when I was fifteen. Some of the shots were my own work, but the majority were prints of Adams, Hyde, and Porter, hanging like a cliché over my bed. "Except it's cleaner."

Lifting my bag over my shoulder, I snorted. "My room was always clean, yours always smelled like gym socks."

"That's disgusting."

"Tell me about it. Why do you think I always preferred the fort," I teased and marveled at the easy smile on his lips, the loose set of his shoulders. I'd missed this. No tension. No eggshells for me to stomp on. "I used to secretly stuff air fresheners in your hockey bag."

"That was you?" he asked, and I cracked up. "I thought it was my mom."

"All me," I said with exaggerated pride.

"The guys used to give me shit for it all the time. They said I smelled like a mix of jockstraps and watermelon."

"Now that's disgusting."

We were breathless with laughter, my cheeks aching, his hand pressed against his stomach, his two dimples on full display.

Rook's amber eyes were flecked with gold, open and alive as he caught his breath. "I owe my mom an apology. I can't believe it was you the whole time."

"To be fair… it was originally her idea," I admitted and bit back a grin when he shook his head.

"I feel so betrayed," he said, but his tone was all humor and comfort.

The air in the room stilled as our laughter subsided. He took a couple of steps toward me, and my heart clenched out a few unsteady beats. I raised my fingers to my collarbone. It was an unconscious movement, a simple, absentminded thing, an itch I didn't think would ever fade, but he noticed, his eyes darting down to the slope of my neck. Rook wet his lips, his chest rising and falling with sharp and distinct breaths. My spine burned with a static charge, and I curled my hands into fists at my side to stop myself from doing something irrational, something that would derail this tenuous truce he'd offered me. My heart had always been imaginative, and I told myself the way he'd looked at me, the way he was looking at me now, meant nothing. It couldn't mean what I needed it to mean. Things between us had changed, but not so much he magically wanted to kiss me, to want me like I wanted him for all these years. It didn't work like that, even if he had discovered something about himself, about his sexuality, it had nothing to do with me. If our friendship was going to work, if coming home, and carving out a life for myself was ever going to happen, I had to stop creating windows where there were impenetrable walls. I was too old to play pretend.

"Do you think your dad would want to be in the feature too?" I asked and started for the bedroom door. Our arms brushed together, his forest and wood smoke scent surrounding me as I walked past him. "He's such a huge part of my dad's life and this town."

"My dad would be honored," he said, and I glanced over my shoulder to catch him smiling. "Thank you."

"Of course, Roger is like a second father to me."

"Luka…"

"Yeah?"

He cleared his throat and shook his head. "Never mind."

"What?" I asked, giving him my full attention. The tightness around his eyes had returned. "What's up?"

"I have the day off tomorrow…" He rubbed the side of his neck, one of his old nervous tics. I had to fight my smile as I waited him out. "Not sure what your schedule looks like, but I thought if you needed some shots of the office or around town for your article, maybe you'd like some company."

"I'd love some company." I didn't even try to hide my ridiculous smile. When we were younger, I used to drag him along on never-ending hikes and adventures. All a ruse to take pictures. He'd never complain or call me on my bullshit. "Maybe we could grab pancakes at The Early Bird before we get started?"

"Pictures and pancakes," he said with a reminiscent twitch of his lips. "It's a good place to start."

I figured he'd meant a good place to start our day, but there might have been a deeper meaning. *A good place to start over. To begin again.* God, my stupid heart was such a fucking liar.

"Your mom sent me up here, by the way," he said. "She told me to remind you no medical stuff."

"Jesus," I whispered and laughed without humor. "Like I wouldn't remember the conversation we had less than an hour ago."

"No medical stuff?" he asked, and I nodded.

"She doesn't want the hospital bed, or any of his medical stuff to make it into the pictures. Like I'm an idiot. I know he wouldn't want everyone feeling bad for him. I want to catch him when he's feeling good. I got a few shots earlier when he was up watching the game."

"Whatever you get will be amazing."

"I hope so."

This project wasn't me proving myself to my new boss. It wasn't landscapes and skylines. This was my dad. His legacy. I couldn't fuck it up.

We made our way downstairs, and as Rook took his seat at the dining room table, I set my bag on the long buffet table by the window. I told everyone to ignore me, to pretend like I wasn't there while they laughed and lived and talked about memories. They were stiff at first, but eventually I dissolved into the background listening, snapping shots while they sipped from wine glasses, and my dad mentioned to Roger, "Remember that time."

After that, it was Dad smiling, eyes watering as he described how Nora used to fit in his arms and, "God, she was so tiny," and "Dad, don't make me cry."

Natalie said, "I wished we could have known you then."

And mom rested her hand on Nat's. "It feels like you did."

Rook's gentle gaze followed me around the room, knowing and calm, as I kneeled to get a better angle. I couldn't remember much of my life before Hemlock Harbor, and sometimes I'd forget we'd ever lived in Seattle. Rook and the Whelans had been a part of every second and every day, and the time before seemed like someone else's life. It had once been suffocating as much as it had been everything. That feeling, it had been one of the reasons I'd left. That not remembering, that unknown. The city buzz that escaped me here. But as I turned my lens, framing Rook's shy smile, it was hard to understand why I'd ever thought leaving had been the right answer.

Later, when my dad was asleep and Rook's parents had gone home, I shuffled through the shots I'd taken. My MacBook was open on my lap while Nora's head rested on my shoulder. Rook was in the kitchen with my mom doing dishes.

"I like this one best," Nora said and lifted her head. "Dad looks… like himself." I'd caught him cracking up about something, my mom smiling at him like they were newlyweds. "You have to use this one."

"I will."

"Can I get copies of everything?"

"I'll send you an email."

She wriggled in closer to me, looping her arm through mine. "I'm happy for you. About the job. I'm jealous you get to be here all the time now."

"Seattle's not that far away."

"I know…" She sighed and bit the inside of her cheek. "It's lonely though. Ever since I moved back from Atlanta, I kept thinking I should have gotten a place here, and now every time I drive back to my apartment it all feels… empty."

"You have friends in the city."

"Not really."

"And a great job."

"I could do my job from here."

"Nora?" I shifted my hips, and she moved her arm. "What's going on?"

She chewed her bottom lip, her eyes glassy. "I want to be here. With you and Mom and Dad while I have the chance."

"You're here. All the time."

"I'm not like you, Luka. I don't need the city." She sank back into the sofa. "I broke up with Julie."

"Shit. What happened?"

"She didn't like how much time I've been spending here. And whenever I asked her to come with me, she'd have some excuse. We weren't a good fit."

"I'm sorry."

"Meh." Nora reached over and stole the MacBook from my lap. She zoomed in on my dad's smile. "She was kind of a bitch."

"You've been dating her for months."

"The sex was good."

"Oh God." We both giggled like we were seventeen, covering our mouths when my dad stirred. "Nora," I hissed.

"What?" Her eyes had gone wide with mock innocence. "She had a very capable mouth. Way better than that guy I dated last summer. And this thing she did with her tongue, I—"

"Please... stop. I will literally throw up."

"Don't be immature," she whispered. "Like I didn't have to listen to you and all your exploits during your sexual awakening. My therapist says I'll never heal from the trauma."

I shoved her shoulder and she laughed. "I never... You are such a liar."

"I'm happy you're home," she said and set the MacBook back on my lap. "It was never the same without you."

She stretched her hands over her head. "I better go spring Rook, or he'll be trapped in that kitchen all night. I bet Mom has him fixing the drain again."

"Again?"

"Yeah, it's been leaking and Dad..." We both stared at his sleeping outline under the covers. "He hasn't had a chance to do it himself."

"I'll go help." I closed the laptop and set it on the coffee table. "You should head home before it gets too late."

"I'm staying here tonight. I have an appointment with a realtor in the morning."

"You're serious?" I asked, feeling more excited than I had any right to be. "You're really going to move back?"

"I think so."

I hugged her until she pushed me away with a breathless, *I can't breathe*, then made my way into the kitchen and almost walked straight into the open pantry door. Rook was standing by the sink, shirtless and wet and laughing while he dragged a towel over miles of warm brown skin and muscle. My eyes snagged on the light smattering of hair on his chest, and how it trailed to his stomach and vanished below the waist of his jeans. He was beautiful and strong lines, cuts and angles, and Jesus, he had abs. I didn't remember him ever looking this hot without a shirt. I tried to rake through all of the teenaged, lustful, jock fantasies I'd had about him when I was younger and came up empty. Nothing could have prepared me for the man standing in front of me.

"Honey?" My mom stared at me, and I forced myself to breathe, to say something.

Unfortunately, all I could muster was a sputtered one-word answer. "N-naked."

"What?" Rook gave me a worried look.

I held my forehead and stared at the wall. "No... not naked-naked, but why?" I waved a hand in Rook's general direction and pinched the bridge of my nose as my face flushed with heat. I'd bet my life my cheeks were the color of a ripe tomato. Fuck. Apparently, somewhere between the living room and the kitchen I'd lost the ability to form a coherent sentence. "Why are you without shirt, shirtless, all..." I waved my hand again. "Like that."

"Are you feeling alright?" By the tone of my mother's voice, I could tell she wasn't sure if she should laugh or be genuinely concerned. I outright refused to look at Rook. "Sit down before you hurt yourself. You've been running all day and—"

"I'm fine, Mom, I was just..." What? Caught off guard? By my best friend's abs? Platonically, of course. "What's going on? Why is Rook all... wet?"

"I might've accidentally turned on the water too soon while he was still tightening the pipe." She gave him a sheepish smile. "You know me, I have the patience of a two-year-old."

Rook set the towel on the counter, and against my better judgment, I turned to look at him.

"The pipe shouldn't cause you anymore trouble," he said and picked up his soaking-wet shirt, wringing it out over the sink. "I added enough plumber's tape to last you a lifetime."

"Let me get you one of Isaac's t-shirts. I'll throw this in the washer," she offered and took the shirt from his hand. "I'll be right—"

"I have a hoodie he can wear," I blurted. "It's in the coat closet."

"Will it fit him?" she asked, and I resented her dubious expression.

I wasn't that small. I had abs, too, damn it.

"It will fit."

It barely fit.

The light-yellow fabric hugged his shoulders and arms, a size too small, but Christ, he looked hot. And there was this complete caveman satisfaction in having him wear something of mine for once. In high school, I'd practically lived in his hockey jersey, and I'd loved how it had made me feel like his. It had been stupid and childish, and I guess I still had some growing up to do because seeing him in my clothes made it feel like he was mine too.

"I'll see you in the morning," he said as we walked down the driveway to his car.

"Around eight?"

"Sure."

He leaned against the driver's side door, and I tugged on the string of the hoodie. "You can keep this."

"I have plenty." He chuckled, and I tried to hide my disappointment with a smile. Like always, he read me like a book. "What?"

"Nothing."

"Do you want me to keep it?"

"No… I… I figured it would be easier." I raised a shoulder, but it wasn't as nonchalant as I would have liked, and he reached for my hand.

He slotted our fingers together. "Say what you mean, Luka."

It's what he'd used to say to me when we were kids, when he could tell I was sad, or worried or afraid of what I had running through my mind. It had been a lot easier to tell him the truth inside our fort with the mask of pouring rain and moonlight.

"I want you to keep it," I said, and he lifted his eyes to mine. "Why?"

The muscle in my jaw clenched as I swallowed. Did he know? He had to know. Maybe my stupid heart wasn't as dumb as I thought. It was dark outside, the clouds covering the moon, the shadows of his face hidden. I couldn't read him, like all those other times, in the pitch black of night, and instead of doing the smart thing, avoiding the truth altogether, I asked him a question.

"Did you like it when I wore your jersey in high school?"

He didn't answer right away, his thumb rubbing two small circles into my palm. The rough touch of his skin raised a riot of goose bumps from my wrist to my elbow. "It made me feel proud."

"Proud?"

"Like you belonged to me."

"I did… I do. I'll always be yours," I said, hoping he could hear the truth this time. Hear it and own it.

"I know."

Rook let go of my hand and clutched me to his chest. I let the familiar weight of his arms pull me in, his scent already permeating the fabric of my hoodie, mixing with my detergent. He smelled like home. This wasn't a hug you gave a friend you'd known since you were nine years old, a friend who was losing his father, or a friend you'd wanted to forgive. This was a free fall and beating hearts. He held our bodies closer, tighter, my breath catching in my throat as he raised his hand to my neck and brushed his lips against my temple. The gesture was too quick and soft, and I thought I might have imagined it.

"I'll keep the hoodie," he breathed, the heat of his breath tickling the shell of my ear.

"It looks good on you." I smiled into his neck when he huffed out a laugh.

Too soon, he pulled away, and the ground under my feet swayed. "Eight o'clock."

"Pictures and pancakes," I said, raw and hopeful.

Rook gave me his quiet smile as he got into his car. He started the engine, and as I walked toward the house, he rolled down his window.

"Luka…" he called my name like he'd forgotten something. "I… I'm yours too."

"Even when you're mad at me?" I asked, my heart dropping in my stomach, and his full lips pulled into a crooked smile.

"Yeah, Luka. Even then."

CHAPTER ELEVEN

Rook

"I CAN'T BELIEVE IT," *Luka nearly shouted, a definite hint of disappointment in his tone I hadn't expected.* "You had sex with her?"

"Jesus, Luka, be quiet." *Forks scraped over porcelain plates while a cook in the back hollered through the small serving window at a waitress about something. The buzz of the diner was loud enough I didn't think anyone had heard, but I sank lower in my seat hoping to disappear into the white-and-green plaid vinyl of the booth.*

"Where? God, not in your car?" *The disgust on his face made my stomach clench.*

"No... not in my car." *I didn't understand the wounded look on his face.* "Are you mad at me?" *The strict lines around his eyes softened as he shook his head.* "Say what you mean, Luka."

"Shit... I'm sorry, I just... Ella Peterson. Really?"

"She's my girlfriend. We've been together since April."

"Didn't realize there was an expiration date on your virginity." *He crossed his arms over his chest, a hard expression tightening his jaw.* "I thought you didn't like her?"

108

"I do… I mean… she's nice, and kind of pretty and—"

"Kind of pretty." He threw up his hands and blew a strand of hair out of his eyes. "You just…" He leaned across the table and lowered his voice. "Gave it up to her because she's kind of pretty. Rook? You did it because those Neanderthals on your team wouldn't stop teasing you about being a virgin."

"No," I argued even though he was skating pretty damn close to the truth.

The pancakes sitting on the plate in front of me suddenly didn't look as appetizing. Nauseous, I pushed my plate away and stared at my best friend, something like embarrassment and regret churning inside my gut. I lowered my eyes, unable to face him. It shouldn't matter to me this much, what he thought, but it did. Luka meant the world to me, and if he thought I'd screwed up, God, maybe I had. I hadn't even liked the sex part that much. It was awkward and took forever for me to get into it, but I liked holding her after, liked just being there with her after something that big. I didn't know if that was weird, or what, and I'd wanted to ask Luka, but now… I didn't want to say anything at all.

"Rook?"

I raised my head and held his gaze. We both sat there, quiet. He picked at the edge of the table, and I fidgeted with my fork. "I like Ella, and sure, maybe everyone is having sex and I was curious."

"Curious? About what?" he asked, sounding more sad than angry.

"If I'd like it."

"Did you like it?"

My face was hot as I shrugged. "I don't know. The guys always talk so much shit in the locker room, and I was expecting something… I don't know, epic. And it…"

"Wasn't epic?"

"No." Despite myself I laughed, and Luka smiled. "Was it for you... when you had sex for the first time—"

"It was pretty damn epic." His cheeks flushed and he hid his face in his hands, peeking out at me between his fingers. "I can't believe we're talking about this over pumpkin pancakes."

"My mom always said if you can't talk about sex, you shouldn't be having it."

"Gross. Your mom talks about sex?'

"All the time." I rolled my eyes when he gasped. "Calm down, just like... she's on my butt about condoms and birth control and I'm always like 'Mom, don't worry I'm a virgin.'"

"Not anymore."

A beat of weighted silence went by as we both took long sips of our lukewarm coffees. I set the mug on the table, gearing up the courage to say what I wanted to say. "Why do you think it's epic for everyone else but me?"

"I wish I could answer that for you." He huffed out a sigh. "Maybe you haven't found the right person yet. You're young and straight, you're destined to have lots of mediocre sex."

I threw my wadded-up napkin at him. "Nice."

"What I mean is... you're special, Rook, you're not like those idiots on your team. You'll find someone..." His voice wavered and he swallowed. "And she'll be amazing, and perfect for you."

"And if not?"

"You'll always have me."

The Early Bird Diner was a town staple, and it didn't matter if it was Saturday or a random Monday, the place was always filled to the brim with people. Luka and I were tucked away in a booth in the back of the small restaurant, stuffing our faces with pumpkin-flavored carbs like we were seventeen again. Nothing in this place had changed, down to the 90's pine, the green-and-white-checkered booths, and all the old sepia photos of sailboats. I hadn't let myself come here much while Luka was gone, too many memories. But sitting here with him, after last night, it wasn't quite the same as when we were kids. This time I thought maybe we were at a precipice, ready to leap into the unknown of a new beginning. I'd had a hard time falling asleep last night, running over everything we'd said in his driveway, the hug. I'd let myself give in to the heat of the moment, something I'd never done before, and it had been whole and right.

I'll always be yours.

Those four words had cast a light on our entire relationship. Every memory a map to something hidden between us. How had I missed it all this time? The way he'd looked at me. The way he'd been mine from the start. This could all be wishful thinking. I could be making something out of nothing, out of hurt and a need to repair the damage of the last five years. The feelings I had for Luka were turbulent, stirring inside a vacuum that was me and him and the revelation of my own sexuality. All the confusion I had, if I would ever belong to someone, if I'd ever want to, had cleared. Like stripes of sunlight breaking through the storm inside my head, he was there. I was an idiot for never noticing, for ignoring the obvious thrum beneath my skin, and now I had no idea what to do, how to figure out where to go from here.

"I thought we could start at the office." Luka spoke around a mouthful of pancake, a drip of syrup sticking to the corner of his lip. "Get a few shots of my dad's office, talk to Charity, and see if your dad would be down to chat as well."

I stared at the sticky spot on his mouth, half wanting to wipe it with my thumb and half wanting to kiss it away. I'd never enjoyed kissing. The wet and sloppy warmth of another person's mouth hadn't ever appealed to me. But I found myself wondering what Luka would taste like. Would he be all nutmeg and maple sugar?

His top teeth sank into the flesh of his bottom lip, nervous and unsure. "Does that sound good to you? Do you think your dad would mind?"

I lowered my eyes to my plate, pushing the remnants of my soggy breakfast around with my fork. "He won't mind, as long as we grab him between appointments."

"You're awfully quiet today," he said, and the concern in his voice made me raise my head.

"I'm always quiet." I smiled and his nose crinkled. "And maybe I didn't sleep great last night again."

He set his fork down and wiped his mouth. The syrup was gone, smeared on his napkin, and a strange sense of loss coursed through me. "Why do I feel like that's because of me?"

"Because you've always been self-centered."

"Ouch." He held his hand to his heart, and I laughed. Luka's smile stretched up and into his eyes, stunning and honest. "You never sugar-coated shit, I missed that."

"I've missed this," I said and rested my foot against his under the table. "Honestly, though…" It took me a second to gather up all the things I'd been thinking about, sifting through everything I was too afraid to say. "It was a little bit about you."

"It was?"

"Do you remember Ella Peterson?"

His brows pinched together as he sat up, spine stiff. "Ella… she's a blast from the past. Why do you ask?"

"I thought about her last night," I said and picked at the cuticle on my nail. "And about that morning when I told you I'd slept with her."

"God… that was ages ago." He reached across the table, stilling my hand. His thumb, a warm anchor, pressed against my skin. "What made you think of that?"

"You were right," I said and noticed his posture had relaxed. This was Luka, my best friend, and no amount of time or miles would change that. I used to tell him everything. I wanted to tell him everything again. "I slept with her because I thought I had to."

"Peer pressure… it's a bitch."

A nervous laugh bubbled up my throat and I turned my hand, lacing our fingers together. "I want to ask you something."

"Okay."

His eyes, those same icy blue eyes I'd known for most of my life, sparked a fire inside my stomach, the burn of it low and settling.

"When I told you about her you seemed… angry. And I always thought it was because you knew that I'd allowed the guys to get into my head. I thought you were mad because you knew I'd done something I didn't want to do. In your own way… you knew me better than anyone."

"I did." Luka's grip was steadfast and heavy in my hand, even though his fingers had started to shake.

"Was there more?" I asked and he blinked, his throat working as he bit his bottom lip again.

"Say what you mean, Rook." He'd thrown my words back at me, and gave me a half smile, pulling the corner of his lip through his teeth.

"Were you angry because I'd let the guys talk me into something I wasn't ready for, or was there something else going on?"

"I was jealous." He shook his head, frustrated. "No… that's not… Why are you asking me this?"

"Luka…" He tried to pull his hand away, but I held on tighter. "Tell me the truth."

"Why?" he asked, his voice pale and unsteady.

"Because there's a wall between us, and I can feel it. I think I've always felt it."

"That day… I… Shit…" He stared down at our hands, his palm clammy. "I was heartbroken." He drew a line along the side of my finger with the tip of his thumb. "I was in deep."

"You never said anything."

"You were my best friend. I didn't want to screw with that. I learned… I learned to shut it out, to love you the way I knew you could love me back." His smile turned sad around the edges, and I would have done anything for a moment of privacy, for dusk, for the fort in the trees, for a room filled with silence. A place where I could tell him I wanted to go back. I wanted to know. I wanted the love he'd been too afraid to give. "Then I got over it. I survived."

I got over it.

"With Graham?"

"He helped."

"California?"

He let go of my hand and I didn't fight him. "I ran away for a lot of reasons. Most of which I've already told you, but yeah, I didn't think I could come back here. I was afraid I hadn't gotten over you at all."

"Looks like you could use some more coffee." Charles, the diner owner, smiled down at us, refilling both of our mugs before either of us could answer. Steam billowed from the pot as Luka and I stared at each other. "Can I get you boys anything else?"

"Just the check." Luka pulled out his wallet as Charles handed him the bill.

"How much do I—"

"My treat," he said, but it sounded flat as he handed Charles two twenties.

"I'll be back with your change."

"Keep it. Thanks."

Charles gave us both a small salute. "It's good to see you boys again, don't be strangers, alright?"

Once he walked away, Luka started to gather his coat, scooting toward the edge of the booth, ignoring me and the fresh cup of coffee in front of him. "We should get a move on if we—"

"Don't do that, don't shut me out again."

"Rook." He sounded tired. "I can't do this with you. I can't… It's too much." He pushed out of the booth and headed for the front door before I could say another word.

"Shit."

It was bitter outside, the wind cutting to the bone as I stepped through the diner door. I shrugged on my jacket as I jogged down the sidewalk. Luka wasn't too far ahead, but when

I called his name, he kept walking. Panic lodged itself in my throat. I shouldn't have said anything, shouldn't have pushed. We'd only just begun to repair the bridge between us. How he'd felt about me when we were kids had nothing to do with how he may feel about me now.

I got over it.

I was selfish. I'd jumped without thinking.

"Luka," I tried again, and he slowed his pace, his shoulders dipping as he exhaled a foggy breath. "Please."

He didn't turn around but stopped at the corner to wait for me. I stood next to him, waiting for the light to change. He didn't speak but pressed his shoulder into mine. The knots in my muscles relaxed enough I could breathe again. A million questions buzzed and banged inside my brain, but I stayed quiet too. I didn't want him to run. I didn't want him to lose any more time with his dad because of old wounds, because of me. Guilt filled the chambers of my heart with every beat of my pulse. He'd stayed away, and even though he'd made that choice on his own, I'd been a variable in that decision.

The light changed, and we crossed the street, the heat of his body harder to ignore with every step. He didn't pull away, hovering as close as he could until we were a block away from the office. Under the awning of the bookstore, he took my hand, the gesture stopping me in my tracks.

"I don't want to shut you out," he said, the trepidation written deep into the furrow of his brow. "I never did. But I had to, with everything, and then my dad. It was… self-preservation."

"I understand… I shouldn't have said—"

"Why did you ask me about Ella? Why now?"

"We're different," I said, the words dizzy inside my head, spinning until my stomach dropped like I'd fallen several feet, like I had thrown myself off one of the nearby cliffs and into the bay. "It took me a long time to understand it, and in some ways, I still don't know how to explain it, how I feel about you. If… if what I want is what you want or ever wanted."

"What do you want?" he asked, and I tugged him closer until we were almost chest to chest. I dropped his hand and raised mine to his neck, his pulse humming beneath my palm. "Rook… I can't…"

I didn't heed his warning, dusting the pad of my thumb along the line of his jaw and his eyes closed for one, two seconds, opening, half-lidded and sleepy. I should have stopped there, I should have pulled away, but I was in deep too. I thought I might have always been. His lips parted, a surrendered soft sound escaping his throat as I leaned in and pressed my mouth to his cheek, to the corner of his mouth, to the spot where the maple syrup had gathered. The contact warmed my cheeks, closed my eyes, and muted the world around me. I was submerged, all the sound fuzzy around the edges like I'd dunked my head underwater, and behind my eyes, all I could see was blue. Luka clenched his fingers into the fabric of my coat, and I brushed my lips over his. He tasted like sugar and falling leaves, like the month of October. He tasted familiar, like how all kisses should have tasted. There was nothing sloppy about Luka's tongue or the way his teeth sank into my bottom lip. It was slow, the way he melted into me, the way he let me in. Every touch was infinite. It wasn't rushing blood and fire. It was finding myself and coming home. It was years of waiting and confusion and forgiveness. I wanted this building pressure, this urge to expose every nerve as his hand slid up my chest to my neck, and his nails scratched my skin.

A moan rumbled in my chest, foreign and loud, and with shiny eyes and pink cheeks, Luka broke away, breathless. "What are we doing?"

I held his face between my hands, the rough texture of his dark stubble felt right under my palms. His lips were this pretty shade of strawberry red, slightly swollen and shaped like a heart. I hadn't noticed that before, the divot above his lip. "I have no idea."

"You can't kiss me like that…" His voice was raw, scraped thin and vulnerable. "You can't kiss me like you mean it if you don't."

"I mean it." I lowered my hands to his hips. I didn't care about the cars passing by, or the cashier staring at us through the bookshop window. "Luka… look at me."

He covered my hands with his, pushing them from his hips, and stepped back, the cold air adding more bricks between us. "I don't want to lose my best friend again."

"You won't."

"You don't know that," he said, his hands in fists at his side.

"I guess I don't." I thought about my failed attempts at relationships, my hesitation toward sex, the loneliness invading my home every time I walked through the front door. "I don't know what I'm doing, or if I can even give you what you need, but hell, Luka, I want to try." I hesitated as he pushed his hands into the pockets of his coat. "Unless you meant it when you said you were over it. Over me."

"You give me what I need every time I look at you. By simply… existing." His bleach-blond hair rustled in the breeze, his eyes, weary and soft, blinked back the brimming moisture dampening his lashes. He wasn't the same boy I'd always known. Time and pain had changed him. But he was mine all the same. He kept his distance and gave me a watery smile. "I don't know what to do… I'll never be over you, Rook, and that kiss…" His voice broke, and he shook his head, huffing out a choked laugh. "It was everything I've ever fucking wanted, and it scares the hell out of me. I don't think I could survive it this time… if it didn't work out."

"Okay."

"Okay?" He raised a brow. "Does that mean… what? What does that mean?"

"It means whatever you want it to, Luka. I'm here, and if that's all you need, if that's enough, it's enough for me too."

"It has to be enough."

Nodding, I breathed through the growing discomfort in my stomach. "Then I can respect that. I shouldn't have kissed you. I shouldn't have assumed that's what you wanted."

"Rook," he said my name with so much regret it was hard to look at him. "I'm sorry."

"Don't… you hate that word. Remember?"

"I don't want things to be weird. I just want my friend, and I feel like I fucked it up again."

"You didn't… I promise…" I gave him a smile that wasn't a total lie. I gave him his friend and reached up to brush a strand of hair from his forehead. "We're good, I swear. Come on, let's go take those pictures."

I started to cross the street, touching my fingers to my lips. The heat of his mouth hadn't yet faded, and as Luka sidled in next to me, I hid my shaking hands in the pockets of my jacket. It didn't matter if, for the first time in my life, a kiss actually meant something, that I actually wanted more than anything to kiss him again. This was who we were, and I didn't want to do anything to lose that. It was enough. It had to be, because more than anything, I didn't want to be someone he needed to survive.

CHAPTER TWELVE

Luka

I WAS SUCH A liar.

I told myself if I stayed busy, I'd forget the way he tasted, like spice and granted wishes. I'd forget how the heat of his lips lingered even three days later. I'd forget how I'd finally gotten everything I'd wanted and promptly pushed it all away. Fucking fear, it ruled me, and I was exhausted trying to fight it all the time. I stared at the screen of my dad's computer, at Rook's smiling face frozen in time. I'd taken the shot on Monday at the office. He hadn't been paying attention, laughing with Charity about something, laughing like he hadn't uprooted every last one of my lifelines, like he hadn't kissed me and opened me up and destroyed me all at once. I didn't know how to move forward. He'd said he wanted to try.

Try.

Try to want me?

Try to love me like I loved him?

Loving Rook was effortless for me. Effortless because I'd always known. It wasn't a maybe kind of thing, or a let's try, it was years of hopeful smiles and subtle touches, disseminating each one and wondering if this time… just maybe… It was hours of talking in the dark shade of trees and knowing that this person, this one man, owned all of my secrets. All but one. And it was a million days of wanting to give him that secret, wanting to give him everything.

I wasn't willing to gamble our friendship, gamble everything on the word try. I touched my fingers to my lips again for the thousandth time since Monday.

"Stop it," I whispered to myself as I flipped through more of the photos and focused my attention on my project. I had to have all the final edited photos to Mr. Burgess and Zach by tomorrow morning and had zero time to wallow. It didn't help that I hadn't seen Rook since Monday, hadn't had the chance to read him face to face. We'd both been too busy, and with this deadline, I had to decline his invitation to lunch today. I wasn't avoiding him on purpose. I wasn't. We texted every night, and I hadn't detected any regret in the tone of his messages. If anything, it was like the kiss hadn't happened at all. Our friendship was intact. Another photo of Rook popped onto the screen and my heart sank, overfilling my gut with anxiety. Fuck. I wasn't very good at this whole self-preservation shit anymore.

I closed the editing program and headed to the kitchen with a plan to eat my feelings. With my mood officially in the toilet, I wouldn't get much work finished anyway. I had all day and night to get it done and figured making sure I actually ate something today was a good enough reason for a break.

I found my mom hovered over the stove, stirring a pot. The scent of carrots and onions in the air had my stomach cramping with hunger. "Smells good."

She wiped her hands on a dish towel and leaned over and kissed me on the cheek, the soft locks of her salt-and-pepper hair tickling my face. The feeling was as familiar as the scent of her perfume. Coco Chanel.

"Chicken noodle soup. I've made some for your father, but there's plenty. Grab yourself a bowl."

"Thanks." I grabbed two bowls from the cabinet and dished myself and my dad some soup. "I'll sit with him if you still want to go to lunch with Nat."

"Are you sure?" she asked, toying with the sleeve of her pastel flannel shirt sleeve. "You've got work to do."

"I need a break." I set both bowls onto the tray Mom set out earlier and opened the loaf of bread sitting on the counter. "And Dad is always sleeping, it will be good to have some awake time with him."

"The nurse will stop by at two, will you have time to—"

"I have time for him," I said, and she gave my arm a gentle squeeze. "I can handle it."

She took the butter knife out of the drawer and tapped my hip with the dull blade. "Let me do this."

"Mom."

"What? I can butter bread." She briskly dragged the knife across the bread, smearing the butter into hectic little waves.

"Mom?"

"I can do it," she said, her voice wavering, spilling over into the deep creases around her eyes and mouth as she fought back her emotion. "I can do it, damn it."

123

I reached for her wrist, and she dropped the bread and knife onto the plate. I pulled her into a crushing hug, and she shook in my arms as she cried. Her tears weren't silent like I was used to. They were loud and big and ugly. Unrestrained, breaking through the solid bone of her chest. It was overdue. Ever since I'd come home from California, all her threads had started to fray like that favorite blanket of hers with loops of yarn sticking out every which way. The worry she'd tried to conceal became more evident as each day passed, and the control she'd held onto with all her might had finally slipped.

"Mom… you can take a break, too, it's okay to step away. You can't take on everything, you can't wrap yourself up so tight." She leaned back and wiped the tears from my cheeks. "Stop trying to take care of everyone else and take care of you."

"What if I leave and…"

"It could happen…" That set off another river of tears. I dipped down to her height and made her look me in the eyes. "But he would never want you to be a prisoner in your own home," I whispered the last part, hugging her to my chest again.

I ignored the guilt I had for allowing this to happen, for allowing my mom and my sister to take on everything. This wasn't about my guilt or what I did and didn't do. I had to be here, be present, and let my mom know she was safe to take a breath. I could deal with my guilt later with a scotch on the rocks.

"Fine… yeah…" she mumbled into my sweater. "I'll call Natalie." Mom rubbed her eyes, her smile sad and shaky. "Thank you. I know you have feelings about staying in California, but your dad wouldn't hear of you coming home." She smoothed her hands over my chest, wiping away the wrinkles in my sweater.

"'Not yet,' he'd say. 'You tell him, not yet.' I wish it was still not yet."

I didn't blink, didn't even flinch. I knew what she'd meant. It wasn't that she didn't want me here. Not yet meant he was still okay. Not yet meant we had more time.

"What did the doctor say yesterday, you never told me."

"Any day now. His labs looked terrible. All we can do is keep him comfortable." She cleared her throat. "Make sure he eats enough, he'll fight you on it, but he has to eat something, alright?"

"Yeah."

"And when the nurse comes, tell her that the soap she used the other day left a rash on his back, and I've left her a bottle of the stuff he likes in the bathroom."

"Okay."

"And tell her to make sure to take his blood pressure on his left side, it's always lower on his right and—"

"Mom… I've got it."

"I'll write it down before I go and leave it on the kitchen counter."

I laughed despite the scowl on her face. "Okay, thanks."

"Thank you." She pressed another kiss to my cheek. "Need anything while I'm out?"

"I'm good, tell Natalie I said hi."

"I will." She gave me another hug on her way out of the kitchen.

A couple of minutes later I could hear her in the den talking to Natalie on the phone while I finished getting lunch ready and headed out to the living room. I set the tray of food on the table next to my dad's bed and switched on the television to his favorite show. He loved all things DIY and my mom had hours of *This Old House* recorded for him. The sound woke him up and he gave me a groggy smile.

"I have strict orders to make you eat," I said. "You have to eat at least half or Mom will never leave me in charge again."

"Where is the Warden?"

"I'm right here," she said, and I laughed as she walked into the living room. "I'm going to have lunch with Nat."

The shadows around my father's eyes parted, another smile breaking through. "That's good, Eliza."

"Please eat," she whispered and kissed his forehead. "For me."

He touched her cheek, the skin on his fingers like vellum. "I'll try. Have fun, okay."

A few seconds passed between them. "I'll be back soon."

Mom left and my dad did as he'd promised. He'd eaten at least half of his slice of bread and the entire bowl of soup while we watched the renovation of some Civil War-era colonial on the big screen. We both balked at the wallpaper choices, critiquing every design choice down to the grout the owners had chosen for the bathroom tile. It was like we'd fallen back in time twenty years. All those Saturday mornings when we'd sit on the couch bundled in blankets, and instead of soup it was Frosted Flakes for me and coffee for my dad. We'd watch the TLC channel and every fix-it-up show we could find until my mom and Nora complained, and we'd give in and watch something else. I remember thinking I'd wanted to be an interior designer until I'd stumbled across a photography show on one of those Saturday mornings, and my life had been altered forever. My dad had seen the light in my eyes and had gotten a camera for me that next birthday. I looked at him now, buried under quilts, his big, full moon eyes, more like crescents as he fought to stay awake.

"Want me to let you sleep?" I asked and he shook his head.

"Stay a while. Unless you need to work."

"I can work out here."

"I'd love…" he stuttered and sighed a trembled breath. "I'd love to see the photos you've chosen for the article."

"Yeah? Give me a second, I'll grab my MacBook."

After I cleaned up the lunch dishes and gathered my Mac-Book and bag from my room, I settled in next to my dad in his bed. Dad had always been an affectionate father and having him snuggled in next to me was nothing out of the ordinary, even though our roles had switched. Here was this human, smaller than he should be, sitting next to me, eager like I'd been when Dad had shared something with me.

"Show me what you got," he said, less sleepy than he had been twenty minutes ago.

"I loved the shots from Sunday dinner, and these…" I scrolled down to the pictures I'd taken at the office. "I don't know. What do you think?"

He stared at the pictures I'd taken of Rook and his dad, of his own office, his desk with papers sprawled across it, untouched like they were waiting for his return.

"It feels… empty."

"What do you mean?"

He shrugged, scrolling away from the office pictures back up to the smiling faces at the dinner table. "Use these. I'm alive in these, the ones at the office… it's like I'm gone already."

"Dad… that's your practice. That's you and Roger. I want to show that."

He tapped the screen, tapped the faces around the table. "This is me and Roger."

"Okay." I nodded as he slid the computer onto his lap. "I'll nix the office shots."

He zoomed in on Nora, then me, then Mom, his eyes misting enough I noticed. "Remember that winter we all went to Vermont. Smugglers' Notch," he said the resort name with reverence and laughed. "You kept begging Rook to go snowboarding with you. He was terrified, but he did it anyway."

"He fell so many times. I thought for sure he was going to break something and that Natalie would bury me alive in the snow." Amused, I reached over and scrolled down to the picture of Rook at the office again.

That smile, the freedom in it.

"He would do anything for you." Dad looked at me then, his eyes shiny and strong. "You know that, don't you?"

"I do… But Dad, it's complicated."

"It doesn't have to be." He wiggled his way up the bed, sitting straighter, and pressed our shoulders together. "You love him."

"I always have."

"I know." He ran a finger along the touch pad until he found the folder labeled 'Rook'. He clicked it open, every memory, every shot littering the screen with color, with a life I'd tried to hide from, with a man I'd never let go of. "Does he know yet?"

"Yeah… I think he does."

Dad nodded, sifting through the photos like they weren't a private diary, like every feeling I had for Rook wasn't on display. "And?"

"*And* I don't know." I exhaled, frustrated with his line of questioning. "It's not important right now. This. Time with you is all I want."

Dad closed the laptop and stared out the sliding door windows. The day was overcast as usual. The hemlocks in the backyard rustled in the breeze, creating a contemplative white noise that seeped through the walls and filled the silence.

I thought I'd put a lid on the conversation and started to feel bad for shutting him out when he spoke again. "Your mom was a lot like you when we first met. Closed off... always second-guessing herself. It took her almost two years to go out with me." It was a story I knew well but loved to hear over and over again when I was little. How my dad had won my mom. "She fought it, thought she knew what was best for me, pretending like she wasn't interested. I almost thought we'd graduate college and never see her again."

"She thought you were too good for her."

"Hmm." He nodded. "That was part of it. But she didn't trust herself either. She didn't trust her feelings... like you." He poked my cheek and I chuckled. "Your mom didn't think I was ready to give everything up for her."

"You didn't have to."

"There is a part of the story I've never told you."

"Oh, is this where you tell me you knocked Mom up and she had to marry you and then over time your love conquered all?"

129

"No." He beamed, and I was brought back to that Saturday morning couch again, DIY, and Frosted Flakes.

"Shit...okay, I'm listening."

"Your mother and I hung around with the same group of people. Her best friend's brother was my roommate. It wasn't a secret I had my eye on your mom since freshman orientation, but it also wasn't a secret my dream was to attend Johns Hopkins School of Medicine. Everyone used to tease me. They'd always told me I might as well go to Harvard if I had to be fancy about it, or asked me what's wrong with being a Husky for a few more years. The University of Washington had a great med school program. But you remember how Bubbe was, and Pop, they were very... particular."

"That's a nice way of putting it."

"They wanted me to have the world. We didn't have a lot, and they wanted to give me the opportunities they never had."

"Johns Hopkins... that's a big deal."

"It was... and Pop never went to college. Bubbe, either. He was a butcher..."

"And didn't Bubbe do hair?"

"She did. And they saved every penny."

"Did you have the grades for a scholarship?"

"Absolutely."

"Shit." I wasn't an idiot. I knew where this conversation was headed. He'd given up Johns Hopkins for my mom. Given up the dream, his parents' hard work. "Mom didn't want you to give up everything for her," I guessed, and he nodded. "But you stayed in Washington?"

"Not at first."

"Wait, what?"

"I'd been with your mom for almost two years when I was accepted to Johns Hopkins. We weren't casual like most of our friends. I would have married her on our first date if she would have let me. But maybe that was a little over the top."

I lightly bumped his shoulder with mine. "You think?"

"I'd spent half of my undergraduate years chasing her, and the other half falling in love, and when it came time to move, I didn't know what to do. I made it a month at Johns Hopkins before I turned around and headed back home. Johns Hopkins wasn't my dream. She was. I took a gap year and reapplied to University of Washington."

"Is that why Bubbe didn't like Mom?"

He laughed and tipped his head back with a sigh. "Bubbe loved your mother. It took her a while, but she came around. I think she blamed Mom for things she shouldn't have."

"Mom wasn't Jewish."

"Hell, Bubbe was barely Jewish." He waved his hand with more strength than I'd seen in days. "The point to this entire story is that love isn't easy. Love is sacrifice, son. It hurts, it's messy, and shit, it will tear you up. At the risk of sounding like one of those greeting cards your sister loves to torture us with, I have to say it's worth it. Love is worth every single hurt it gives. It's worth it because it's fucking living, and you deserve to live it."

I hadn't realized I was crying until he threaded his fingers through mine. "I'm afraid. What if we don't make it and I lose him?"

"Impossible."

"I left. He deserves better."

"You left. You made mistakes. But you love him, and you're here now. Mom decided her self-worth and gave away two years to that choice. You know what she said to me last night. She said she'd give anything to have those two years now. You aren't guaranteed anything, Luka. Tomorrow you could walk out that door and get hit by a bus."

"Jesus."

"Well… Macabre as that may be, it's reality. Don't you think you've thrown away enough years? You don't get to say you're not worth it. That's up to him, and I have a feeling he thinks you're everything."

"I want that more than anything."

He let go of my other hand and rested his head on my shoulder. "Then go get it."

CHAPTER THIRTEEN

Rook

"PORTLAND?"

Luka leaned against the trunk of the tree, ripping up blades of grass between his fingertips, brutal and nervous. The shade of the fort casting shadows across his face. He looked different today, older.

"It's a good school, Rook. Pacific Northwest College of Art has one of the best photography programs on the west coast. It's only a two-hour-and-fifty-seven-minute drive from the University of Washington."

"That's very specific."

"I looked it up and it's not that far."

"That's pretty freaking far, Luka." I plopped down next to him and ignored the ache in my chest. If this was what he wanted, I wouldn't give him shit for it. "What am I going to do without you?" I asked, hiding my heartbreak with a smile I definitely didn't feel. "Three hours feels like a thousand miles when I'm used to having you next door."

"It's basically the same length of time as The Fellowship of the Ring.*"*

"That's a long-ass movie."

"I recall you saying it should have been longer."

"They left out Tom Bombadil."

"You're never going to let that go, are you?" His lips broke into an easy lopsided grin as he bumped my shoulder.

"I love Tom," I half whispered, and we both started to crack up.

"Shit… I'll miss this."

The corners of my eyes started to sting. "We still have this summer."

His hand found mine, his skin warm and soft against my calloused palms. "I promise. Every summer will belong to you."

Luka's name lit up my screen, filling my bedroom with a quiet blue glow. I stared at the text message, not sure if I should respond.

Are you awake?

He'd kept his distance this week, but it wasn't anything I wasn't used to. Ron said I should be mad, but it was hard to muster the ire. Luka and I were good at being us. We'd perfected our dance over the years. He'd run, and I'd pretend like it didn't hurt getting dropped into the dust storm he'd left behind. It started the day he'd told me he'd chosen to go to Portland for college. The simplicity of our relationship had become burdened with some unspoken weight I hadn't ever been able to fully bear. We had changed. He'd promised me every summer, but in the end, he'd given them to someone else. He had changed. He loved me, and it was more than friends. We were two people connected by old and intricate branches, and that weight, that secret he'd held, it had reshaped every memory of him I'd ever collected. I couldn't be angry at him, not when the burden I'd thought I'd carried had been the anchor keeping him at sea.

Resting my back against my pillows, I thought about the kiss, about the boundaries I'd needed to keep in place, and hesitantly swiped my thumb across the screen of my phone.

Me: I can be. Everything alright?

Luka: I'm outside.

"Outside?" I sat up and tossed the sheets off my legs. My feet hit floor with a loud thud, and Maribelle's head popped up from where she slept in her dog bed by the dresser. "It's okay, girl. Go back to sleep."

I gave her a quick scratch behind her ear and peeked through the blinds of my bedroom window. Luka's VW sat in my driveway, steam rising from his exhaust pipe, idling with the headlights off. A rolling sensation rocked inside my stomach, a mixture of worry and something else, something I had no name for.

Me: I'll be right there.

I grabbed a t-shirt from the top drawer of my dresser and tugged it over my head as I headed down the stairs with Maribelle on my heels. A soft knock had me hurrying to unlatch the

135

lock, my pulse building, rising like a surging tide ready to drown me. I knew before I saw his face. I could feel it, that drum, that thread pulsing between us stripped and bare.

"Rook." Luka's lips trembled, ashen like the alabaster of his wet cheeks. Dull blue, almost gray eyes stared through me, unseeing as Maribelle whined. She nudged his hand with her snout, but he was unmoved. "Rook... he... he's gone. God, I can't go home." His head fell forward, and he swayed on his feet.

"Shit... Come here." The words scratched their way up and out of my throat as I pulled him into my arms. His entire body thundered and quaked against me, and I fell apart with him. We stood in the doorway, huddled together, my hand on his neck, his fingers twisted into the fabric of my shirt. "I've got you, I'm right here." His broken sobs stole my whispered consolations, but I repeated them anyway.

I said the words over and over into the chilled night air, into the crook of his neck until he believed me, until time seemed to stop and there was nothing else but this loss and the cracks in our veneers, exposed and sharp.

"I can't go back there," he said, his hot breath on my shoulder. "I can't go back..."

"Then stay here. Stay with me, Luka."

He didn't say yes or no but took my hand and I led him into the house, closing the door behind us. Maribelle nipped at our linked fingers, and Luka laughed, this wild and unsure, sad sound. For a second, he took a breath, rubbing his bloodshot eyes with the heel of his free hand. But then a fresh wave of tears brimmed over his lashes and his shoulders shook. "I'm so fucking lost. I knew it was coming, I knew, but I... I thought I'd have more time."

"Luka…"

"I-I don't know what to do," he whispered, brittle and scared, like a young boy waking up from a nightmare. "What do I do now?"

I was lost, too, and this time I had no idea how to fix this. And it hurt, God, it hurt too much to look at him, to watch him break.

"I don't know," I said, and Luka sank into me again. I held his weight, held him together, all his pieces crumbling through my fingers. I told myself to stop crying, to hold him steady, but I only managed the latter. "I wish I did."

"He's gone."

He tipped his chin and muffled a scream into my collarbone, grasping fistfuls of my t-shirt. I let him scratch at my skin and soak my chest with his tears. The sour scent of mourning hovered between us, and I buried my nose in his hair, desperate for the familiar smell of his shampoo. I needed something to remember, something tangible, something to stop my own seams from tearing open one by one. I needed to be his roots, his refuge. His pain had always been my pain. Every breaking sob, every heaving breath belonged to me, belonged to us. I kissed his forehead and wiped his cheeks with my thumbs. I held him close and told him he never had to let go. I told him I was here, right here, and I wasn't going anywhere. I told him how much I loved him, how much I loved his father, his family, how much he meant to me. I rambled and cried with him, our wet cheeks pressed together, until there were no more words, only our fingers clutching fabric, pulling tight, sealing off any space until we were one person, one heartbeat aching, tied up in grief and silence.

"I feel bad… leaving Mom and Nora there, but I'm so fucking tired. And I can't… Everyone is too quiet… it's unbearable," he said, and I rubbed the goose bumps from his arms as he pulled away. "All I want to do is sleep, but I don't know if I'll be able to."

"You need to try." His exhaustion had carved itself into the dark circles under his swollen eyes, his gait unsteady as he tried to take a step toward the couch. "Come on, let's go upstairs. You should lie down."

"Yeah."

We made our way up the stairs, and as I opened the guest bedroom door, Maribelle pushed her way inside. "There's an extra blanket in the closet if you want it. I know how cold you get at night."

His lips parted in a quiet smile, softening the sorrow around his eyes. "Thanks." Luka sat on the edge of the bed and kicked off his shoes. Belle snuffled her nose against his socked feet and his smile widened. He leaned down and scratched the top of her head as I hovered in the doorway. When he raised his gaze again, his humor faded. "I don't want to be alone."

"Do you want me to sit with you for a while?"

"Until I fall asleep?"

"If that's what you need."

"I'm afraid to fall asleep. What if I forget he's gone, and I have to remember all over again when I wake up? I feel like if I stay awake eventually it won't hurt as much."

"I think it will always hurt, Luka."

He swallowed, his lips trembling again and exhaled a ragged breath. I walked toward the bed, and he grabbed the side of my shirt, pressing his forehead into my stomach. "Stay with me."

"I will." I ran my fingers down the long line of his neck. "As long as you need."

He scooted to the other side of the mattress, and I pulled the covers back, a swell of nostalgia filling my stomach. We were kids the last time we'd slept in the same bed. Two boys talking about books and dreams, when the future had been as far away as the stars in the sky, and the worst things to worry about had been report cards and making it home by curfew. There was no heartache, no loss, just life to be lived, trees to sit under, and a hand to hold in the dark. Here in this bed, there were miles between us. We stared at the ceiling, our heads on our pillows with heavy hearts beating inside our chests.

"We had a good day," he finally said after several minutes, and I turned to face him. "We watched DIY shows and had lunch together. We talked about you… and what a fucking idiot I am." His laugh clogged inside his throat. "The nurse came, and he showered, and she said everything was fine. He took his medicine and put on that ugly sweater Nora had gotten him as a joke. Jesus, I can't even remember what it was for." Luka went still and scrubbed a palm over his face. "Maybe that should have clued me in, maybe he knew… But Mom came home and started on dinner. It was like any other normal fucking afternoon. He was awake the whole time, Rook. He looked like himself again. He did. He looked so good. And after Nora got there, we all ate together." Luka stared at me, the tears on his cheeks glowing in the moonlight pouring in from the open blinds. "Dad insisted on watching that stupid movie he loved…"

"*Airplane*."

"Yeah… and we all gave him shit, but of course, we watched it because it's Dad, you know, and we all secretly love that stupid fucking movie." Luka swiped his hand across his face and curled onto his side. He reached for me, fiddling with the sleeve of my shirt, and I brushed that perpetual strand of his hair off his forehead. "Dad fell asleep about halfway through the movie and…" He choked on a sob, his face contorting as he fought to find the words. "When… when Mom tried to wake him up to say good night… Rook… he didn't wake up. He didn't wake up and it was chaos. I've never seen my mom cry like that, and I… Nora…"

I drew us together until his heat was my heat, and his breath was on my skin. I kissed his cheek, kissed the tender skin below each of his eyes as he closed them, kissed the tip of his nose, and carded my fingers through his hair. He shivered and snuggled into me, his hands tied up between us.

"Your dad was basically my second father," I managed to say, my heart stuttering as I tried to hold myself together for my best friend. "Your family… my second home. And I… I…" My nostrils flared, the lump in my throat doubling in size making it next to impossible to speak. "Luka…" I said, my voice wavering. "Christ, I'm so—"

"Don't say you're sorry. Please." His jaw clenched, and he wiped a tear from my top lip with the tip of his finger. "It won't fix anything."

"I know."

Seconds ticked by with his eyes on mine, my fingers trailing down his neck and along his spine, I'd completed the circuit a few times until he closed his eyes again. His breathing evened out and I thought he was asleep. I debated on whether or not I should stay here like this or go back to my own bed, and decided I didn't care about right and wrong anymore. I didn't care about the kiss or those fucking boundaries, or the feelings I had to work through. I needed to be here for him, and maybe I needed him too. I didn't want to be alone either. I didn't think I could stay away after having him this close again. Another piece of his hair had flopped over his brows, and I gently pushed it to the side. Luka appeared to be at peace, the tension in his face relaxed. Even though I probably shouldn't, I rested my forehead against his.

"Rook," he whispered, startling me. I attempted to pull away, but he captured my face between the palms of his hands. "Kiss me again."

"Not like this, Luka."

"I need to feel something besides this hole in my chest. It hurts to breathe." Vulnerable, glittering blue eyes held me hostage as my heart stammered out a few clumsy beats. "I need to feel it. I need to know you meant it. When you kissed me before…" His lips were feather soft against the corner of my mouth as he moved closer. We were nose to nose, his thumbs digging into the line of my jaw. "I don't want you to *try*, Rook. I need you to know… Like I've known since that first day when you held my hand in the woods. I was yours then, and I'm yours now."

I didn't understand this urgency building inside the tips of my fingers, this static need crackling like a wildfire inside me.

I was yours then.

"Do you really want this?" he asked. "Do you want me?"

I'm yours now.

"Yes."

"Yes?"

"I want you." More tears spilled over his lashes, and he was all salt and breath as I kissed his top lip. "I didn't know… but I always have."

Luka and I were like two rivers, raging toward the same open sea, and there wasn't a thing in this world, not death or distance or time, or even my own naivety that would keep us apart.

CHAPTER FOURTEEN

Luka

I WANT YOU.

I always have.

Those two sentences, those six words, were like a dream. I was floating, light under my own skin, the only thing holding me to the earth was Rook's warm mouth as it covered mine, unsure and slow. His lips were wet with tears, his cheeks too. I didn't know if this was smart, or if I was opening myself up for more hurt once the sun was in the sky and tomorrow offered me no relief from yesterday. The only relief I had was right now, with Rook and those six words and his mouth and the way he cradled my face in his hands. I was fragile, but he'd always known how to carry me. I grasped his hip, dragging our bodies together as a rush of heat spread through me. Lighting me up, it burned away the images of the day, and I opened my eyes to find Rook's open too. Our lips parted as we looked into each other's eyes, my thumb brushing small circles above the waistline of his sweats, his fingers tracing shapes on the back of my neck.

"Luka." He leaned in, leaving less than an inch between our lips. "Luka," he whispered my name again, and I shivered as his mouth claimed mine.

Somewhere in the fog, the truth of this day lurked, waiting to ambush me, but I couldn't think, and I didn't want to. All I wanted was him. I deepened the kiss, pulling Rook's bottom lip through my teeth. His groan shook me to the core. I'd known this man my whole life. He was the first boy I'd ever wanted, the first man I'd ever loved, and I never thought I'd get to have him like this, never thought I'd be the one to unravel him. The blunt tips of his fingers sifted through my hair, holding my head, controlling the kiss as I moaned into his mouth. He tasted like toothpaste and memories. Every nerve ending in my body was ready to combust, and I pressed my hips into his, needing to feel him, to feel the weight of the man I'd craved since I'd understood what it meant to want. Rook's breath hitched as my eager and clumsy hands found their way to the ties of his sweats and pulled them open.

"Wait." He stopped me, grabbing my wrist. "Luka, we shouldn't… you're not—"

"I know what I need right now."

"Do you?" he asked.

"I don't want to think about anything except us." I kissed his chin, nuzzled the line of his jaw, drinking in his scent, smokey pine and earth, and I was home. "Please."

"You're hurting… I don't want you to regret anything."

"I'd never regret you," I breathed. "Never." A quiet concession flashed across his eyes as he released my wrist. "I need you, Rook. Just you."

"I need you too."

He brushed his knuckles across my right cheek and leaned down to kiss me. My fingers skimmed underneath the elastic of his sweats, my nails skimming the trail of hair that disappeared below his boxer briefs. Rook shuddered and rolled me onto my back, pinning my body between his powerful thighs. He straddled me, his hands splayed under my shirt and over my stomach. I counted five of his breaths, his chest rising and falling deeper and deeper with every second that passed. With him like this, in the dark, it was easy to believe there wasn't a nightmare waiting for me outside. I sat up and helped him out of his t-shirt and stripped mine off as well. The air was dense, filled with a chilled electricity, and I struggled to catch my breath as Rook traced the lines of the tattoo along my arm and up to my shoulder and collarbone.

"This is our fort," he whispered, his fingers pausing over the shaded blue sky. "Our tree."

"It is."

He cupped my cheek, his thumb swiping across my parted lips. I linked my arms around his waist, reveling in the feel of his skin, in every etched muscle of his back. Our mouths met with a needy crash of teeth and tongues. It was overwhelming. This was Rook. My best friend. And as far as I knew he'd never been with a guy before. Feeling like a selfish asshole, I broke the kiss, and he reached up, sweeping the back of his hand across my sternum. He turned his palm and rested it in the center of my chest. Rook was breathless, his amber eyes two pools of fire and wonder. And even though I'd always wanted him like this, and needed him now more than ever, I didn't want him to do anything he wasn't ready for. And he would, I realized, for me. He would do anything.

"I don't want to rush you," I said and touched my forehead to his shoulder. I turned my head and tasted the crook of his neck. His hand slid down to my stomach, his finger hooking through one of the belt loops of my jeans. "I wouldn't want you to do something out of guilt or pity."

"This has nothing to do with guilt or pity, Luka." I held onto him tighter, keeping myself moored. "We could go to sleep right now, if that's what you wanted, and I'd be content, but..."

He swallowed and his throat moved against my lips. I could hide like this, buried in the curve of his neck, or I could face him. Face whatever he had to say, take whatever he had to offer. Being with Rook in any capacity was all I'd ever wanted. I lifted my head, and he pushed the ever-present strands of my hair out of my eyes.

"You need a haircut." He gave me a wistful smile.

"Yeah, I know."

"I've never felt like this before," he finally said. "I've always forced my way through attraction, but with you... I want this. I want to see where it goes. I want to be with you, but I..." He lowered his eyes and huffed out a quiet, embarrassed laugh. "I'm a little out of my depth."

"Hey..." I lifted his chin, kissed the side of his mouth. "We can go at whatever pace you need. I just want to be close to you. I don't need anything else."

146

Rook grasped the back of my neck, drawing us together again, his kiss intense, like he'd been holding it in his whole life, his tongue at war with mine. He unlatched the button on my jeans, and I leaned back onto my elbows. "Can I touch you?" he asked, and I nodded, unable to speak.

I was too struck by the beauty of this man, my friend, and how I'd envisioned something like this probably about a billion times, and it was happening at last. That dark shadow looming in the corner of my thoughts was still there, all the things I'd refused to process tonight waiting for when I closed my eyes and let sleep have me. But as Rook blanketed my body, his skin soft and warm, the shadow faded enough I didn't notice it anymore. Desire coiled deep in my belly, burning hotter as he kissed the top of my tattoo on the edge of my collarbone, the divot between my pecs, the ridges of my abs, and pulled my jeans and underwear to my knees. Rook's breath stuttered as my cock sprung free, a nervous glint sparking in his eyes.

He rubbed the tops of my thighs, his breath uneven as he crawled down my body and lowered his lips to my hip. He lingered there for three, four, five seconds before he kissed the top of my pubic bone, my belly, then back to my hip. I skated a hand over the back of his head, the rough feel of his clipped hair a satisfying scratch under my palm. Trapping my bottom lip between my teeth, I couldn't find my breath, couldn't move, he was breaking me apart with tiny kisses and soft touches, exploring every millimeter of my skin with his mouth. He nestled his nose against the junction of my inner thigh, his fingers shaking where they'd settled on my waist. I was out of my skin, almost ready to beg when he pressed his cheek against my thigh, his hot breath washing over the base of my cock as he closed his eyes.

"Tell me what you like."

"This," I said, a little too enthusiastic. "I like this."

He opened his eyes and lifted them to meet mine. "I'm not sure what I'm doing."

I raised myself up onto an elbow and ran my fingers along the curve of his jaw. "Are you sure about that," I said, and smiled as the brown color of his cheeks deepened. "You're making me crazy."

"I am?"

"I was about two seconds away from begging you not to stop."

"I don't want to stop." He shifted, and my hands fell to my sides, my fingers curling into the sheets as his lips brushed the head of my cock. "I've never done this, but I want to. I have this need... to keep going, and I've never had that before."

My back bowed off the mattress as his tongue licked along my shaft. "Fuck..." He licked the bead of moisture from the tip, a low sound rumbling in the back of his throat. "Rook... please."

He took his time studying my body with careful touches, grazing his cheek up the length of my cock, turning his nose into my groin, inhaling as he gripped my base with strong fingers. A moan parted my lips as he stroked me, his thumb pressing into the sensitive spot below the crown with every pass. My body took over and I lifted my hips, fucking his fist as he watched with a scorching fascination. The blood in my veins thrashed, rebelled, racing faster and faster as he finally took me into his mouth, the wet heat too much, with every shallow, uncoordinated taste, with every pump of his fist, and I forced myself to slow down, to breathe through the intense pleasure. Rook's cheeks hollowed, working me to the back of his throat, and I choked on a ragged groan when he gagged.

"Shit, are you okay?" I asked, and he came up for air. "I'm sorry… I… Shit, I'm sorry."

"I'm okay," he said.

"If you hate this, God if you do…" I sat up and brushed his cheek. "It's alright… Rook, it's—"

"I don't hate this." He kissed me, and I could taste myself on his tongue, and it was fucking perfect with inevitability, with us, and it was enough to wake me up, to let go of the last pieces of myself that I'd hidden away, that I'd protected just in case. In case he realized this wasn't what he actually wanted. In case he realized I wasn't for him. "Luka… I don't hate this at all." He drifted his thumb over my cheek, along my jaw, his mouth following along the same path. I whimpered as he sucked on my neck, biting my shoulder hard enough I was sure it would leave a bruise. "I want you." He took my hand in his and lowered it to the rock-hard evidence of his desire. "This all feels so different from anything I've experienced. Being with you, it means more… you mean so much to me. I—"

He didn't finish his sentence, pushing me down onto my back. I kicked my jeans off the rest of the way, while working his sweats over his hips. Once we were both naked, and skin to skin, I could breathe deeply again. Our bodies aligned, clicked into place, my hips fitting into his, his hands fitting my cheek, our mouths moving in sync, like a dance we'd somehow already known. My legs wrapped around him as we rutted together, seeking, needing. Rook held one of my hands above my head, threading his fingers through mine, and the quiet, cold night caught fire with the sound of our bodies, our moans as we lost ourselves in each other. My heels dug into the backs of his thighs, my free hand grasping the firm curve of his ass, needing him closer, harder. I rocked my hips, grinding into him. We were both slick and sticky with pre-come and sweat and I was losing my battle, the urgency of his thick cock sliding against mine, it was too much. I needed to come, I needed to scream, I needed to keep going and never stop.

"Luka," he said my name in a hoarse whisper, his hips jerking once before his entire body went rigid.

His head dropped, his mouth open and panting above my lips as he came in hot bursts onto my stomach. My hand slipped from his grip above my head, falling to his hips as I teetered over the edge, writhing underneath him until I cried out his name too. The pressure of my climax washed over me, rooted me to this man above me, this man I'd always loved and thought I'd never have. I held onto him, my legs shaking, my eyes burning with humiliating tears. I blinked a few times but couldn't stop the traitorous moisture from trickling down my cheeks.

"Luka... What's wrong? Shit, did I do something you didn't want?"

"No, God..." I shook my head, the absurdity of crying after sex made a strangled chuckle bubble up my throat. "I'm... Jesus. I don't know why I'm crying."

Rook kissed my tears, my lips, the heat of our orgasms quickly fading, drying on our skin. He rolled onto his side, and I moved onto mine, facing him. He picked up his t-shirt from somewhere and cleaned us both before tossing it back into the oblivion of the room. A place that didn't exist to me beyond this bed, beyond him and me, and what we'd done.

Rook was all anxiety and concern as his serious, dark eyes assessed me. "You can cry. You just lost your dad." He sighed, kissing my forehead and held my face in his hand. I leaned into the touch. "I shouldn't have… we shouldn't… Shit… I didn't want you to regret it, but I understand if you—"

"Stop. I don't regret a fucking second of what just happened." I looked him in the eyes and covered his hand with mine. "Truthfully, I'd do it again, and again, until we couldn't feel our lips if you were up for it, and not because I lost my dad, and I'm a fucking mess, and I'd rather get off than deal with it, but because I need my best friend. Because… I love you."

"I love you, Luka. You know that."

"I know." I dropped my hand to his chest, trailing my fingers through the hints of hair there. "But it's always been different for me, and maybe I got a little emotional because I can't believe I get to have you like this."

"I always thought I'd end up alone," he said after a few tense seconds and scooped me into his arms. And like the needy guy I was, I snuggled deeper into his hold. "I've been confused for a long time."

"Confused about your sexuality?"

"Yes, and how I never fit with anyone like other people do." His fingers sketched the plunging line of my hip bone and the curve of every one of my ribs. "Nothing has ever come close to this, to tonight. Sex has always been an expected step, something that was unavoidable if I wanted to be romantically involved with someone. Sometimes it was okay, but I never had a chance to get to know the women I dated on the level I needed to let myself be vulnerable with them. And they'd get annoyed, or think I wasn't attracted to them, and then it was over before I could get to know them well enough to really want sex. The closest I ever came to something real was with Elle, but we were too young."

"And you never thought about dating men?" I asked, and he smiled, seeing through my passive-aggressive jealousy.

"There was this guy I thought was attractive in college. We got along pretty well, and he was into Magic, but he had a girlfriend. I think the attraction I had for him was just a reflection of how much I missed you. Missed what we had together."

"I missed you every day I was gone."

"Even when you had Graham?"

"I missed you more when I had him. He was never going to fill the void. And I feel like a dick for saying that because I did care about him." Rook's fingertips distracted me, tickling their way up my spine, leaving wakes of prickling goose bumps on my skin. "He wasn't you," I said and kissed the quiet dimple in his cheek.

"I'm nervous. What if I disappoint you?"

"No one is perfect, Rook. I know that."

"But..." he hesitated, avoiding my eyes, every raw nerve we'd exposed tonight left uncovered and stinging between us. "It's been difficult for me, in the past, and there's no one I'd rather be with, but I can't promise..." He exhaled, exasperated, and I rested my palm on the small of his back, and he relaxed under my touch. We were connected, his knee touching mine, his hand on my neck, our feet tangled. "I can't promise sex will always be easy."

"This wasn't easy," I said, and Rook held my gaze. "And it shouldn't be. If I wanted it easy, I could have found some guy on Grindr. But I don't want that anymore. I want to fall asleep like this. I want to stay wrapped up with you until you complain about it being too hot." He laughed and I shrugged. "You've always hated getting overheated."

"You're oversimplifying."

"I don't have the mental capacity to under simplify."

"I should let you sleep," he said, and I tucked my head under his chin.

"Rook."

"Yeah?"

"I like sex. But I love you."

His chuckle ruffled my hair. "Love you too."

"I don't need you to make me any promises."

"Alright." He skated a gentle palm down my back, and I yawned.

The smell of Rook's skin permeated the air, but somewhere in the background I heard the jingle of Maribelle's collar. The sound of reality biding its time. The pain I'd evaded snuck around my heart with every beat of my pulse, and my mother's voice whispered in my ear, *he's gone. He's gone.* I closed my eyes, and focused on Rook's touch, on the heat of his body, like bright sunlight, and it was safe and comfortable and mine.

CHAPTER FIFTEEN

Rook

"UGH, YOU'RE LIKE AN *octopus," I groaned and tried to untangle myself from Luka's hold. The small tent was overheated, sunlight bleeding through the hole in the rainfly, the humidity heavier than it had been the day before. Sweat beaded across my forehead, on my back, and across Luka's chest. "Come on, man. I'm dying."*

He didn't budge, muttering something about being cold, while his sleeping bag stuck to the side of his damp face. I suppressed a laugh when he squeezed me tighter, snuggling against my chest. I stole the opportunity to count the new freckles on his nose, to be close to him even if I was melting from the inside out. This was the last chance we'd have to camp before school started, the last chance we'd have like this before we started ninth grade.

High school.

It made my stomach feel empty. I was probably stupid for being worried, and I thought maybe other kids would be excited about starting a new grade and a new school, but it made me sad. Things were shifting, moving forward, and I wasn't ready. Luka had started to put some distance between us lately. He had always been affectionate, and I never minded it. It was just our way. But some of our friends gave us crap, him more so than me, and recently, he'd started to pull away. Even when we were in private, he'd choose to sit on the floor instead of next to me on the bed or couch when we watched movies or went over our next D&D campaign. Maybe it was part of growing up. Maybe he didn't need me like he used to. I figured when he finally woke up, he'd be embarrassed about clinging to me like a koala, but if this was my last chance to hang out with him like this, sweating my balls off or not, I'd take it.

Luka stirred again, groaning, and wiping his wet strands of hair from his forehead. "Are you awake?" I asked and laughed when one of his eyes popped open.

My humor didn't last long. As soon as he realized he was strapped to me like a backpack he rolled away immediately and sat up. "Shit, sorry. I…" He stared down at his knobby knees and shook his head like he was trying to shake away the sleep from his eyes. Luka cleared his throat, his cheeks red as he stood abruptly. "I gotta take a piss."

He was out of the tent before I could even tease him about the way his hair was sticking up on the back of his head. Things were definitely different, and as the cool air from outside washed over me, stealing the remaining heat Luka had left behind, I shivered.

My alarm on my phone went off around five-thirty, and I expected Luka to be stuck to me like a sucker fish like he used to do when we were kids, but his side of the bed was empty and cold. I stood on wobbly legs, rubbing my bleary eyes with my fists, and yawned. I grabbed my sweats from the floor and pulled my phone from the pocket, silencing the alarm. Half asleep, I shuffled and stumbled through getting dressed, remembering at the last minute, the shirt I'd had on last night was a lost cause, and tossed it. I didn't bother with getting a clean shirt, too worried about Luka. The kitchen light streamed down the hallway, Maribelle's collar jingling and I followed the sound. I found Luka sitting at the kitchen table in a pair of my sweats, with Belle's head at his feet. I would have smiled at the fact he'd helped himself to my clothes, and that his hair was sticking every which way like the old days, but Luka's eyes were swollen and red like he hadn't slept at all.

"Hey," I whispered and bent down, kissing his temple. "You didn't sleep, did you?"

"About an hour." His smile was weary. "You have to work today?"

"I'm going to text Charity, if my dad hasn't already, and tell her what's going on. I don't have any inductions scheduled today, and it's not a big deal to move appointments around."

"Inductions?"

"Scheduled deliveries. Babies and all that." I gave him a crooked smile, and it cracked through the sorrow, his lips lifting up at the corners.

"And all that. Sounds fun." Luka raised his brows with a half-hearted effort, and I sat down next to him, pressing the sides of our thighs together. I stared at the intricate ink on his arm, the details of our childhood etched with permanence into his skin.

It was beautiful. I wanted to reach out and touch it again, but I didn't know if he'd want me to. Luka beat me to it though and took my hand in his. He laced our fingers together, keeping his eyes on the table. "Are we… I mean, are you freaking out about last night?"

"No. Are you?"

"No." He lifted his eyes, his thumb rubbing deep, nervous circles into my palm. "I think I'm processing… all of it."

Everything that happened last night lingered against my skin, phantom touches and kisses on my lips and jaw. I could feel every mark, every moment, and I didn't regret anything. I'd gone so long without understanding how it could be, treading water in a gray and empty sea, getting momentary glimpses of light, but nothing I could ever grab ahold of, nothing I ever wanted. And then Luka. Luka, whom I'd known and loved, he broke through all the gray and showed me how amazing touch could feel, how a kiss was supposed to taste, how losing yourself and letting go wasn't a perfunctory obligation, but vivid fireworks in a clear sky.

"A lot has happened."

"I'm trying to separate it all in my head. The good and the bad, and it all feels like one big fucking mess, and I don't want to feel that way, not about you." He swallowed, his voice gruff as he spoke. "Not about us."

Maribelle moved under the table, her tail thumping against the floor as she stretched her head across both mine and Luka's legs. I ran my fingers through her curls as I worried about what to say, or that I might say the wrong thing and push him away. Last night had happened fast, and it was unexpected, but it was

157

everything I hadn't known I needed. Every sexual experience I'd had before last night seemed like a lie. I thought being intimate came with the baggage of a relationship, when in reality the one thing that had always been missing, I'd already had with Luka. We'd been intimate in a way that hadn't ever been related to sex, and it had taken me forever to get it. All those years and memories, it was a turn on. His smile, I knew it like the back of my hand, his smell, his laugh, these were all things that made him attractive to me, made me want to open up and share myself with him. I was safe with Luka. There wasn't another person in this world who knew me better than him, and I wanted him in every way. It was foreign, this feeling of desire, and I had to find a way to balance it with what Luka needed from me now. His father had died, and the last thing I wanted was to become another complication in his life.

"Luka, you can't help how you feel. I get it, you need time to figure out if this is what you want. You're grieving, and I don't want to be another thing you have to worry about."

"What? No… You're the only good thing in this whole situation. I can't go backward."

"I can't either."

He leaned over and brushed a soft kiss across my lips. "I didn't think we'd ever get here."

"Promise to tell me how you feel from now on," I said and grazed a finger across his cheek. "And I'll do the same."

"I can try. But it's hard breaking habits. I have a lot of experience hiding how I feel from you."

"I'm sorry you never felt like you could tell me."

"I knew I could tell you, and if you didn't feel the same, you'd have been kind about it. You wouldn't have let it ruin our friendship, but I was terrified I would, and I almost did. These past five years, I was such an idiot."

"I know." I smiled and pulled him into a hug, Maribelle groaning as her head slipped from our laps. "But we're not going backward, remember. What's done is done."

Holding my face in his hands, he kissed me with reverent lips, long and deep, igniting the dormant flame inside me, and I was alive with it. Awake, that gray ocean dissipating into the thick air as Luka's teeth sank into my bottom lip.

"I don't want to face this day," he whispered, and we were nose to nose, his forehead pressed to mine.

"I won't leave your side."

"Promise?"

I heard the click of his throat as he swallowed, felt the heat of his hand on the back of my neck.

"I promise."

It was barely seven when we walked into Luka's house. His mom and sister were already up and making tea in the kitchen, though the stark circles under their eyes made me think they hadn't gotten much sleep either. Guilt pinched at my chest as his mom gave me a sad smile.

"I'm glad you're here," she said, and I hugged her.

She didn't cry, just squeezed me tight like I was the one who needed the comfort. My eyes might have started to burn. "Eliza, God."

"He was an amazing person," she said, her voice too calm. Too steady as she released me from her embrace. "He didn't deserve to have his life cut this short."

"No, he didn't." Luka pulled his mom into his arms, and her shoulders started to shake. Nora looked away, her glassy brown eyes overflowing. "I'm sorry I left last night... I needed—"

"Don't be." His mom wiped his cheeks, and then her own. "You did what you had to do."

"Are you okay?" Nora asked, and Luka nodded.

"I mean, no, but yeah." He looked at me and his lips twitched as he took my hand. "I think I will be."

"He's not suffering anymore." Eliza stared at the empty hospice bed. "He had a good day...went on his own terms... He—" She cleared her throat, tucking her hair behind her ears. "If you'll excuse me, I need to use the bathroom."

His mom left the kitchen as the tea kettle on the stove started to whistle. Nora stood stock still, and Luka stared at it like he'd never seen the thing before. I let go of his hand and removed the kettle from the heat. I opened the cabinet, grabbing Nora's favorite lavender tea, and Eliza's Earl Grey. I set the bags in the mugs already waiting on the counter and poured the hot water. I moved around the kitchen like it was my own, in some ways it was, and pulled out the creamer from the fridge and the sugar from the rack above the stove. I moved around the bodies in the room like they were ghosts—watching me—the silence overhearing, quelled only by the soft thud of a cabinet door closing and the brusque slide of the silverware drawer as it opened.

"I can't remember if you like sugar in your tea?" I asked Nora and she sucked in a breath like I'd broken her from a trance.

"Um... yeah. Thanks."

I stirred in a few teaspoons and handed her the mug. She set it on the counter and tackled me into a hug. Big, wet sobs cracked through her chest, and I stared over her shoulder at her brother who was on the verge of falling apart himself. For a second, I felt like I didn't have the right to be there, like I shouldn't have come at all, like maybe I was some strange voyeur to all this heartache that didn't truly belong to me. But then Luka linked his arms around the both of us, and we all cried for the man who had been a father to us all.

For the first few days after Isaac died, I'd stayed with Luka as I'd promised. Maribelle was all too happy to serve as the happy distraction, while my folks helped keep everyone fed. Nora and I cleaned while Luka and my dad helped Eliza with the funeral arrangements. There wasn't much for them to do since his dad had already set up most of it when he first got sick. Which I thought must have been a terrible thing to have to think about on top of a cancer diagnosis. It put into perspective how fleeting everything could be. One minute you're making meatloaf, and the next you're planning your own funeral.

Every day had been the same as the one before, long and hard fought, all of us floating around one another. The nights were worse. I could hear Eliza crying through her bedroom door, and Nora disappeared inside the photo albums that had been left out on the coffee table downstairs. Luka was in his own world too. During the day, he'd leave for an hour or so with his camera, no doubt losing himself behind his lens somewhere in the murky light of the forest, and at night, once we were alone, he'd allow himself to break down. Every day I told myself it wasn't too much to bear. Luka was my family. But I couldn't deny the slight relief it had given when my cell phone rang around eleven Sunday night. One of my patients had gone into labor, and I'd just ended the call with the hospital when Luka walked into the bedroom with a towel tied around his waist. I didn't want to leave, but I thought maybe a break could be good for the both of us. He needed space to think, and maybe I did too.

He gave me a quiet smile as he rubbed another towel through his hair. I watched the rivulets of water drip down the planes of his chest and abs, each drop taking a leisurely stroll along his skin until they disappeared in the soft trail of hair below his belly button. My body heated and I averted my eyes.

"Everything okay?" he asked, and I pushed my phone into my back pocket.

"Yeah... I have to head to the hospital. My patient's water broke."

I wasn't used to the sensation of arousal, at least not like this. Luka took care of his body. He was lean muscle and lithe limbs with broad shoulders that tapered down into narrow hips. These were all things I used to think were objectively attractive, nothing I would have ever cared about. But after last Thursday, after what had happened between us, there were times I couldn't stop myself from thinking about his mouth and his hands, and the way he'd touched me—the way he'd made me feel. Nothing had happened between us since then, and I hadn't expected it to. I was grateful to get to be there for him, grateful to sleep next to him, and hold him until he fell asleep.

"Oh..." His shoulders slumped, but he tried to hide it, turning to throw one of the towels into the laundry basket by his closet. "I guess it's back to life."

I stood and the springs in his mattress creaked. He watched my reflection in the mirror above his dresser. Wrapping my arms around him from behind, I kissed him below his ear. His skin was hot from the shower, his pulse throbbing beneath my lips. "Hopefully it won't take long."

"You're coming back?" He turned in my arms, his blue eyes hopeful.

"I have to, you have my dog," I teased, and he shoved me in the chest. "Where is she, by the way?"

"Nora's room. She's a pet thief."

"Maybe she needs someone too."

He draped his arms around my neck, his mouth sliding over mine with a soft sigh. "I guess I am the lucky one. I have you."

I hummed against his lips, and he parted them for me. If I didn't have to leave, I would stay like this for as long as he would have me, his skin under my palm, his sweet tongue in my mouth. But babies were not accustomed to waiting for people to deliver them, and I had to leave or chance having another provider, or one of the nurses, catching this kid.

"I have to go."

His fingers bunched in the cotton of my hoodie, and he kissed me again, urgent, once, and then again, before tearing himself away with the cutest, sulkiest expression on his face. "I'll be okay."

"It's good, Luka. To have some time for yourself. It's healthy."

"I know you can't stay here forever, and you need time, too, but it's been nice. Makes me think about all the summers we had as kids, without all the pubescent stink."

"We were inseparable."

"Yeah."

"Hey…" I pressed a kiss to his cheek and pulled my keys from my pocket. "I'll be back soon. I can stay here as long as you need me to. But I think you need to spend some one-on-one time with your mom and sister too. I want to be here for you, but you need to process with your family."

"Maybe. But it's easier when you're here."

"I'm not a crutch, Luka. I'm your friend."

"Just a friend?" he asked and leaned in, running the tip of his nose along my throat.

"I don't think we've ever been *just* friends." I cupped his cheek, tracing the curve of his lip with my thumb. "You're not alone. Nora is down the hall. And I think your mom would love some company."

"They make it all feel too real."

"It's real, Luka… Your dad… your family… me…" I hugged him to my chest, and he squeezed his arms around my ribcage. "I'll come back as soon as I can."

"I love you," he said, the words wet and shaky. "You're right…" He raised his eyes. "Maybe tomorrow you can stay at your place. Mom wants to finalize the memorial, and… maybe it'll be a good time for all of us to just… mourn him."

"I think that's a good idea." I leaned down, resting my hands on his shoulders as I looked him in the eye. "You're stronger than you think you are."

"Sure."

"You are." I gave him another quick kiss, and he lowered his arms to his sides. "Get dressed, or better yet, don't. It will give me something to look forward to while I'm gone."

A real smile split his face, his cheeks flushing with color for the first time since Thursday. "Rook... you can't say stuff like that and then just leave me here."

"Bye, Luka."

"Wait," he grumbled. "Rook, come on." I waved at him over my shoulder as I opened his bedroom door. "You're the worst," he said, but there was too much humor in his tone to take him seriously.

"Love you too," I said and heard him laugh as I made my way down the hallway.

It was pure, like all the years I'd known him, genuine and bright.

All of this was real. But it was ours to bear.

And the fear, the anxiety of how the hell we'd make it through this loss, that heavy weight I'd been carrying around all weekend, fell off my shoulders and tumbled to the ground.

CHAPTER SIXTEEN

Luka

TIME EBBED AND FLOWED. The last week had been the longest and shortest of my life. I wasn't sure how it was already Friday, and how I'd found myself sitting on the couch, in my parents' home, surrounded by people I hadn't seen in years, with a copy of *The Harbor Herald* laid out in front of me on the coffee table. Everything was a blur. The droning, polite conversation spilled around me and buzzed inside my brain. I yanked at the tie around my neck, attempting to take a breath. My collar was damp with sweat, my fingers shaking as I stared at the photo I'd taken of my father in black and white on the front page of the newspaper. Hometown Hero was scrolled across the top of the page, but in a much smaller italicized font beneath the bold headline was the truth added by the editor. *Dead at sixty-seven. Gone too soon.* My tribute to my father had turned into a full-page obituary. I wasn't sure how that made me feel.

Mostly empty. Mostly sad.

"Are you hungry?" Rook sat next to me on the sofa and pressed his knee against mine. "You should eat something."

"I don't think I can," I said. "My stomach is off."

He looked good. I hadn't seen him in a suit since his college graduation. He was all tailored and put together, and I had a toothpaste stain on my tie. Part of me felt ashamed for caring about trivial shit on today of all days. I buried my father this afternoon.

"Maybe some water?" he asked, and I nodded.

"Yeah, that sounds good, actually." I tried for a smile.

"I'll be right back."

The couch shifted as he moved, and the low hum of chatter broke through my bubble. I looked up from the paper and scanned the room. It was a sea of people with frowns and finger foods, whispering to each other about my dad while shooting furtive glances at me and my family. Rook's parents flanked my mom, keeping her in a protective cocoon while these same people offered forced smiles and pity. It was all so barbaric. Why couldn't we mourn alone as a family? Why did we have to entertain like we'd had a wedding and not a funeral? It wasn't a celebration of life, it was a free meal and a way for people to insert themselves into others' misery, like the same way most people stared at car accidents as they drove by. They wanted to get a glimpse of tragedy, something interesting to talk about over dinner, a way to feel better about their own lives, all to say, "God, I'm glad that wasn't me."

I checked my watch and sighed. We still had an hour left of this nightmare. I stood, abandoning the paper and the picture of my father. I needed a reprieve from my own thoughts, from the heat of the room, and the watchful eyes. It was all too much. The day too long.

I started for the front door and made it halfway before Nora stopped me. "Escaping already?"

"I need some fresh air."

She popped a stuffed mushroom in her mouth and grimaced. "I've eaten about a pound of these. And they're not even good."

"How can you eat right now?"

"Some people get drunk, some cry, I eat. It's the only thing that helps."

I noticed the dark smudges under her eyes, evidence of her tears and the lack of the waterproof mascara she'd begged me to buy the night before. "I might get drunk later."

"Sounds like a solid plan." She tucked a lock of her dark hair behind her ears. "Maybe after I drive Anders and Ethan to their hotel, I'll join you."

"I can't believe your old boss and his husband flew all the way from Atlanta for this."

"I can. Anders would do literally anything to support his friends."

"He didn't know Dad."

"It doesn't matter. You didn't know him, but you still came with me to his wedding."

"Not the same thing."

"I miss working for him sometimes," she said and tossed another mushroom into her mouth.

"You haven't found a house yet. You could go back to Atlanta. I bet Anders would give you your job back."

"No…" Nora placed her empty plate on the sideboard table and tucked her hands into the pockets of her navy-blue dress. "Mom is here, you're here, and after… after everything, I guess you never know how much time you have. And I want to spend it with people I love."

"Yeah… me too," I said, regret niggling through my ribcage. "I wish I would have figured that out sooner. If I could go back, I wouldn't have ever moved to Los Angeles."

"You're here now. Make the most of it." She leaned in and kissed my cheek. "Love you, big brother." Her voice trembled and I pulled her into a hug.

"If you see Rook," I whispered. "Tell him to meet me in the blue. He'll know what I mean."

She wiped at her eyes as she pulled away, making the smudges even worse, and sniffled.

"Um… yeah, sure."

Outside, the sun had almost set, and everything was bathed in a dull blue blanket. I had to hug myself to stay warm as I walked down the path between my house and Rook's parents' house toward the forest. The trees stood at attention, watching over me like the sentries I'd imagined them to be when I was a kid. This forest, and all of its secrets, were ancient to me now. Like the life I'd lived here had happened centuries ago. If I closed my eyes, I could see it all unfold, see the sulky nine-year-old who never wanted to move in the first place, the pre-teen who had learned something too big and too scary about himself, the young man who'd fallen in love with his best friend, and the idiot who ran away from it all. But I kept my eyes open and stared at the fort that was barely a skeleton of itself after all these years, and wondered how all this time had passed me by.

"Why are you hiding up here?" my father asked, and I quickly swiped at my eyes with the back of my hand. His head peeked through the treehouse trap door, his smile falling. "What's the matter?"

"Nothing."

"Want to try again?"

Our gazes caught for a second before I dropped mine, staring at my knees like they were the most interesting thing in the world. "It's nothing, Dad. I needed some air."

"Don't you think you're getting too old for tree houses, son?"

I shot him a dirty look and he chuckled.

"I see." He waited, and when I didn't say anything, he wriggled his way through the small space and sat next to me. "Rook and his girlfriend just got here. Should I tell them—"

"Tell Rook I went out."

"Luka…"

"Please, Dad. I can't… I don't feel like going to the movies. Not tonight."

"You care about him," he said, and my heart threatened to shatter. "More than a friend?" My throat burned, too tight to speak as I nodded. His big hand enveloped my knee, and he leaned his back against the wood wall. "I thought so."

"You did?"

"When you came out to me and your mom… I wondered. I don't know. You're different with Rook than you are with anyone else. He lights you up. You make each other shine."

"Well… he's straight and has a girlfriend. Nothing shiny about that."

"He cares about you."

"Not like he cares about Ella."

"Maybe." Dad smiled at me, bumping me in my shoulder. "Rook's always been a patient kind of soul, you know what I mean? He takes his time. Maybe he hasn't seen it yet."

"He'll never see it," I said, slumping into my father's side. I rested my head on his shoulder. "I need to move the hell..." I cleared my throat, and he raised his brows. "The heck on."

"Do what you need to do, but I'm telling you, that boy cares for you." He patted my knee, then folded his hands in his lap. "Love takes time."

"You're so cheesy." I laughed, and he grinned. "Love takes time... God, where do you come up with this shi..." I cringed. "I mean... stuff."

"Your mother," he said and playfully shoved my shoulder. "She gives me all the good lines."

"I want what you guys have."

"You will."

"Yeah?"

He mussed my hair with his hand, and I groaned.

"Yes. Now go inside and tell your friend yourself you don't want to go to the movies. You can't hide your life away out here. You'll freeze to death."

"Luka..." A warm hand on the nape of my neck brought me racing back to the present. Rook's lips brushed the shell of my ear as he folded his arms around my waist. I pressed my back into his chest and dragged the damp air and his woodsy scent into my lungs. "Are you hiding?"

"Not from you."

"I thought you wanted a glass of water?"

"I needed this more."

Rook kissed the slope of my neck. "I wish the fort wouldn't collapse the minute we'd try to crawl in. Everything was easier when we were inside those four walls."

We both stood silent and stared at the ruins of our youth. I never thought I'd be here like this with him. With his arms around me, his lips pressed against my skin, his nose buried in my neck.

"My dad knew... even back then," I said low enough I wasn't sure I meant to say it out loud.

"About?"

"He knew how I felt about you... It was forever ago. When you were with Ella. You'd invited me to go to the movies with you, and I didn't want to go. He found me hiding out here. He knew.... He told me *love takes time*." A wet laugh wracked through me. "And I told him he was cheesy."

"Sounds like you."

I elbowed him in the ribs, and he laughed.

"Ow."

"You're supposed to be the supportive boyfriend today, not a jerk." Rook went quiet, and I realized what I'd said. "You know what I mean. I know we're not ready for all of that, and I don't expect—"

"Luka..." He placed his hands on my hips as I turned and faced him. He had a hint of a smile on his lips and shook his head. "What do you think this is?"

I chewed my bottom lip, too afraid and wary to say what I wanted. We hadn't spent the night together since last Sunday, and we hadn't done anything sexual since that first time beyond kissing. I realized that it wasn't really the ideal week to start exploring a sexual relationship with your best friend of twenty-three years. My emotions were all over the place, and I wanted to make the right choices this time. I didn't want to scare him away. "This is new for you."

"Is it?" he asked and cradled my chin between his thumb and forefinger. "I think we've known each other, loved each other, long enough that a word like boyfriend doesn't scare me. This is us, Luka. But more."

"Better?"

"Much," he said, and I kissed him, the sun fading somewhere behind the trees.

I hid my hands inside his suit jacket, holding onto his waist, wrinkling his well-pressed shirt. He slipped his fingers into the back pocket of my pants and pulled me closer. His hot breath tickled my lips as he spoke. "Are you okay?"

"I'm making it through."

"It's weird in there," he said, looking back and nodding toward my house. "Who the hell are all those people?"

A wild laugh broke past my lips, and my head tipped toward the sky. "Fuck if I know. I swear people from three counties over showed up for the stuffed mushrooms and cheese ball."

"I don't think they're here for the food. Your dad was a well-respected doctor. He was loved."

"He was," I said and swallowed through the gathering sentiment lodging itself in my throat. "I don't think I can go inside again. At least not yet."

"Want to go for a drive?" he asked. "We could check on Maribelle, and then come right back."

"Yes… please get me out of here."

"Then let's go."

On the way over to Rook's place, I shot my mom and Nora a text letting them know we were on our way to check on Maribelle, and that I promised to be back in time to clean up. Nora told me to take my time, Mom sent a one-word reply. *Lucky.* It gave me some peace knowing my mom, at least on the surface, had been handling everything well. She'd kept her humor all week even though there'd been times I was certain she'd wanted to throw something. She'd said to me this morning on the way to the church, "It's hard preparing for death. I don't think anyone is ever really ready, but at least we had some sort of warning. I sometimes wish he would have died suddenly, like a heart attack or something, instead of suffering as long as he did. He's not in pain anymore, and I have to remember that, even if my pain hasn't yet passed."

With time, maybe the pain would fade to the background, but there would always be holidays and birthdays and some days simply having breakfast without him. I hadn't said anything then, but I'd thought that the pain we all felt was here to stay.

Much to my chagrin, it didn't take very long to get to Rook's place even though he'd gone the long way around the park. He cut the engine and we both stared through the windshield. All of his windows were dark, except for the front where Maribelle stuck her nose through the curtains. Rook's chuckle drew my attention and he smiled.

"She's waiting for us."

"I'm worried once we go inside, I won't ever want to leave."

"You don't have to," he said, his amber eyes suddenly serious.

"I have to go back and clean. My mom will kill me if I leave all that mess for—"

"That's not what I meant," he said and shook his head. "When you're ready... you could stay here with me. If you wanted."

"Live together?"

"If you'd rather use the guest room, that works too. It just makes sense having you here." His certainty made me dizzy. "When you're ready," he reiterated.

He'd said it like it was this easy thing, like I'd thrown a penny in a well and said I wish, and the universe decided to grant me everything all at once.

"I want to say yes, but the practical part of my brain says maybe we should go on a few dates and, oh, I don't know, tell our parents about us before we move in together."

"Since when have you been the practical one?"

"Since now..." I said, and he pursed his lips like he did when he was overthinking something. "What are you brooding about over there?"

"This house... it's mine and I like it... but it's never been a home. It's felt lonely for a long time, and maybe it's too fast, and with all that has happened this past week, I shouldn't have mentioned it. But I liked falling asleep next to you, having you here with me, and then spending those nights with you at your parents' house. Coming home alone again, it didn't feel right. The house was too quiet. I haven't slept more than a few hours a night. Worried about today and you, and selfishly, worried I wouldn't be able to fill this vacancy in my chest without you. I've missed you for too long, and maybe I'm scared you'll leave again without your dad as an anchor. I don't want to miss you anymore. I want you here," he said, and a tear escaped the corner of my eye. It trickled down to my jaw and then he wiped it away, a soft, hopeful look in his eyes. "I don't think there's a timetable that fits us, there isn't a list of things we need to check off. I don't know a lot of things about relationships, but I know you, and I know I'm in love with my best friend. And I'm ready, Luka… if you are."

CHAPTER SEVENTEEN

Rook

WE LAID OUR BIKES *near the dock by the lake's edge and kicked off our sandals. Luka didn't wait for me, running full steam ahead into the dark water. His scream scattered the nearby birds hiding in the trees and made me laugh. He sounded like his sister when she was yelling at him about one thing or the other. I probably should have warned him, but knowing Luka, he wouldn't have listened to me anyway.*

"It's t-too c-cold," Luka stammered, rubbing his arms. "No w-way am I g-going b-back in t-there."

"It's not that bad," I said, and he plopped down onto the sun-warmed grass. I handed him a towel from my backpack. "It's still early, the water always feels warmer at the end of summer break."

"That sucks," he pouted, wrapping himself into a Luka-sized burrito. "I wish we had a heated pool."

"That would be awesome."

"When I grow up, I want to be rich. I'll have a pool and go on vacations all the time and live in California. What about you?" Luka stared at me, his eyes big and curious.

"I like it here."

His face screwed up and his nose wrinkled. "You want to stay here forever?"

"What's wrong with that? I want to be a doctor like my dad."

"I'm not smart enough to be a doctor," he said, and it made my stomach hurt.

I didn't like it when he said stuff like that about himself. Luka had only moved in next door a year ago, but he was already my best friend. He always told me everything he was thinking even when the teachers had told him to stop being a chatterbox. He never complained about hanging out in the fort, and sometimes he slept out there with me. It was easier to fall asleep when he was there. It was weird to think he hadn't always been around, and when he said mean things about himself, I wished he could see how much happier he'd made me by just being here.

"You are too," I argued. "You always know all the answers in math."

"Math is easy."

"Not for everyone. My dad has to help me."

"I can help you if you want, when school starts again."

I smiled and picked at the blades of grass between my feet. "I'd like that."

He leaned back, the towel falling down around his arms, his pale skin covered in goose bumps.

"You really never want to move?"

"I don't think so."

"I bet you'd live in that fort if you could." He cracked up, and I threw the torn pieces of grass I'd collected at his face.

"You're the one who said we should live out there all summer."

"It could be fun," he said and picked a speck of grass from his lips. "Having like a month-long sleepover."

"Do you think our parents would let us?" I asked.

Luka jumped up, shaking out his wet swim trunks with a grin. "Only way to find out is to ask." He ran toward the bikes before I could even stand.

"Wait. Right now?"

"Come on."

Laughing, I pushed up and onto my feet, almost tripping as I took off after Luka. Once I caught up to him by the road, I was out of breath. "What's the hurry?"

"My dad will be home soon, and I think he'll say yes."

"And if he doesn't?"

"Then you can sleep over at my house. And then tomorrow I can sleep at yours."

"Every night?" I asked, feeling more excited by the minute.

This was going to be the best summer ever.

"Why not?" He shrugged once and grinned before racing down the dirt path toward our neighborhood.

"I don't want to miss you anymore either." Luka stared up at me, confusion warring inside his eyes. "My dad… he wasn't my only anchor. I want to spend every night with you. Every fucking night. I think I've been ready for this since I was a kid. All those sleepovers…" His lips lifted at the corners. "I never wanted them to end. This weekend, it was like I was myself again. I haven't slept for shit either. And yeah, it's a lot about my dad, but it's you, too, Rook. I have you back and I don't ever want to let go. But… I also need some time. I can't up and leave my mom alone in that house with all those memories."

"I know…" I cleared the lump from my throat. "I don't mean tonight or tomorrow. Or even next week. Like I said, you have a place here, anytime you need it."

"Nora is moving back. She's looking for a house and she's going to stay with Mom until she finds a place," he said and reached across the console to thread our fingers together, settling them on his thigh. "Maybe once she's here I'll feel better about having a more permanent sleepover."

"Take your time, Luka. Be with your family. My offer stands. I'm not going to change my mind." I gave his hand a gentle squeeze and let it go. "I don't need an answer right now, and besides…" I looked at the house and suppressed a sigh. "We should let Maribelle out before she destroys the blinds she's currently chewing."

He shot his gaze to my front window and huffed out a laugh. "Shit."

"Thank God I had the forethought to buy an extra set the last time she destroyed them. She gets excited when I leave her alone for too long."

"And with a face like that, how could you even be mad?"

Maribelle had her nose pressed to the window, her tongue lolling out of the side of her mouth. "You'd think so, but when she chews up your favorite pair of shoes for the first time, I'll remind you of this conversation."

"Oh."

"Yeah." Laughing, I opened the car door. "Come on."

180

The blinds were a loss, bent and broken in several places by the time we made it inside. At least the throw pillows I'd bought a couple of weeks ago were still alive. Belle was a good dog for the most part, she only got wild when she was anxious or overly excited, which didn't happen very often. At the moment, however, she was in a full-blown spin out, barking and jumping with more enthusiasm than I'd witnessed in a while. Her behavior wasn't surprising seeing as she'd been alone all day.

"Shh, it's okay, baby. It's alright." I quickly moved for the back door, and she darted around me, nearly cutting me down at the knees. "Jesus."

"She can come back with us," Luka offered, picking up the pillows from the floor and tossing them on the couch. "My mom loves her, and most of the people will have cleared out by the time we get back."

Maribelle barked somewhere in the distance, and I sighed. "I better check on her. When she's like this I can't trust her to be by herself, she may chase an imaginary animal all the way to Puget Sound. I won't be long."

"Don't stress about it. I'm not in that huge of a hurry to get back." He dropped a quick, chaste kiss to my lips. "I'll wait in here, though, it's cold as fuck outside."

"I'll be right back."

I closed the door behind me and shoved my hands into the pocket on my jacket as I walked toward the dock. The wind had picked up, the soft roar almost blotting out Maribelle's distant yapping. I whistled for her, and she came running, kicking up the dirt and damp grass behind her. She leapt in the air, then circled me a few times. I got down on her level and she panted as I dug my fingers into her fur. "You want to go with me to Luka's?" I asked and she snuffed her hot breath in my face. I'd take that as a yes. "Alright then, go potty."

I stood to my full height as she trotted off into the trees, waiting for her to do what she needed to do. Out here, in the clean, crisp air, it wasn't as difficult to process the conversation I'd had with Luka without his scent clouding my thoughts. It was easy to forget myself in the familiarity of him, in the possibility of us. What would my life look like with him at my side? We'd had a lifetime to know each other already. But not like this. The intimacy of friendship was bicycle chain-grease-stained fingernails and scraped-up elbows and knees, it was sleepovers and Saturday morning cartoons, and knowing what kind of milk he liked with his Frosted Flakes. It was stinky socks and swearing because it made us feel older. It was leaving and homesickness and writing essays alone in a dorm. This heat I had, this constant pilot light burning inside me when I looked at Luka, when his lips were on mine, it wasn't something I recognized. It was different and real, and I wanted it to become a part of our history as well as our future. He was made for me. And I was his too. I knew that now, knew it as well as I knew my own way through my house with the lights off. The way I knew he had changed, but he was still my home.

Maribelle licked my fingers, breaking me from my whirling thoughts, and we went inside. Luka wasn't in the kitchen, or the living room, and the bathroom downstairs was empty too. I filled up Belle's water bowl, and when I headed upstairs, I found Luka sitting on the edge of the guestroom bed.

"Are you okay?"

He raised his head, the low light of the room making it hard to read his mood. "Did you sleep in here all week?"

"What?" I diverted, embarrassment leaking into my cheeks, my face flushing with heat. I hadn't made the bed this morning and the sheets were bunched into a tangle. The pillow Luka had slept on when he'd stayed over was situated in a way it would be hard to deny I hadn't snuggled the hell out of it the last few nights. "Uh…"

Luka stood and crossed the room, his cocky smile making an appearance. These past few days it had felt like I'd never see it again. "Your bed is still made."

"You went in my room?" I asked, not because I cared, but more because I was trying to evade the truth.

He stepped into my space, backing me into the hallway.

"The door is open."

"Oh…"

He rested his hands on my chest, and it was as if his palms were charged with electricity. My heart stumbled over itself, warmth pooling inside my stomach—the air pleasantly thin as he craned his neck to look at me.

"My bed doesn't smell like you," I admitted, unable to hide the longing in my voice.

"Maybe we should change that."

Luka nuzzled his nose into my neck, and my hands pressed into his lower back. "Now?" He lightly bit the lobe of my ear, sending a jolt of sparks down my spine. I clung to the fabric of his shirt, hesitant to start something after the day he'd had. "Shouldn't we get back?"

"We have time." He kissed my jaw and pressed his mouth to the curve of my Adam's apple. "I need this. Need you."

183

"Luka," I hedged, and he pulled away, the desire in his eyes dying, his pupils constricting until all I could see was a sea of watery blue. "It's been a hard day, and I know you want to escape it but—"

"That's not what this is about." He pushed out of my hold, the crease between his brows a deep gash of hurt. "You know what? Forget it. You're right, we should go."

He turned to leave and was almost to the stairs when I found my voice. "Luka…" I didn't realize. I thought maybe he needed a way to forget, a way to remove himself from reality. And I could. I could be that for him again. But I wanted more. "Say what you mean."

He spun around and scrubbed his hands through his hair. His tie was askew, his dress shirt rumpled. He was a mess and all I wanted to do was kiss him. Kiss away all that frustration and anger. "This isn't about *escaping*. I haven't had a chance to be alone with you all week. All I wanted was a moment to be with you, and I get it… Fuck… You think I'm using you, and—"

I didn't let him finish the poisoned thought, grasping the back of his neck, I pulled him into a bruising kiss, drinking away the words. Without breaking the kiss, he shoved my jacket over my shoulders, and I wiggled my arms. We were all teeth and tongues, and biting lips until it fell to the floor, both of us tripping on it as he backed me into my room. Stumbling, we bumped into the doorjamb. He laughed against my mouth, and the sound of it went straight to my groin. He was himself again, light, and stunning, and tasted sweet on my tongue. Any apprehension I had melted away with our ties and shirts and shoes where they laid discarded somewhere by the foot of my bed. Luka pushed me onto my back, crawling over my body like he couldn't wait one more second to touch me. I ran my hand over his stomach, over the dips and valleys, resting my palms on his hips, my thumb tracing the sharp V above the waistline of his pants. He stared down at me, mesmerized with a lopsided grin, his mop of hair almost covering his eyes.

"I want to taste you," he said, and my grip on his hips tightened. "I want to show you what it can feel like when it's with someone you trust."

Nerves rocked through me, and he bent over, kissing the hollow of my throat. My hands slid up his ribcage as he kissed his way down my chest. He spent time licking and sucking each of my nipples, my breath catching in my throat with a hoarse moan as he nibbled the skin. My cock ached, the feeling so unfamiliar I shook with it. I lifted my hips, needing something, anything, and everything he could give me. Luka looked up at me through his lashes with the sexiest smile I'd ever seen.

"You still with me?" he whispered, peppering wet kisses over my belly. His soft lips dusted against my skin as he spoke, my back arching into the husky confidence of his voice. "You can tell me to stop anytime."

"I'm with you," I breathed, and he unhooked my belt.

He stripped my pants down my legs, and I toed off my socks, my erection flagging under the weight of the moment. I was bared to him again, but this time it was different. The shadow of grief wasn't present, that curtain dismantled even in the wake of all that had happened today. This was us. Luka and me. And his familiar blue eyes devoured me as he straddled my thighs. My heart was in my throat, my skin a live wire, and when he wrapped his hot hand around the base of my softening shaft, my entire body convulsed. My fingers dug into the comforter, every muscle in my body twitching with a painful mixture of need and anxiety. What if I did this wrong? What if I couldn't stay hard? What if I ruined it like I had so many times in the past?

"Rook." His voice was calm and steady, his hand splayed across my chest as the heat of his body covered me. He reached up and cupped my cheek, bringing our lips together in a slow, deep kiss. His tongue searching for mine, the pressure of his hand on my heart, grounding me. "There you are," he said as he pulled away, a quiet smile on his wet lips. "We can stop, or we can just lie here for a little while. Naked cuddles work for me, too, you know."

"I don't want to mess this up. Do something wrong."

"You couldn't…" I started to stare at the ceiling, feeling like I'd failed him, but he gripped my chin and held my gaze. "Hey… this is me and you," he said, mirroring my thoughts from earlier, and some of that nervous energy abated. "You have nothing to be worried about. This is new for you. For us. We can slow it down."

The minute he said it, I knew I didn't want to slow down. He understood me when no one else had. He'd been a presence in my life, even if sometimes it was merely a flicker. Luka's heart had always been mine, and it was all I needed to remember to feel free under his touch.

"I want to keep going," I murmured and reached up, framing his face in my hands. "I want you to touch me."

He leaned down and I kissed his bottom lip, his hand slipping between us. Luka ran soft fingers along my half-hard cock.

The touch was almost not enough and too much. Over and over again, a ghost of fingers and nails, gently raking over the sensitive skin, around the crown, until I was harder than I thought possible and moaned into his mouth with parted lips.

"Luka… God…" I gasped and let go of his neck.

He left sloppy kisses across my chest and stomach as he situated himself between my legs. I'd spread them for him without thinking, my fingers mindlessly running through his hair. He licked the bead of moisture where it had gathered and dripped over the rim of my cockhead, his hand firm around the base, and I grunted as he pumped his fist. It didn't seem real, this building inferno, scorching its way through my veins. It was next to impossible, but I forced myself to keep my eyes open. I needed the connection, needed to see Luka, watch him as the damp heat of his mouth enveloped me, while he swallowed me down to the root.

"Holy shit," I shouted and fell onto my elbow, my fingers twisting into his hair.

These unbidden, unknown feelings of desire Luka had tapped into, his hands and lips and breath on my skin. He was relentless, taking me into his throat again and again before he gagged and stole a moment to breathe. His eyes watered, spilling onto his cheeks and I brushed it away with my knuckles. He kissed his way back down my shaft, leaving no inch unexplored, and when I begged him, asking him for something I didn't know I needed, he worked me back into his mouth. I lifted my hips, unable to stay still. His cheeks hollowed out, and I watched my cock disappear past his pink lips. They were full and slightly swollen, and I couldn't stop staring. Every pump of my hips was slow and deliberate, and when he groaned, I noticed his hand was between his legs. I wasn't sure when he'd unbuckled his belt and pushed his own pants down, too overwhelmed by the feel of his mouth, and teetering on the edge myself. But the sight of him was almost enough to take me straight over, to come apart, and let go.

He worked himself fast and hard, and I grit my teeth, reeling and writhing beneath him. His hands moved in tandem, his moans vibrating down my shaft with every dip of his head.

"Shit… Luka… Don't stop. Fuck. Don't—" My back hit the mattress as I came, my fingers brutal in his hair.

He swallowed my load and the head of my cock, and I cried out, my limbs locked, suspended in an overwhelming and indulgent tension. Luka gasped as he lifted his head and sat up on his knees, his own cock stiff in his hand. The head was swollen, and he dropped his other palm to my chest as he jacked himself with short, rough strokes. His lips were the color of strawberries, slick and puffy, his cheeks splotched with red. His hair was a tumbled nest, the muscles of his abs contracting as he moved. Luka pinned his bottom lip between his teeth, the color of his eyes completely eclipsed by the dark black of his pupils. We stared at each other as I reached for him, and slid my hand under his, wanting to take over, wanting to give him what he'd just given me, everything, he deserved everything.

"Rook… I'm close. I'm—" Luka's hips jumped and jerked, and it only took a few seconds for him to fully unravel.

His release poured over my fingers and shot onto my chest. He rubbed it into my hot skin as his body trembled above me. Luka's head fell forward, and our mouths met in the middle.

Tasting myself on his tongue was the headiest thing I'd ever experienced. I smelled like him, like spunk and sex, and I never wanted to shower. I wanted to stay like this, our bodies wrung out and sated, and kiss him until tomorrow. I wanted him to look at me like this, with lust-drunk eyes every day. I held my clean hand to the back of his neck and ran my fingers down his spine as he licked the seam of my mouth, kissed the curve of my top lip—the dimple in my cheek.

"I don't want to move," he said, and chuckled as I squeezed his hip. "But I guess we should at some point."

"I'm thinking if we don't, our moms will eventually show up wondering what happened to us."

"Wouldn't that be a shocker for them?" he asked, and I laughed, my pulse spiking as his face broke into a huge sunshine smile. "I suppose we should get dressed."

He sat back, still straddling my waist, and glanced down at the drying evidence of his orgasm.

"I'm filthy."

"Isn't it great?"

I sat up and kissed the spot under his ear. "It's epic."

CHAPTER EIGHTEEN

Luka

BY THE TIME WE'D gotten back to my parents' house most of the guests had left. There were a few stragglers vying for my mother's attention when we walked into the living room, all of whom I didn't recognize. Mom didn't even realize we were there until Maribelle skirted past us and nudged my mom's hand with her nose. She gave us a smile, and a sort of *help me* wide-eyed look, and I wanted to laugh.

"Sorry it took us so long," I said. "Um… Maribelle had to get some of her energy out."

Lowering his eyes, Rook rubbed the back of his neck, and my mom's perceptive eyes didn't miss the movement. "Sure… Or maybe you both thought you'd get out of cleaning?"

"No, ma'am." Rook nodded toward the kitchen. "We'll get started on it right now."

"Don't worry about it," she said, and one of the people she'd been talking to gave her a quick wave. "Thank you for coming. It's nice to know how loved Isaac was."

"Let us know if you need anything?" A man with dark hair and a white beard reached for my mom and pulled her into a hug.

Her smile faltered a little, but it recovered by the time she pulled away. "Will do."

The small group turned to leave, and she let out a sigh of relief. "God, I thought they'd never leave."

"Who was that?" I asked.

"I have no idea," she said, and we all started to laugh.

The dark valleys below my mother's eyes lightened as she giggled, the wrinkles around her mouth softening. All day she'd looked the picture of the perfect widow. Not a salt-and-pepper hair out of place on her head. Her black dress immaculate and wrinkle free. But as she ran her fingers through her bangs and kicked off her shoes, I finally recognized the woman under the shroud of grief. It was the first time I'd seen her smile, like an honest to God, sincere smile, since I'd moved back from California.

"What a day, huh?" she asked and flopped down on the couch. The dog climbed onto the cushion next to her and rested her head in my mom's lap. "Are Natalie and Roger still here?"

"I haven't seen them," Rook said, and gave me a private smile. "Maybe they're in the kitchen. I'll go check."

I refrained from leaning in and kissing him on his cheek before he retreated toward the kitchen. We'd discussed telling our parents about us tonight, but figured it wasn't the most opportune time, and decided maybe we'd wait a few days to let everything settle. I didn't think our parents would be shocked, to be honest. My mom hadn't been subtle about her feelings on the matter of me and Rook ever being a couple. In her eyes, Rook had always been my soulmate. I was excited to tell her she'd had dibs on saying, "I told you so," but it felt too big, too monumental, and I didn't want to detract from today, from my dad and the gaping hole his absence had left behind. I hoped he knew somehow that Rook and I had taken this step together. He'd be happy for us, and I could picture all of the teasing he'd rain upon us for taking this damn long. It hurt to imagine it, but it was a happy feeling too.

"Have a seat," Mom said, wielding that discerning gaze in my direction again.

I could feel her scrutiny as I sat on the couch beside her, Maribelle's head popping up to stare at me too.

"How are you holding up?" she asked as Maribelle nuzzled her head under my mom's hand.

"Well enough, you?"

She leaned back deeper into the overstuffed sofa cushion. "You know… I am. Today was tough, but it went well, I think."

"Dad would have loved Roger's story about the sailboat incident."

Her smile was sad and soft. "He would have. I can't believe those two never sank that damn boat."

"Jameson and sailing do not mix."

"Very true." She eyed me, a curious smile forming on her lips.

"What?"

"Did you leave your tie at Rook's?" she asked, the mischievous lilt to her tone hard to miss. I grabbed for my nonexistent tie, and she laughed. "Did you two find some time to let off a little steam while you let Maribelle *get out her energy*?"

"*Mom.*" Blood rushed to my cheeks. "Don't."

She pressed her lips together and shooed her hand at me. "I'm not stupid. I just hope this means you two are done dancing around each other."

I blamed this day as my eyes started to burn, and I blinked a few times to stop myself from getting teary. I was so sick of crying. At least these tears stemmed from a happy place. "Yeah... I think we are. We were going to tell you and his parents in a few days. We didn't want to—"

"Steal Dad's thunder?"

"Well... exactly."

She patted my knee and leaned into me, resting her cheek against the side of my shoulder. "He would have been overjoyed to see you two finally pull your heads from your asses."

"*Mom,*" I said and laughed when she snorted. "Are you sure *you* weren't stealing sips of Jameson today?"

"Nope. This is pure exhaustion, my love." She lifted her head. "I'm happy for you." She cupped my cheek. "I think it's about time you got a taste of happiness."

"Oh God, why is Luka crying again?" Nora asked as she walked into the living room.

Before I could answer, Rook walked in as well, with Carter and Ron behind him. "Looks like these two cleaned up everything," he said as Ron tucked my sister under his arm and hugged her.

"You didn't have to do that," my mom admonished, but the relief in her smile gave her away.

"Yes, ma'am, we did." Carter stood tall and swept a tattooed hand through his long beard. The thick silver chain on his neck dipped beneath his dress shirt. Rough-boy-next-door-meets-business-casual. The whole look didn't make sense but was kind of sexy all the same. "Nat and Roger are packing up a few food items, but it's all done. It's the least we could do."

"He's right. If you need anything, Mrs. Abrams, don't hesitate to call us, or have Rook or Luka give us a ring." Ron looked down at my sister and squeezed her tighter. "You, too, Little Abrams. Anything you need, alright?"

Nora scrunched her nose. "No one has called me Little Abrams since high school."

Carter reached over and mussed his hand through her hair, and she swatted his arm. "And you're still the size of a hobbit."

"I'm not that short." She smoothed her hair behind her ears, her face flushing crimson. "I hate you sometimes."

The whole interaction was tripping me up. I had no idea Nora was that close to these guys.

"Little Abrams?" I asked and Nora shrugged.

"It was a thing," she said and sat down on the other side of the sectional. "It's not a big deal. I dated one of Carter's friends my junior year, and it stuck, I guess."

"Who?"

"Sarah," Ron said and hid his laugh behind a fist.

"Cool it," Carter rolled his eyes. "You're such a child."

"I feel like I'm missing something," I said, and my mom laughed.

It was everything light and I couldn't stop my own smile from spreading.

"Sarah was my ex," Carter said and shook his head as Ron chuckled.

"And oh, how his ego was shattered when Nora swooped in." Ron playfully punched his friend in the shoulder. "It was kind of a humbling moment for you, wasn't it?"

"I didn't like Sarah that much anyway." Carter postured and we all cracked up again.

There were smiles on everyone's faces. The black clouds had parted as we teased Carter and Nora, and when Roger and Nat found their way back into the living room, the mood lifted even more. We all sat on the oversized sofa, Rook's warm body pressed into mine, our hands covertly clasped, and told stories, remembered, and even though Dad wasn't a part of all the stories, he was there in every way. Maybe it was my mind playing tricks on me, my own way of keeping my dad close, but I could have sworn as the night went on, I heard his laugh a few times too.

After the night of the funeral, the next few weeks blew by. Each day that had passed had its challenges. Some days worse than others. Going through my father's things with my mom and sister had been a lot harder than I thought it would be. His clothes had still smelled like him, a mixture of Gain detergent and Old Spice cologne. It hadn't felt right boxing them away and sending them to Goodwill when that piece of him still lingered. But it was cathartic in some ways as well. Letting go of the thing but not the man. It wasn't his suits or his t-shirts that held him in my heart. It was the pictures on the wall, those moments in time and the memories I carried that kept me going through the process. Healing was hard, but I'd kept myself busy with work and making sure my mom was taken care of. Between work, running errands, and keeping up with the honey-do list my father never finished, I had little time for myself, or time to wallow. Rook had been busy too. He'd had more deliveries this past month than he had in the entire history of his practice. He had attributed it to the weird lunar eclipse last year, apparently it was some type of love moon. It sounded like a bunch of nonsense to me, but I kept to that to myself. I thought it was adorable how Rook blamed the moon for everything. It was something I hadn't known about him, something he'd picked up in college, and I sort of loved learning new things about the man I'd thought I already knew everything about.

As predicted, his parents were not surprised that we were together. They'd actually seemed relieved when we told them over dinner a few days after my dad's funeral. Nora couldn't stop teasing us, and as much as I'd wanted her to move in, it wasn't ideal having her in my business all the time.

Even with her there, though, I hadn't had a chance to sleep over at Rook's. Nora was always in the city or visiting a friend or away on business. I suppose we all grieve in our own way, but I didn't love leaving my mom alone in the house for too long. Rook had stayed over with me a few times. It was strange adjusting to his schedule, to the middle-of-the-night calls, but when he was there, he made the grief more bearable, made the long nights seem manageable. I wanted him there all the time, especially on those nights my mind wouldn't stop racing. It was incredible feeling safe in his arms, having his scent on my skin. We hadn't explored each other as much as my libido would have liked, but in truth, spending time with him, kissing him, falling asleep with the heat of our bodies pressed together, these moments were all precious to me because these were all the things I never thought I'd get to experience with him. The sex stuff could wait. I wanted to give myself to Rook in every way, but first, I needed to feel whole again. I didn't want him to be an escape route every time I woke up from a bad dream.

"Abrams," Mr. Burgess called through my open office door, startling me enough I almost dropped the proofs I'd been looking through. "Shoot, I'm sorry, didn't mean to scare you."

"It's okay," I said and set the pictures on my desk. "What's up?"

"I wanted to catch you before you left. I had an idea," he said, and made himself comfortable in the chair on the other side of my desk. "If you're up for it."

He rolled his mustache, a nervous habit I noticed when I started coming into the office more regularly. It usually meant I wasn't going to like whatever he had to say. Last week he'd wanted me and Zach to do a feature on Betty Weinstock. Her family had owned the apple orchard on the outskirts of town for the last fifty years. It would have been a great story, and I would have loved shooting all those old craggy apple trees, but the lady was a hermit, and surly as fuck, and told us in no uncertain terms she wasn't interested, and that we should get the hell off her property. I surmised that if it hadn't been for her sons, that orchard would have gone under years ago. The story didn't happen, and we ended up interviewing Dot about her bakery instead. I never thought a picture of a cupcake could make the front page of a newspaper.

"Why do you look so nervous?"

He shifted in his seat, avoiding my eyes as he sighed. It was more like a harrumph, his swollen belly shaking with a nervous laugh. "I'm not nervous. I'm more worried about whether or not you're going to want to participate in something this big."

I leaned back in my chair and crossed my arms over my chest. "Color me intrigued."

His smile was back in full force. "What would you say about doing a feature on Reese? Another hometown hero piece."

"Rook's brother?"

"The one and only. It's not every day a small town like ours can claim an NHL star. And Vancouver is doing quite well this season." He cleared his throat again and lowered his voice.

"And let's be real, the man is thirty-four years old. This could be his last season. Best to strike now while the iron is hot."

I didn't bother asking why he hadn't thought about this years ago. He hadn't had an in like he did now. But Reese was a private person even if his persona was larger than life sometimes. He was two years older than Rook, and they'd played hockey together as kids and had hung around in the same circle of friends, but they weren't as close as they'd used to be. Rook didn't care about hockey like his brother did. Reese's dream was to play for the NHL, and when his potential started to show, and his hope had looked more like a reality, he'd spent as much of his time as possible cultivating his talent. He hadn't come home very often after he'd gone away to Michigan State, and things hadn't changed much with time. He hadn't even come home for my dad's service. Which wasn't a surprise to me, he was a professional athlete and most likely didn't have the time, but it stung, nevertheless.

"Um… I'm not sure that's—"

"Wait." He held up his hand and sat up straighter. "I have a pitch."

I laughed. "Let's hear it."

"Obviously the paper would pay for your travel expenses, and Zach has a contact, a sportswriter friend who can set up the official interview. It wouldn't be like we're calling in a favor because you know him. You'd simply be there to take pictures."

"Very convenient."

"I'd like to think so." He smoothed a hand down his tie, a proud smirk peeking out from under the hairy caterpillar above his lip. "Take your boyfriend with you. I'm sure he'd love to see his brother."

"How did you—"

"The whole town knows you and Rook are together now." He chuckled and my face heated. What the fuck? "Brie from the bookstore saw you two kissing. I mean, you were on a public street corner. She didn't think it was a secret."

I pinched the bridge of my nose trying like hell to gather some patience. "And how did you find out?"

"What? Are you worried I would care? I'm all about equality and loving freely."

"Um… sure, but—"

"Stacey told me when I stopped by to pick up my prescriptions the other day."

"From Rhett's?"

"I guess Brie was so surprised by the whole kiss and told a few of her friends, and word got out. This isn't exactly a big city. Anyway, I think Dot told Rhett who told Stacey." *Jesus fucking*

Christ, this town. "The whole town knows how hung-up Stacey's been on Rook. That wasn't much of a secret either. Needless to say, she was heartbroken."

Heartbroken.

I had to force myself not to roll my eyes. Part of me wanted to ask him why the love life of one of his employees was something he deemed appropriate to chat about at the checkout counter of Rhett's Pharmacy. But this entire conversation was giving me heartburn, and I thought it best we get back on track.

"About Vancouver," I said. "I'm not sure I want to leave my mom for that long. It's too soon."

"I thought about that." Of course, he did. "And I spoke to Natalie."

"You spoke to Mrs. Whelan?"

"To get a feel for the situation… To see if she thought Reese would be receptive to my plan. She thought it was a great idea and assured me Reese would be honored to participate."

Nat could be persuasive, and I was sure Reese wouldn't have had the chance to tell his mom no. But I wasn't sure what the hell that had to do with me or my mom. "That's great, but that doesn't change the fact I'm not comfortable leaving my mom."

"I understand, I do," he said, giving me a fake sympathetic smile. "But Natalie told me she would make sure your mom was taken care of while you're gone. You wouldn't have to go until next weekend. It's basically a paid vacation for you and your boyfriend." He waggled his brows, and I exhaled an annoyed breath. "Think about it and let me know tomorrow." He stood before I could answer. "This could be a big opportunity for you. The team manager said they wanted to sign off on any photos you take. That's exposure."

Fuck.

I hated that he was right.

"I'll think about it," I agreed, but when I got home thirty minutes later, my mom was waiting for me in the kitchen.

"You're going," she said by way of greeting.

"Christ." I set my camera bag on the counter. "Please tell me my boss didn't call you and convince you to let me go to Vancouver. Because I swear to God, this day has been a day, and this town… I can't—"

"It was Natalie," she admitted and slid a mug of tea in my direction.

I lifted it to my lips, the lavender scent calming me as I inhaled. "Is this a bribe?" I asked and sat down on the barstool.

"Maybe." She smiled over her teacup. "Promise me you'll listen before you say anything."

"I'm listening." I waved my hand for her to continue.

"I'm feeling good." She held up her hand as I opened up my mouth to argue. "I'm getting there. I am. It's hard and I'm sad, but every day is a little better than the day before. And Nat and I feel—"

"Nat and I…"

"Luka Abrams, can you please shut up for one second in your damn precious life." Her hand slapped the granite countertop and my heart jumped. "Please." She sounded exhausted.

"Wow."

"I'm not a child. I do not need to be watched or taken care of. I appreciate you being here. I do. But you are a grown ass man, with a grown ass boyfriend and you both need time to yourselves. You don't think I haven't noticed how little time you've given yourself to heal? You need this."

"Mom, I'm fine."

"I'm not asking you, Luka. I'm telling you. Roger can cover Rook's patients, and Nat and I can spend some much-needed time together. I'm not fragile. Stop treating me like I'm about to break every goddamn second. It's suffocating." Her eyes glittered with unshed tears. "Every time you look at me like I'm about to shatter it makes it harder not to."

"I thought I was helping."

"You are," she said and moved around the counter. She held my face in her hands. "You do, but you need to take care of yourself. You and Rook… it would be good for you to get away. You two need time together. You've hardly seen him since the funeral, and don't tell me it's *fine*. It's not. You need to live your life just as much as I need to live mine." Mom lowered her hands, leaving her words to swim around inside my head.

Having a whole weekend alone with Rook without any interruptions, without my mom and sister in the other room, without the shadow of the last month looming over me, would be more than amazing. God, it didn't seem possible. It felt selfish to want it this bad.

"I feel guilty, like I'm running away. I promised Dad I wouldn't run away."

"Taking time for yourself isn't running away. It's healthy." Her smile stretched up and touched the corner of her eyes. "Go to Vancouver. It's one weekend. I think I can manage on my own."

One whole weekend with Rook.

A slow, burning excitement coursed through me.

Two nights and three days without anything looming over us.

"Okay," I said. "I'll go."

CHAPTER NINETEEN

Luka

"THERE'S A DOOR..." WILL held up his hands and twiddled his fingers as his eyes widened. "With a green light emanating from the crack beneath and around the frame…"

"Shut the fuck up," Ron shouted, and the entire table laughed. I was obviously missing something. "Not that jelly cube thing again. What is it with you and amorphous gelatinous beings?"

"I'm sorry, what?" Ry, whom I'd met for the first time tonight, furrowed his brow. "Why did we decide not to play Magic?"

"Because Rook thought it would be fun to do a D&D campaign and let this idiot be the DM." Ron shoved his character sheet toward the middle of the table. "Anyone else need another beer?"

"It's getting late," Will said and shook his head. "I have to work tomorrow."

"I'm good," Rook and I said in unison, and we shared a secret smile.

"I'll have one." Ry stood and stretched his long arms over his head. He scratched his thick blond beard, his ice blue eyes narrowing as he yawned. "Well, maybe not. I'll grab a bottle of water though."

"Grab me a water too," Will said and leaned back in his chair as Ry and Ron headed into the kitchen.

"Where's Travis tonight?" I asked.

After the conversation I'd had with my mom about Vancouver, I'd arrived late. If my mom hadn't insisted I come over here, I would have canceled altogether. I didn't want to be the asshole who kept showing up mid-game. But they'd been in the middle of making Ry's new character and hadn't minded throwing one together for me as well.

"He's on a date." Will rolled his eyes. "Traitor."

"Let the man have some fun," Ron said as he sat back down and handed Will a bottle of water. "God knows he needs it, and Stacey is a good chick."

"I thought Stacey was into Rook?" Ry asked, and Will threw an unsubtle elbow into his ribs. "Ow… what did I say?"

The whole table got quiet, and Rook shifted in his chair. I'd assumed everyone here knew about us. The whole fucking town did, according to my boss, but I hadn't had a chance to talk to Rook about that fiasco. He stared at me, and I noticed Ron fighting a smile. Oh yeah, they all knew.

Rook's foot pressed against mine under the table and I nodded. He swallowed, clearly more nervous than he needed to be. He tore the label off his empty beer bottle, avoiding all the eyes that were now swung in his direction. "I wasn't sure how to tell you guys... or when... but I suppose now is a good time." God, he was cute when he was flustered. "Luka and I... we... we're..."

"Together?" Will asked, but it sounded more like a statement and not a question.

Rook was greeted with an entire table of knowing grins. I chewed the corner of my lip, trying not to smile too wide. He had no idea how sweet he looked at that very moment. All that vulnerability and hope, it made my fucking heart swell.

"You all already knew?" he asked.

"The entire Harbor knows, apparently." I lowered my voice. "My boss mentioned something about our kiss in front of the bookstore..."

"Oh," he said, wide-eyed and adorable.

"Yeah, oh." Ron chuckled. "I can't believe you didn't tell me."

"Hello... What about me?" Will asked, more offended than anyone. "I didn't even know you were gay."

"I'm not." Rook shook his head, ready to explain when Ry cut in.

"But you and Luka..."

Ron playfully shoved his shoulder. "Aw... you have so much to learn."

"It's always been hard for me to define it... How I've felt about relationships, and women, and I don't know... I'm pretty sure I'm demi-sexual... which is kind of under the gray asexuality umbrella. I don't really care about the label though. I've been questioning things for so long, wondering why I wasn't like you guys, or why it was hard for me to connect with someone... I'm just happy I understand myself more. All my confusion … I have an answer for it now."

"Asexuality…" Ry's brows dipped. "I think I've heard of that, but…" I could picture wheels turning in his head. "Does that mean you're—"

"He's Lukasexual," Will said with a snort and Ron groaned. "Why are straight people so ignorant sometimes?"

"Hey." Smirking, Will held up his water bottle and pointed it violently in Ron's direction. "I am not fucking ignorant. I can't vouch for Ry though… I don't know him that well."

Ry's face pinked up, his eyes sparking with laughter. "Fuck off. You knew me well enough when you referred your dad to my office for an echo."

"How did you meet these guys again?" I asked Ry as I caught my breath. It had been too long since I'd laughed this much.

"He's a cardiac surgeon at the hospital." Rook finished peeling the rest of his label off of his beer. "My dad and I met Ry at a conference right after he moved here from Oakville."

"Wow," I said, impressed. "That's kind of cool."

Ry was a big guy, definitely over six foot, with broad as hell shoulders and big hands. It was hard to place him doing something as delicate as operating on a heart.

"Only kind of?" Ron teased. "This man heals actual fucking human hearts for a living."

Ry blushed again as Ron gave the back of his neck a friendly squeeze. "It's intense, but I love it."

"Can we circle back to the sexuality thing?" Will asked. "Does Travis know?"

"I think so." Ron coughed out a laugh. "That's why he asked Stacey out."

"Everyone in town really knows?" Rook looked at me, and for the briefest of seconds, I thought he might've been worried.

"It sucks, not being able to come out to people on your own terms. I get that, but in a way you did." The humor in Ron's eyes turned serious. "You guys kissed on a public corner, in a small ass town, and everyone knows, and from what I can tell, they're all chill about it. It could be worse. And if anyone does give you shit, I'll set them straight."

Rook shared a look with Ron that was private, some unspoken thing between friends. Instead of feeling jealous, I was happy he'd had someone like Ron in his corner all this time.

"I'm sorry," Ry said. "If I sounded ignorant earlier. I didn't… I guess I do have a lot to learn."

"Don't be sorry." Rook gave him a soft smile. "I just recently learned about the ace spectrum. Google is very helpful when you're having a sexuality crisis."

"Or your friends," Ron said.

"Yes…" Rook exhaled, the tightness in his shoulder releasing as he sank back into his chair. "I'm lucky to have such great friends."

"I think it's cool." The sentiment in Will's voice surprised me. "I'm happy for you both."

"Thanks," I said and tried to let go of the old hurts he'd caused me.

It was obvious Will had changed. He wasn't that playground bully anymore.

"Should we see what's behind the glowing door?" he suggested, and everyone groaned.

"Fuck… let's do this." Ron set his beer down, picking up his character sheet, and I didn't miss the hidden smile on Ry's lips as he stared at him.

"Are you going to open the door or flee?" Will asked the room and the game continued.

About an hour later, we'd wrapped up the campaign for the night. Ron and I worked side by side at the sink while Rook walked Will and Ry out to their cars. The silence wasn't necessarily uncomfortable, but I could tell he was holding something back as he placed the last dish in the drying rack. I wiped my hands on the towel looped around the handle of the stove and Ron turned to face me. Crossing his beefy arms over his chest he said, "If you hurt him…"

"I wouldn't… not intentionally."

"That's what I'm worried about." He let out a slow breath and lowered his arms, opening up his posture. He didn't seem as scary when he relaxed. "Listen, we don't know each other as well as we should, but I know what it's like to be in love with someone who might never love you the way you hoped they could. I know how awful it can be to think you're finally getting what you want, and then have it…" He shook his head. "What I'm trying to say is, I know you love him, and I know that's why you stayed away. But if shit gets bumpy, you have to stick it out this time, because Rook fucking loves you. And I don't think he'd recover from it if you left him like that again."

"I'm not leaving. Not again. This is my home." Those three sentences, the truth of the words resonated in the air, in my chest. *This was my home.* "I've never loved anyone the way I love that man. He's been my everything. My whole life is wrapped up in him. He knows me. Every moment I've breathed has belonged to him, to us, in some way or another. I messed up. I tried to cut him out of my life, but it was like cutting out half of my heart. I was barely surviving in California. I love him. And I appreciate you protecting him, but you don't have to anymore. Because I will."

Dark blue eyes stared straight through me, piercing and deliberate, like he was weighing what I'd said, measuring the honesty of the words. After a moment, he nodded, a slight smile growing on his lips and clapped me on the shoulder. "That's good. Because that man deserves the world."

"I can't argue with that."

"What are we arguing about?" Rook asked as he walked into the kitchen.

I curled my arm around his waist and kissed his cheek. "Nothing, we were just talking."

"I should get going," Ron said and grabbed his keys from the countertop. "I told Ry I'd go running with him in the morning before work."

"I think Ry is into you," I said, and Ron's head tipped back as he laughed.

"Not likely."

"I don't know," I pushed. "For a lumberjack type, he sure did blush every time you paid him any attention. I'm thinking baby bi vibes for sure."

"Maybe he's questioning," Rook added. "He's never mentioned what happened with him and his ex-wife."

"Cut it out." Ron waved his hand with another baritone laugh. "You two are terrible. He's new in town and wants to make friends. Besides, I've spent enough of my life lusting after a straight guy. Unless the man shoves his tongue down my throat, I'm not interested."

"So, what I'm hearing is that there's a chance?" I asked and he rolled his eyes.

"See you guys later," he said, dismissing me. "We should grab lunch this week. Give me a call."

Once the front door slammed shut, I pulled Rook to my chest and kissed him. His hand found the nape of my neck and my fingers twisted into the front of his hoodie. I heard Maribelle traipsing down the stairs, but I didn't break from Rook's lips. His tongue swept into my mouth, and I moaned. God, I'd missed him this week.

"Stay with me tonight?" he asked.

My mom was right. She didn't need a babysitter, and being here with him, I felt a million pounds lighter.

"Okay."

We let the dog out one last time before we all headed upstairs. Maribelle wasn't invited into Rook's bedroom, and we both laughed when she whined at the door.

"Go lie down," he hollered as he let go of my hand, and we heard her nails clacking against the wood floor, slow and despondent, as she found her way into the guest bedroom.

"I feel bad."

"Don't," he assured me. "She has a dog bed in the other room too."

"But she normally sleeps in here?"

He shrugged and lifted his hoodie over his head. "She'll be fine." His undershirt clung to the muscles of his chest and shoulders, my gaze snagging on his strong hands as he started to unbuckle his belt. "I need to take a shower. You should join me." He pulled his t-shirt off, and I lost my reply.

The beauty of Rook's body continued to slay me. His was miles of flawless, soft, tawny-brown skin. Every sweep and curve of muscle defined beneath it. And with him standing there, shirtless, his pants hanging open in the front, it was like he'd stepped out of one of my many fantasies. Except I wasn't a horny teenager anymore. I was a full-blown adult with a very gorgeous man waiting for me to get undressed.

"Luka?" he asked, and the grin on his face told me he was well aware of what he was doing to me. "Shower?"

"Uh… yes… yeah, let me…" I ripped my long-sleeve shirt over my head and made quick work of my belt buckle.

He shoved his pants and underwear to the ground, and I watched him as he walked into the bathroom. The firm globes of his ass flexed with each step and, Jesus, my entire mouth went dry. I was completely hard and hungry for him by the time I joined him under the hot spray of water. His shower was large, all glass and gray and white tiles. With his back to me, I was able to stand behind him with plenty of room but nestled my dick in the crease of his ass anyway. Rook backed into me, and I snuck my arms around his waist, my palm splaying across his belly. I kissed his neck and sucked the wet skin between my lips.

"Hi," he said and turned his head to kiss me.

I reached down with my right hand, holding him against me with my left, and a flash of embarrassment heated my cheeks when I wrapped my fingers around his soft cock. Here I was poking him with my ridiculous boner, and he wasn't even into it yet.

"Sorry, I—"

He covered my hand with his, his teeth nibbling my bottom lip, and stroked himself slowly. The velvet of his skin against my palm, the way he panted in my mouth, I struggled not to spin him around and take control. He needed to pace this. Rook's arousal was something new to him, and as much as I wanted to be everything he needed, I didn't want to rush this either. His cock gradually thickened in my hand, and his mouth fell open as I teased the crown with my thumb.

"That feels good," he panted and licked a drop of water from my lips.

He wasn't fully erect, but he didn't seem to care as he turned in my arms and framed my face with his hands, his kiss rough and commanding. My back slammed against the shower wall, and I might've yelped at the cold tile on my ass. His forehead rested against mine and we both laughed. "Shit," I said. "Didn't mean to break the moment."

He pulled back, his amber eyes blazing, his hands holding my face like I was something to treasure. "*This* is the moment, Luka. This." He kissed my lips, my jaw. "Being here with you. I like touching and getting off, but I love this. Love you, more."

We made out until our fingers started to prune, exploring each other's bodies, without taking things too far. He covered me in his soap, and I basked in the idea of having his scent all over my skin. I washed his body, too, massaging my fingers into the muscles of his ass and the back of his thighs. He rested his palms flat against the shower wall, his head falling forward like a statue of a god in prayer. I thought about what it would be like to be inside him, how it would feel, if he would even want to try. Lost in the thought, I kissed a slow path down the arc of his spine, biting the top of his right butt cheek. He hissed and I stood to my full height.

Rook looked over his shoulder, his dark gaze pinning me in place. Every sharp rise and fall of his chest came quicker than the last as I slid my arm around him, taking him in hand again. He was still half-hard, but his eyes were hooded, his skin tinged with heat, his lips chapped from the stubble of my five o'clock shadow. He thrust into my fist, and I grasped his hip with my left hand. Finding the right angle, my cock slipped between his legs. He moved, hugging my shaft with his thighs, and I whimpered into his mouth as he kissed me. I wasn't sure if it was the friction or the sound I'd made, but his dick swelled and hardened in my palm, his hips stuttering as I tightened my grip.

With his skin still soapy and slick, I fucked between his thighs, keeping the same rhythm as my hand, working him until he swore, his breath catching in his throat, his fingers grasping at the slippery tile wall and failing. I held him up the best I could, my quads burning with every pump of my hips. I was close to losing it, and when he arched his back, and squeezed his legs together as he came, I let out a strangled cry.

"Christ." My legs quaked, my release sticky between his legs. I wanted to stay buried there all night. I nipped the crook of his neck and he shuddered, his hand finding mine on the side of his hip, his come washing away in the lukewarm water. "If I could, I'd fall asleep right here."

Rook chuckled and turned in my arms, pressing against me. "I think our skin would slough off eventually."

"Gross."

He left a soft kiss on my lips, and with a dopey smile on his face, he ran his thumb along my jaw. "We should get dried off. The water is getting cold."

"Fine," I complained, but kissed him thoroughly before reaching behind him to turn off the faucet.

We were both dried off and naked, snuggled under his covers when he rolled onto his side and cuddled me into his chest. Brushing the hair from my eyes, he said, "I didn't think I'd ever find someone who I could truly share myself with like this."

"I knew you would. I just never thought it would be me. Anyone would be lucky to have you." He curled my hand with his, resting them between us. Nervous, I focused my gaze on the small patch of dark freckles near his hairline. "But you'd tell me, right? If you didn't like something I did. I don't ever want you to feel pressured…"

"I would tell you," he said and let go of my hand, only to hold my chin instead. "Look at me." I did as he asked, my bottom lip stuck between my teeth. "I will always be honest with you. Like I said in the shower, I don't always need to get off. And sometimes, all it takes is for you to make a certain sound and I'm ready to explode. It's our connection though, that's what I want more than anything."

"Me too." I kissed the warm skin at the center of his palm, and it settled me.

"I'm glad you're staying tonight," he said and draped his arm over my hip. "I don't have an appointment until nine, we could sleep in, or grab pancakes at The Early Bird."

"That sounds good to me." His fingers skated along my spine. The quiet intimacy of his touch lulled me to sleep. My eyes started to drift close when I remembered I hadn't asked him about Vancouver. "Oh my God." I laughed. "I almost forgot to ask you. My boss wants to feature your brother as a hometown hero. And I have to go to Vancouver next weekend, and I was hoping you'd come with me."

Rook chuckled, the wrinkles around his eyes so familiar my heart shimmied. "I was wondering when you'd get around to asking me about that."

I sat up on my elbow, incredulous. "You knew?"

"I already cleared my schedule with my dad. Sorry. My mom told me about it today but made me swear I wouldn't say anything to you until you asked." He grazed his knuckles across my cheek. "Are you mad?"

"No," I said and sank back into his hold. "I like how she conveniently left out the part about the entire town, including my boss, knowing we were together."

"My mom prides herself on getting in other people's business, but just enough it's not obvious to the unsuspecting."

"Mine, too, together they're terrible." I wriggled in closer, needing his heat. "You know what my mom told me today? She said I was suffocating her."

"Damn."

"Right? She basically said she didn't need a babysitter and gave me her blessing to get the hell out of the house."

Rook met my gaze. "Does that mean you can move in soon?"

"After Vancouver, if everything goes okay, and she's still of the opinion she has it all handled, I guess I don't see a reason to stay there anymore. Is that too soon for you?"

He drew the tip of his nose along the line of my throat and smiled against my skin.

"No… I think it's perfect timing."

CHAPTER TWENTY
Rook

"I'M GOING TO FALL." *Luka couldn't stop laughing as he held onto the side of the ice rink. "Shit." He looked like a newborn calf trying to figure out how to walk for the first time. "Oh my God," he shrieked, and his legs shot out from underneath him as he fell on his ass. He shot me a vicious glare and I cracked up even harder.*

"Are you okay?" I asked as I caught my breath. I gripped the rink's edge and bent over to offer him a hand that he playfully swatted away. "I'm sorry. I didn't know you—"

"Suck at life. Oh, I did." Luka found his footing again and brushed the slush from his backside. "I can't believe I let you talk me into this. I'd rather be at a stupid football game taking pictures for the yearbook."

His smile didn't falter though, and when he slipped on the ice again, I caught him. Chest to chest I held him steady. "Just stand still for a second, get your bearings."

"I'm trying. We can't all be amazing hockey player, skate gods." He blew out an exasperated breath and the hair above his eyes shift-

ed, revealing his narrowed blue eyes. It almost made me laugh again, but Travis skated by and whistled, making a kissing face at us both. Luka pushed away from me too quickly and almost toppled over, his arms spinning like a wild windmill. He caught the wall's edge in the nick of time. I heard a few of my teammates laugh as they skated by. Luka wasn't smiling anymore.

"Fuck, can we leave?"

"Hey… they're just playing. Trust me, Travis trips over his own stick if he isn't paying attention."

Luka pursed his lips, his cheeks pink from the chill of the rink, or maybe he was that pissed? This was my first year on a high school hockey team, and Luka was my best friend. I'd wanted him to be a part of this with me, to include him. And when the school hosted this open skate night, meet the team thing, I'd thought this could be fun. The guys could be jerks sometimes, but for the most part they were cool and just messing around, and I wanted them to see me with Luka, to get to know him like I did. If they didn't like him, then they sure as hell didn't need to be in my life. I loved hockey, but not like my brother, Reese. I played because it was fun. It wasn't my whole life. But Luka… I looked at my best friend, his eyes gleaming, his breath puffing out in aggravated little clouds, and my stomach got all warm. He was more important to me than any of this would ever be.

"Let's get out of here," I said.

"For real?"

"Yeah, I made an appearance. Coach won't care." I hooked my arm through his. "If you hold on to me, we'll get out of here quicker."

"Go slow," he said, wobbling as he let go of the wall. "And don't let go."

"I won't," I said and held him tighter. "I swear it."

The lights of Vancouver twinkled against the water that surrounded the city and its snow-capped mountain backdrop. I could almost see the entire North Shore range from the floor-to-ceiling window of our hotel room. It was a strange juxtaposition to the sounds of sirens in the distance and all the cars buzzing through the grid system below us. One minute I felt claustrophobic, with the towering buildings cloaking the sky, and then the next, if I remembered to look up, look past the glass and steel, I'd get a glimmer of something that reminded me of home.

"Are you ready?" Luka whispered, draping an arm around my waist. "We should get going if we want to meet Reese at the rink."

"Yeah…" I inhaled the citrus scent of the hotel shampoo as I turned my head and kissed his temple. "Are you sure we shouldn't invite Zach to dinner?"

"Nah, he's meeting up with some sportswriter guy he used to date. The official interview isn't until tomorrow. After we shoot a few photos at the rink tonight, it's just us."

I hadn't had a just us night with my brother in years. He was my family, and I shouldn't be nervous to see him, but he didn't know about me and Luka yet. I didn't think he was homophobic. Reese had always been good to Luka and hadn't batted an eyelash when he'd come out in high school, but I was his brother. Would that change things? Would he accept it? Accept us?

I exhaled and Luka stared at me, those knowing eyes my ever-present anchor. "It's going to be okay," he said. "Reese loves you."

"I know. I shouldn't be this anxious but—"

"Coming out is scary." He grinned. "But I bet you my left kidney your mom already gave him a heads up. She sucks at secrets."

I laughed and felt safer in my skin. "God, you're probably right."

"If she didn't tell him, I'll kiss you in front of him and then he'll find out like everyone else did."

I wish I could have stolen some of his confidence and made it my own. "And what if he's disgusted?"

Luka took my clammy hand in his. "Let me ask you this... does it matter? If he doesn't accept you as you are, will that change anything? Would you walk away from this? From who you are?"

"No. Of course not."

"There's your answer," he said and pressed a chaste kiss to my lips. "I know it's not that simple, but if he chooses to walk away from you, that's on him. All you can do is trust in the people who love you, no matter what, to be there for you when it hurts the most. You have that. You have so many people who care about you. He's your brother, but you don't owe him anything."

I cupped the back of his neck and brought our heads together. Nose to nose, his toothpaste-minty breath fanned across my lips. "Thank you."

Luka closed the distance and kissed me, our mouths melding together in a way I'd started to crave. He ran his hand up my chest and I lowered mine to the small of his back. Our bodies came together, and he deepened the kiss, groaning as my tongue caressed his. I could forget the world, all my anxiety and worry, when we were like this, wound up in each other, my heartbeat crashing inside my ears.

"Feel less stressed now?" he asked as he reluctantly pulled away. "We could always text him and tell him we'll meet him at the restaurant later?" Luka curled his finger through one of my belt loops. "Or we could cancel altogether and meet him for lunch with Zach tomorrow."

"You need to get shots of Reese on the ice," I reminded him, and he shrugged.

"Way to be responsible."

"One of us has to be." I kissed the tip of his nose and took a step back to admire him. He had on this cozy-looking green sweater that changed his eyes to the color of sea glass, and dark-fitted jeans that hugged his thighs. He was beautiful in this effortless way, and as easy as it would be to hide away in this room all night, he had a job to do. "Come on, you need these pictures."

"Do I, though?"

"Yes." I laughed and took his hand, dragging him toward the hotel room door.

"Wait…" He chuckled. "I need to grab my camera."

With the rush-hour traffic, we arrived at the practice facility about ten minutes later than we should have. My anxiety had come back in full force by the time we made it inside and the smell of ice stung my nose. The team was hosting an open practice and had invited one of the local youth hockey teams to come and meet the players. The place was crowded with fans and parents trying to get pictures of their own. I followed behind Luka as he flashed his press pass to security and told them we were here for some promotional shots of the team. A serious-looking guy with more muscles than anyone needed kept his eyes fixed on us while he radioed to someone on his walkie-talkie.

After a minute he nodded and stepped to the side. "Down that way, last door on the right, you can check in there."

"Thanks." Luka looked at me over his shoulder and gave me a nervous smile. "This reminds me of high school…" he said as we made our way down the long concrete hallway. The scent of rubber and sweat had me reminiscing too. "When I used to do the sports photos for the yearbook."

"Remember that time I made you come to my team's open skate?"

"Oh God, and I humiliated myself," he said, his tone comically annoyed. "How could I forget?"

"I felt terrible. I knew you couldn't skate, but I thought you'd figure it out… and then, Jesus, Travis was such a dick back then."

"I told you." He laughed. "Will was worse, though."

"He was," I agreed and rubbed the back of my head. "Out of everyone, though, he's changed the most."

The door to the rink suddenly swung open, and Reese barreled into the hall in full gear. His smile stretched across his face, and he whacked Luka in the ass with the blade of his stick.

"You're late."

"Nice to see you, too, Reese."

My brother lumbered toward us, pulling Luka into a side hug. His watchful eyes never left mine. "Long time no see, little brother." He released Luka from his hold and yanked me into his chest. "Did you shrink?"

"You're on skates, asshole."

"Excuses, excuses." His laugh boomed down the corridor as he pulled away. "Come on, let's get this over with, the quicker we get out of here, the quicker I can eat. I'm fucking starving."

As we followed behind him, Luka leaned over and whispered into my ear, "He hasn't changed at all, has he?"

"No… not at all," I said, and everything I'd been worrying about didn't feel as scary.

Reese introduced us to his coaching staff before showing us where Luka could set up. My brother was beyond excited to have us here, and I couldn't help but regret that I hadn't been to more than a handful of his NHL games during his career. He'd been traded a few times, and with work and building my practice, it never seemed possible to travel around a lot. Here I was worried about him accepting my and Luka's relationship, and he was just happy to see me at all.

"What's the matter?" he asked and lightly punched my shoulder. "You alright?"

"I'm good… It's…" A boulder had lodged itself in my throat, and I struggled to formulate a sentence. Luka stood next to me, and I unconsciously laced his fingers through mine. Reese didn't even notice, or if he had he didn't make a thing out of it. "I'm sorry it's been forever since we've seen each other. I should have come to more of your games."

"And I should come home more, but what can we do? Life is life, right?" His lips parted into a crooked grin. "I don't follow you around while you deliver placentas and shit, why should you follow me?"

"Placentas?" Luka cringed.

"That's different."

"Not to me. I love hockey, that doesn't mean my entire family has to. You, and Mom, and Dad, supported me when I needed it most, and I've benefited from that. I mean, if you can make a game every now and then, sweet. If not… I'm not crying about it, alright? You worry too damn much, always did." His gaze fell to where Luka's hand was linked with mine. "You two have something you want to tell me, or is this one of your weird friendship things?"

"Um…" I hesitated and he waved a gloved hand.

"You know what… Save it for dinner. There's a story here, and I have to get back on the ice."

At that same moment, one of his teammates came to an abrupt stop in front of the boards. "Bro… we're being accosted by six-year-olds, we need back-up."

"Bryson, this is my brother, Rook, and his…"

"I'm Luka… it's nice to meet you." He held out his hand and nodded toward the ice. "Those little munchkins are relentless. They've been skating circles around you since we got here."

"No joke." Bryson took off his glove and shook Luka's hand, his Canadian accent leaking through as he spoke. "If I had half their energy I'd never lose."

"Don't let him fool you." Reese swung his legs over the side of the boards. "This guy never quits. We're lucky Tampa traded him up."

Bryson slipped on his glove and tapped the top of Reese's helmet. "Yeah, yeah, let's skate. Good to meet you both."

"Same," I said, and Luka reached into his bag for his camera.

Skating backward, Reese grinned at us, and Luka grabbed a few shots before my brother turned and disappeared into a swarm of children.

A couple hours later, the three of us were tucked away in a shadowed booth in the back room of one of Reese's favorite breweries. It was loud, with tall ceilings and drafty ductwork. Nineties rock music blared from the overhead speakers, while a huge widescreen television played a rerun of last Thursday's hockey game. The place was busy, but the staff was attentive, refilling our waters twice before we'd even had a chance to order. A perk of going to dinner with an NHL player I assumed.

"Did you get all the shots you needed?" Reese asked and set his menu to the side.

"You guys were too cute with those kids." Luka beamed. "I think I took about a thousand pictures."

"One of the upsides of being in the League, we get to do cool shit like that all the time. Some of the guys hate the charity stuff, but I think it's fun. We make a lot of money, and yeah, we kill our bodies, but it's nice to give back. Without our fans, we don't have a job." He took a sip of his water, watching us from above the rim. "It's story time, boys." He placed his glass on the table and stretched his arms across the back of the booth. "What's going on with you two?"

"Mom didn't say anything?" I asked and he shook his head. "I figured she would have."

"Shit." His posture changed, his shoulders slumping forward. Reese scrubbed a palm over his hair. It was longer than he usually kept it, the tight curls falling over his forehead. "I didn't think... I'm so sorry, Luka. About your dad. I wanted to be there, but—"

"Thank you, and don't... I understand. My mom got your flowers, she loved them."

"I'm an asshole," he grumbled.

"We weren't close, not like—"

"You and my brother." That look returned to Reese's eyes, like he was waiting for some revelation. I still couldn't believe my mom hadn't said anything. "Seems like you guys patched up everything... Last time I heard, you were in California."

"He moved back," I said. "And yeah... I guess we patched things up." I turned to look at Luka and smiled. "We're together."

"I can see that." The humor in my brother's tone grabbed my attention. "Like boyfriends?"

"Yes."

"Is that a bad thing?" Luka asked, and his defensive tone surprised me.

It surprised my brother, too, and he laughed. "Calm down, tiger. I'm not a bigot." He swallowed and fiddled with a straw wrapper, tearing it in two. "Rook... when we were younger, I thought maybe you'd come out to me at some point, and when you didn't, I figured I was wrong to assume shit."

"I didn't know then."

"No?" he asked, and his dark brows slanted into a crease.

"It's not always black and white," Luka explained. "For me, sure. I knew I was in love with your brother the minute I understood what it meant to be attracted to someone, but for some people it's not that straightforward."

"You're in love with my brother?" A slow grin spread across Reese's face.

"I am."

"I love him, too. This is… it was confusing for a long time." I held my brother's gaze. His eyes the same blue color as our mom's. "I didn't understand it back then… but when I'm with Luka… I feel like myself. I don't have to talk myself into being with him."

"You don't have to explain it to me," Reese said, his voice as soft as his smile. "If you're gay then you're gay… If you're straight, bi… whatever. You're my brother and I love you, alright. Who you're attracted to has nothing to do with that." I rubbed the sting from my eyes with the back of my free hand, and Luka scooted closer to me, pressing into my side. Reese touched the tip of my sneaker with his and shook his head. "I swear to fuck, if you make me cry right now, I'll tell my publicist you're not allowed to print any of those pictures."

"Wow." Luka laughed. "He doesn't play fair."

"Not on the ice." Reese knocked a fist on the table. "And not in life. Play dirty or don't play at all, that's my motto."

He winked at the waitress as she approached our table and flirted with her while he ordered half the menu for himself. Over dinner we talked more about the charities my brother's team worked with, and the photoshoot and what Reese could expect for the interview tomorrow with Zach. I didn't miss my brother's fascination every time Luka and I found ways to be close or kissed each other. He'd tried hard not to stare, but I'd caught him. This time when Luka kissed the back of my hand before excusing himself to go to the bathroom, I said something.

"It's weird for you?"

"I don't think weird is the right word." He sighed. "You were never affectionate with any of the girls you dated. It's different."

"The connection I have with him is deeper." I pushed my empty plate to the side of the table. "Attraction for me… it's not about sex or gender, it's about the person. I didn't know those girls like I know Luka."

"But did you want to know them?"

"Maybe I could have… but they never stuck around long enough. It's not easy for me like it is for you."

"Shit." He laughed. "For me… Relationships are far from easy … trust me."

"Luka makes me feel safe… and that's what does it for me."

"I want that too. To be with someone who isn't after me for my job or status." He lifted his drink to his lips and glanced toward the bar. He gulped down the rest of his beer and wiped his mouth with the back of his arm. "But all these fucking people… I don't know. They want something from me. Maybe when I retire…"

"Are you thinking about it?"

"This is the last year of my contract. I'm a thirty-four-year-old D-man with bad knees. There's no thinking about anything. This is my last season."

"Retirement could be nice… finally settle down somewhere, give Mom those babies she's always harassing you for."

He scoffed. "I think you're closer to that goal than I am. Do you think you two will get married? You've known each other forever, wouldn't be too much of a leap."

"Maybe? I don't know. Being together like this… it's new," I said. The idea of it, having Luka for forever, maybe having kids of our own, I hadn't thought that far ahead yet.

But I was in my head now, with every I love you, every touch and kiss Luka and I had shared since he'd come home, and there wasn't a fiber in my body that didn't yearn for it. Yearn for him and a future I couldn't fathom without him.

CHAPTER TWENTY-ONE

Rook

IT WAS TOO QUIET, *and I couldn't think. Luka was stretched out on the floor in front of me. He was supposed to be doing the same math homework as me but had spent more time texting than he had on actually working. The blue light on his phone lit his face as he smiled, and irritation rankled itself inside my gut. I shut my eyes and took a breath. I didn't know why I was so frustrated.*

"Wake up, sleepyhead."

"I'm awake," I grumbled. "I'm just… I hate geometry."

"Want to copy from me?"

"I'll fail the test," I said, more annoyed than I should have been. "I'll figure it out." I shut my book and leaned back against the footboard of his bed. "I just need a break."

"A break sounds good." Luka dropped his phone to the carpet and rolled onto his back. "I can help you, if you want."

"Maybe later."

"Want to watch a movie?" he asked.

230

I glanced at the clock on his dresser. It was almost ten.

"I have to go home soon."

Luka laughed and turned to look at me. "Your parents won't care."

His phone lit up again and I stared at it. "Better get that."

"What's wrong?"

"Nothing," I lied. I knew Luka had a life outside of our friendship. I did too. But lately, with my hockey schedule, I hardly had time to hang out with him. I missed him, and I didn't know if that was a weird thing to feel. "I'm tired, I guess. We've had a lot of late practices this week."

"I know, I've hardly seen you," he said and sat up with a dramatic frown. "I miss us."

It was silly, but that made me happy.

His phone pinged again. "Who is that?"

"Just some guy." He turned off his phone and rested his head in my lap. "He's not important." I ran my fingers through the soft strands of his hair, and he closed his eyes. "Promise me you won't run off to the NHL like your brother wants to."

"I promise," I said, and he smiled.

"Good." Luka opened his eyes, and I stared down at him. "I wish… I wish shit didn't have to change."

"I feel it too. Like time… I don't know… everything feels too fast." I laughed at myself. "Shit… I'm tired. I don't even know what I'm saying."

"It makes sense. Next year we'll be seniors and then…"

"And then?"

"Fuck, I don't know… but I hope whatever happens we'll be together. I hate missing you."

"We'll be together," I said, and he grinned. "Whatever happens, Luka… I don't ever doubt that."

~~~~~~~~~~

Luka held my hand as I pushed open the hotel room door. We were both dead on our feet after a long day of traveling, and then the rink and dinner with Reese. We'd left him with a promise to meet up for an early breakfast. He wanted to make sure he had enough time to take us around the city to do touristy things before his interview tomorrow. It was our only real chance to spend more time with him since he had to fly out for a road trip at six that same evening. But as selfish as it was, I would have loved to sleep in with my boyfriend instead. I wanted a day without a schedule. A day to be with Luka like we used to. To lie around and watch a movie and make out and enjoy each other. We hadn't had much of an opportunity to be together without something looming over us, and even though he was right here in front of me, and we had this whole weekend, it didn't feel like enough time.

Luka unhooked his watch and set it on the desk in the corner of the suite. The city lights spilling through the window danced across the angles of his face, and when he turned and found me watching him, he smiled.

"What?"

"I wish I could keep you all to myself this weekend," I admitted as he sat on the edge of the king-size bed. "We haven't had a lot of time together."

"We have right now…"

"Are you tired?"

"I should be," he said. "What about you?"

My exhaustion couldn't compete with the buzzing under my skin. Luka's eyes were hooded as I walked toward him, hazy with a look that I'd learned meant he wanted to kiss me.

I held his chin between my fingers, and he looked up at me. "No… not anymore."

He rested his hands on my hips as I bent down to kiss him.

"You know what I want to do?" he asked.

"Hmm," I hummed against his lips. "What?"

"I want to watch a movie on that ridiculous television in the bathroom while we take a bath."

I laughed as I stood to my full height, and he grinned up at me. "What movie?"

"Shit… I have no idea. I don't even care. As long as you're naked and the water is hot, I'm happy."

The idea sounded perfect to me, and once we were both settled in the tub, we'd picked a movie neither of us had seen, some new thriller he'd heard about from Nora. The bathroom was almost the size of the suite itself. The tub could have fit at least three people, and with the jets on, it was more like a jacuzzi than bathtub. The entire thing was surrounded by gaudy marble, but one wall was a full-length mirror with a television inside of it. I'd never seen anything like it. Luka was situated between my legs, his back to my chest, his hands running a slow circuit up and down my legs. The lights were dimmed, and with the low vibration of the jets, and citrus scent bubbling around us, I could almost fall asleep like this. Luka rested the back of his head on my shoulder, and I kissed his temple. I should've been paying attention to the movie, but I was too distracted. My fingertips skimmed across the smooth planes of his abs as I tracked the beads of condensation trickling down his neck, to his nipple.

"I can hear you thinking," he said.

"This is nice."

"I feel like we're in my room back home, like all those times we'd watch movies and I'd pass out in your lap. Except… we're naked."

"And I want to kiss you."

He turned his head and smiled. "Back then I always wanted to kiss you."

"Sometimes I think you should have."

"I don't know… You weren't ready."

He was right. But looking back at my life, at all the little things, all those moments we had between us, it was obvious to me now.

"I'm ready now, though."

Luka sat up and I spread my legs as he turned to face me. On his knees, he slowly leaned forward, his eyes on my mouth. The intensity of his blue eyes, the way the silence charged around us, there was nothing but his mouth, and his skin, and the warm touch of his hands. One breath, and then another, and finally his lips were on mine. I groaned as his tongue pushed into my mouth, unsure of who grabbed who first as we became a tangle of arms and legs. The water around us slapped the sides of the marble, splashing onto the floor as he straddled me with strong thighs. His stubble chafed my skin, his teeth marking me as I claimed him with mine. My hands traced the curve of his spine, and I was a thousand dandelion seeds drifting away in the summer heat of his skin. I ached for his touch, my cock filling for him, throbbing as we rutted together. Everything was slippery, falling away too fast, and I held on to his hips, held him as he whispered against my mouth between kisses how much he needed me, wanted me.

"I'm here," I said. "I'm here."

The words were lost in the steam, my muted grunts buried in the crook of his neck. We grasped with frantic hands. Closer and not close enough. I kissed our secret message inked into the skin of his shoulder, traced the line of his tattoo with the tip of my tongue. I craved every goose bump I tasted, every etched muscle under his pale skin. My hands shook with awe as they slid over his chest, down his ribs and below his ass. He leaned back, the flushed head of his cock leaking against his stomach as he lifted onto his knees. The water had started to cool, and he shivered as he stared down at me.

"Are you ready to get out of here?" he asked, and I nodded.

We barely dried off, unable to stop kissing long enough to get the job done properly. Luka's hair was still wet when his head hit the pillows, and as I crawled on top of him, his hand slid to the back of my neck.

"Are you cold?" I asked.

"A little."

"Should we—"

Luka dragged me down into a blistering kiss, my entire body covering his. We moved together, our cocks sliding between us, and after a few minutes, we were both panting and sweaty.

"Fuck," he moaned and rolled us both, holding me down beneath him.

He took his time kissing his way down my neck and chest, and I was a mess of need and nerves. He swallowed my cock into the obscene heat of his mouth, and I almost came right then and there. I was turned on and edgy, the sensation still new, and I wasn't sure if I wanted relief. It was too good, too surreal, having something like this, having Luka.

"Rook." His cheeks were red, his eyes hazy as he came up for air. He was breathless, his fingers curling against the hair on my thigh. "I… I want to be inside you… but if you don't—"

"I do." I sat up and he leaned back onto his knees. I cupped his cheeks, my thumb dipping between his parted lips. He'd given himself to me. He'd let me explore and touch and feel on my own terms, and I wanted to keep going, going until there was nothing unknown between us. "I want to give you everything."

"I want to make it good for you." He smiled against my lips. "Epic."

"I trust you."

"I love you."

He fell into my arms and our mouths met in another messy kiss. I fell back onto the mattress, and Luka tumbled down next to me. We slowed down, taking a few breaths, and when he kissed me again, I could taste the words he'd spoken. *I love you.* It was painted against his tongue, against mine.

"Give me a second," he said and brushed my cheek with his knuckles.

I waited for him as he rummaged through his bag that he'd put in the closet after we'd checked in that afternoon, and a nervous wave of energy coursed through me. I wanted this, wanted him, but by the time he crawled back into bed, a few of those

236

same old insecurities had come crashing forward. Would I be enough? Was I what he needed? He set a bottle on the night-stand, before pulling me back to the present, into the heat of his hold. His kiss was tentative at first, slow and deep pulses of tongue and teeth. His touch was gentle, his fingers reacquainting themselves with the slope of my shoulder, the line of my hip. We were both on our sides, and as he tugged me closer, the warmth of his body absorbed some of my anxiety.

This was Luka.

I took a breath between kisses.

I trusted this. I trusted him.

"Hey…" he said and raised up onto his elbow. "Everything still okay?"

"Yeah…" I kissed his fingers. "I want this… I want to know what you feel like."

"God," he groaned. "Hearing you say that…"

He pushed me onto my back, his lips capturing mine. Luka poured everything into this kiss. Every year we'd spent together, every word we'd never said, every blue hour and every sunrise. There was no doubt or reluctance, my body was his to have. He took his time, bringing me to the brink again and again, with his mouth and hands, and I was dizzy with the scent of his skin, with the feel of his lips on my thigh.

"Spread your legs for me," he whispered.

Luka reached for the bottle he'd left on the nightstand and popped it open with the tip of his thumb. He slicked up his fingers, and my heart took off like a hummingbird. I could feel my pulse in my fingertips, in the shaft of my cock as his mouth closed around the crown. He brushed my knee with his shoulder, and I spread my legs wider. My face flushed at the first touch of his finger, the intimate pressure almost too much. I moaned as he slipped the pad of his thumb into my hole, and I grabbed the backs of my thighs on impulse. Luka pressed in deeper, whispering praise into the private hollow between my hip and thigh, and switched out his thumb for a finger. I gave into the pinch of pain, melting into something more, something I needed.

I needed.

And it was all him. Always him.

He worked me open, unlocking my body, inch by inch, until I wholly surrendered myself to him, until every ember inside my body had ignited. He was three fingers deep, and I was sweating, coming out of my skin, nothing more than a body of bones and want and...

"Ah... fuck... Luka..." I arched my back, my fingers twisting in the duvet, my climax suddenly way too close. "Holy shit."

"That's your prostate," he said, and if I wasn't so close to falling apart, I would have laughed at the smug grin on his face. "Feels good?"

"Too good."

He kissed the inside of my knee.

"You think you're ready?"

I swallowed as his fingers slipped from body, leaving me empty. "I'm ready."

He crawled over me, and the relief I felt with his lips on mine again, was too much to bear. His mouth was warm and tasted like me. Every muscle in my body was relaxed, almost wrung out from everything we'd done up to this point, but that need he'd stirred up inside me, it swelled inside my core, and the longer he drew out this kiss, the more I needed him, needed him to fill me, to take away that empty want building inside me.

"Do you want me to use a condom?" he asked and kissed the corner of my mouth. "I get tested regularly, but if you want me to I will."

"I don't think we need it, unless you do."

"You haven't been with anyone in—"

"Years, Luka. It's been years."

"Then we're safe."

The city was sprawled out below us outside our window, continuing at its rapid pace while we lost ourselves in the slow dive of our bodies. Luka grabbed the bottle of lube again and took my hand in his. He poured the liquid into my palm, and after he clipped the cap shut and tossed it aside, I slicked up his cock with a few strokes. He kissed me with tender lips, pushing me back onto a pillow. He slipped inside me, gradual at first, his eyes a sure point through my daze, through the feel of his body taking mine. Full and stretched, I panted as he stilled and lifted my legs, draping them into the crook of his elbows. He traced quiet circles on my skin, waiting for me to catch my breath.

"Tell me…" I didn't recognize the husky, spun out, sound of his voice. His jaw clenched, his breath ragged, on the edge of control, as he said, "Tell me if you need me to stop."

"Can you kiss me again?"

He lowered my legs and held the weight of his body above me with his forearms, his mouth covering mine. The familiar taste of him, the prickly stubble on his chin, it brought me home. It reminded me this man had dotted every moment of my life with memories I never wanted to forget, with his smiles and laughter, and his eyes, the same bright blues that watched me now as he moved his hips with slow shallow thrusts. I dug my heels into the backs of his legs, and he inhaled my gasp, taking small pieces of me inside of him too. The twinge of pain faded, sending pulses of pleasure to the base of my cock, to my spine, our bodies breaking against each other, my fingers in his hair, his teeth sinking into my shoulder. A low sound trapped itself in my throat as Luka leaned back onto his knees, changing the angle of his hips, hitting me deeper, finding that same spot that had me spinning earlier. Luka swore, his cheeks blushing red, and my world had been narrowed down to this room and how it was steeped in the smell of sex and Luka and that citrus bath soap, to that sticky wet sound of our bodies, to the moans Luka gifted me, to the dry, perfect scratchy feel in my throat as I fought to breathe.

"Luka…" I gasped his name instead of what I needed to say, what I wanted to say.

Please, tell me how, how to let go, how to give in.

And he knew. Without the words he knew, like he'd always known, and gave me what I wanted. He leaned over me, threading his fingers through mine above my head. The full weight of his body held me to the bed, trapping my cock between us. Every rock of his hips, every slide of his belly, skin on skin, along the length of my cock, pushed me further and further, and I wanted to give in, to let go of that precipice and fall. Fall into the desperation as he fucked into me, as I pleaded, as he swallowed my moans with uncoordinated and delicious kisses. Strung tight and sensitive, I came without his hand ever touching me, my hot release never ending, pooling on my chest, my stomach, and in my belly button. Luka shouted, some sort of strangled expletive, my head too clouded with my own climax to decipher it. I felt it, though, the moment he slipped over the ledge too, felt the heat of him filling me, spreading through me, and as he dropped his shoulders, burying his nose in my neck, our chests heaving together, I wrapped him up in my arms with a plan to keep him, just like this, until morning.

CHAPTER TWENTY-TWO

Luka

WITH MY CHEEK ON his shoulder and my nose nuzzled in his neck, I never wanted to move. I was boneless, saturating myself in the scent of sweat and soap and something purely Rook. His hand trailed up my spine, nothing more than a barely there brush of fingertips over my fevered skin. He tickled my neck, combing his fingers through my hair, and I shivered.

He started to move, trying to reach for the duvet, and I groaned. "No… this is good. Can't move yet."

His chuckle puffed against my skin, and he kissed my temple. "You can stay like this as long as you like."

"At some point, we'll have to at least clean up."

"Let's not get carried away."

A huge smile stretched across my lips at the sleepy, sexed-out sound of his voice. I indulged in it, in the way his body fit underneath mine, seamless and decadent. Rook had opened up for me, and I felt lucky, honored to be the one he trusted enough to love, to show him how good it could feel to fuck, to let go, to be the one he allowed inside of his body. I wanted to be the only one. I wanted to spend the rest of my life making him happy, making up for the last five years, even though he'd tell me I didn't need to. I wanted to show him, like those stars we'd spent so many nights counting, my love for him was infinite.

I slid my hip to the mattress and burrowed into his side. "Tell me what you're thinking."

A laugh rumbled in his chest, and he turned to look at me. I stared at his full lips and traced them with my finger.

"Are you fishing for compliments?"

"I'm checking in," I said and pinched the dimple in his cheek. "Smart ass."

"I was thinking about how different that was."

"Good different?"

"Yes," he said, and kissed the side of my jaw. "It was… consuming. If that makes any sense?" He swallowed and bit the side of his lip. "I didn't have to think about how I should be feeling, or what to do, my body just took over. It hasn't ever worked like that for me. It was sort of liberating. I can admit, at times, I worry I won't be enough for you, but then I remember it's you. And how much I care about you, and how I never want to stop touching you and kissing you and it's…"

"Consuming." I grinned.

"Yeah." He tucked me under his arm. "Is it like that for you?"

"It is now," I answered honestly. "With you it's not just a release, or something that feels good. I enjoyed sex, I'm not saying that I didn't. But with you it's more. We're sharing something

243

that only belongs to us, and it's more than our bodies. I've never had that with anyone else. What we have... it feels boundless. It feels like forever."

Rook rolled me onto my back and kissed me like forever started now. We made out like we should have when we were teenagers, wrestling with each other, jockeying for position, laughing, and grinding together like we had all the time in the world. My chin was raw, and my lips chapped, but I didn't give a shit, and when we were both unbearably hard again, I gave him my body. Straddling his hips, I prepped myself while he watched with complete adoration, his amber eyes hidden behind wide pupils. I hadn't bottomed in forever, but I wanted to give him this, give him every experience, give him myself entirely like he had for me.

"Luka... Do you know how sexy that is... damn." He sat up, his grip rough and eager on the back of my neck as his mouth collided with mine.

We were chest to chest, his hand holding the base of his cock as he slipped inside me, the sharp stretch giving way to a fullness that was indescribable. We were touching in every way possible. My thighs against his hips, his hand on my neck, my lips at his temple, his body fully seated inside of me. I knew I wouldn't last long riding him like this, with the pressure of his fingertips digging into my ass cheeks. I lost control, the sweet edge of our first time fading with every forceful snap of his hips. This time was fast and dirty, and I loved it like this, needed it as much as I needed the tender touches too.

"Yes..." I gasped, his teeth sinking into my bottom lip, my mouth parted and open as my head fell forward. I gripped my shaft, stroking my dick with quick and aggressive strokes, trying to catch the flame licking up my spine, to soothe the ache building inside me every time he hit that spot, that fucking spot, and…

"Fuck, Rook… I'm…" My orgasm burst through me and I cried out, spilling my load onto his chest and stomach.

My ass spasmed around his cock and he growled, the heat of his release pouring into me. I held onto his shoulders, riding out the trembling aftershocks as he leaned in and kissed me with lazy lips, both of us sucking down air like it was water.

"Holy fuck," I panted, and he blinked at me with sleepy eyes. "You look a little wrecked."

His smile turned shy. It was my favorite of all of his smiles. "I feel a little wrecked."

I admired the mess I'd made of his chest. "Do you want to take a shower?"

"I just want to sleep," he said. "And honestly, I like smelling like you."

I wasn't going to argue with that. I liked smelling like him too.

"We can shower in the morning."

I leaned over and grabbed the box of tissues on the nightstand and cleaned us both up enough we wouldn't totally ruin the sheets. Rook held my waist the whole time, his thumbs brushing back and forth across my ribs. Once we were snuggled under the sheets, he rolled toward me and stared at me through his dark lashes. He ran his finger down the bridge of my nose and across my cheek. "Do you have a preference?" he asked. "When it comes to sex?"

"I prefer to only have it with you."

His laugh was soft. "You know what I mean."

"And that's my honest answer. I don't care. As long as it's you." I threaded his fingers through mine and rested them against my chest. "I love being with you, in any way, if you prefer to bottom, or top, or neither, it doesn't matter to me."

"It doesn't matter to me either." He kissed my knuckles, his lashes fluttering closed once, and then a second time. He was fighting that post-orgasmic crash and losing. "Only you, Luka… that's all I want."

His eyes stayed closed, his breathing eventually evening out, and I watched him sleep, because this was better than any dream waiting for me when I closed my own eyes.

* * *

"Why hockey?" Zach asked and Reese grinned.

"Because it's the best fucking sport there is," he said. "You could drop me onto a baseball field, or a football field, and after a little while I'd figure it out. Maybe I wouldn't be a pro, but I could fill in for a game. You can't do that with hockey. There are too many skill sets to master."

"Cocky much," I muttered, and Rook laughed. He handed me another blessed cup of coffee. "Fuck, I love you."

He pressed a kiss to my cheek and leaned against the wall next to me. "He's right, though."

"I know, but he's supposed to sound like a humble hero, not some dude bro asshat."

"Wow, tell me how you really feel." He stared at me, and I sighed.

"I'm tired and cranky because a certain hockey hero felt the need to drag us across the entire city of Vancouver this morning."

"Or..." He turned to whisper in my ear. "Are you cranky because we slept in too late and didn't have time for that blowjob you offered me in the shower?"

"That might be part of it... and my feet hurt. I can't believe I'm going to say this, but I like how small Hemlock Harbor is. I can make it from one side of the town to the other without breaking a sweat."

"Small town for the win?"

I snuck an arm around his waist and rested my head on his shoulder. "Definitely."

The interview took less than an hour, which gave me lots of time to do my thing. I took a few candid shots of Reese talking with Zach and just shooting the shit around the arena with Rook. A couple of his teammates had shown up later, and I couldn't miss the chance to grab some pictures of all that homoerotic brotherly team affection. I'd forgotten how fun it could be, doing a shoot like this, getting to capture a moment without artifice. On the sideline, through my lens, I got to frame the world the way I saw it. I loved taking pictures of nature, snapping the moment the sun kissed the horizon, or the moment it turned the world to gold. But catching a smile, a touch, a hug, and a welcome home, there wasn't anything better than that. And these guys together, it was hard not to feel their energy. Bryson and his goofy smile, the way he hung on Reese while the other guys teased them. They were juvenile, grown men without a care in the world. I could stay here all day trying to catch all of their secret handshakes and jokes, but we had to wrap up around three, right before the team had to head out to catch a flight to Denver.

"You guys need to come visit again," Reese said as he smothered his brother with a goodbye hug. "Preferably during the off season, I'll have way more time. You could stay a week or something."

"Or you could come home to visit," Rook said. "Mom would love that."

"Maybe. You know me… I get antsy if I'm in the Harbor too long." Reese pulled me into a side hug, wrestling with me until he had me in a headlock. He leaned down and whispered in my ear, "Don't you fucking break my brother's heart. You hear me?" I shoved out of his hold, and he laughed. I smoothed a hand over my hair, my face hot as he stared me down. "Yeah… you heard me."

"I did."

He pointed two fingers at me. "Good."

"Cut it out, Reese." Rook's lopsided smile was enough to quell my aggravation.

Reese was a meathead, but he meant well. "Don't forget to send me a wedding invite," he said as his ride pulled up to the curb. "I throw a wicked bachelor party."

He blew us a kiss as he got into the backseat.

"A wedding invite?" I asked Rook as his car pulled away.

"He's messing with us," he said, but the playful gleam in his eyes made me think there was more to that story. "What did he say to you when he had you in that headlock?"

"He told me not to hurt you." I laced our fingers together as we headed back inside the facility. "The whole protective big bro thing. I get it…"

"Luka," Zach called my name, his eyes on his phone as he walked toward us. "I have news."

"What's up?"

"The team's management loves all of the photos you sent from the other day, and they want you to sign off on a few for them to use as promotion."

"That's awesome."

"Yeah, man, and wait till they see what you took today." He rapidly swiped his thumb over his screen, holding up one of the pictures I'd taken today. I'd sent them to him via email about ten minutes ago. "These are great. Like quality stuff."

"Um… thanks."

Zach wasn't one to dole out praise, and maybe I didn't realize how much I needed to hear it, but it sure as hell felt good to know I didn't totally suck at what I loved doing. I'd spent so much time chasing this idea of what I thought I wanted to be, chasing a career that had been more like a dream than a reality. With every failure, I'd started to believe maybe what I saw through my lens was a distortion of truth, and I wasn't cut out for this after all.

"I'm serious." Zach dragged his eyes from his phone. "I want to show these to my ex, Dale, that sportswriter guy I was telling you about. With pictures like this, and the right connection, you could get a job with a team, or a sports magazine, in a heartbeat. Your talent is wasted at *The Herald*."

"You think so?"

"I know so. Let me see what I can do."

"You don't have to do that… I'm happy at—"

He held up his hand and tapped his phone once, and then again. "I forwarded everything to Dale, he'll get them into the right hands."

"Thank you... I mean, wow... Really, I appreciate it, but I'm not looking to—"

"Don't sell yourself short. Let's see what we see," he said. And shoved his phone in his pocket. "Do you guys have plans for dinner? We could meet up later."

"Um…" Stunned by the entire conversation, I hadn't noticed Rook had let go of my hand. "Yeah… we—"

"We planned on staying in," Rook said, his tone too quiet. "But thanks."

"No problem. I guess I'll see you back in Washington, and I'll let you know if Dale hears anything."

"Thanks," I said. "And send me whatever I need to sign so the team can use those photos."

"Already did."

Zach left with another, "see you later," and Rook and I made our way outside in a weird stagnant silence. Flurries and fat flakes started to float down from the gray sky above us, and I zipped up my jacket, scowling at the traitorous precipitation. My fingers were instantly cold, and I wanted to reach for Rook's hand again, but he had his phone out, likely looking for a nearby ride.

"Anything close?" I asked and he pocketed his cell with a long exhale.

"Three minutes."

"Not too bad, we shouldn't freeze to death before then."

Rook cracked a smile, and the heaviness in my chest became less distinct.

"Just so you know…" I said. "I don't want a job at a big sports magazine." He turned to look at me, the concern in his eyes cutting me open. "I don't."

"Luka…" He swallowed and turned to stare out into the street. A couple of cars honked their horns, the snow falling even harder as I waited for him to speak. "You heard what he said. You're wasting your talent working for the newspaper. And he's right. I see you… how excited you were yesterday and today. You were in your element. How happy will you be taking shots of the bay every day, and Main Street and cupcakes for the rest of your life?"

"I tried, Rook. I did. I did the magazine thing in Portland, and then L.A. and I wasn't happy. I'm happy at *The Herald*." I held his hand. "I'm happy with you."

He faced me again, lowering his eyes, and rubbed his thumb into my palm.

"I can't be the reason, Luka… You'll resent me later. You have to mean it. You have to be sure."

"I'm sure. Christ, Rook." I lifted his chin. "Why are we fighting over a hypothetical job offer?"

"We're not fighting," he said and swept his lips over mine. "We're having a discussion."

"It feels bigger than that."

"I don't want to be the reason you throw away an opportunity."

"I'm pretty sure I'm capable of making my own choices. I told you. I can take pictures anywhere." He wiped the snow from my shoulders and pulled me into his chest, placing a soft kiss to my forehead. "I will always choose you, Rook. End of story." I snuggled into his arms, partly to hide from the wind, but mostly because he needed to know I wasn't going anywhere. I refused to make the same mistake again.

CHAPTER TWENTY-THREE

Rook

THE RAIN WAS MORE *like a mist as it seeped through our clothes, the muddy water staining our legs and backsides as it whipped up from our bicycle tires. I never liked playing in the rain much. It was cold and my fingers were numb, but Luka was thrilled, hollering and shouting at the sky as we made our way down the steep hill behind the Village Market. The park wasn't much farther, and I would have turned around and headed home if I was with anyone else. But Luka loved the rain even though he'd said he hated it not more than three minutes ago when the clouds had rolled in. He did that a lot, said he hated or loved something when he really didn't, and I wasn't sure why. I thought maybe it was because he was still getting to know me, or sometimes just to make his mom mad about one thing or another.*

"That was amazing." He was out of breath, rain dripping down his face. "Want to do it again?"

I curled my cold fingers and stared up the huge hill, dreading the hike back up, but when I turned back to tell him we should head home, I found him smiling so big it made me smile too.

252

"Sure. Sounds like fun," I said and realized maybe Luka wasn't the only one good at twisting the truth.

~~~~~~~~~~~~

"Sorry I'm so late," Luka called out, and the jingle of his keys sent Maribelle running toward the front door. I lowered the heat on the stove and stirred the mixture of meat and peppers I'd been cooking as Luka crooned at the dog. "Hey, baby." I had to laugh at his high-pitched tone. "Did you miss me?" Luka and Maribelle made their way into the kitchen, Luka all smiles and sweet talk as the dog jumped and circled his legs like he'd been away for days when he'd only been gone since this morning. "Hi." He snuck his arms around my waist, drawing my back to his chest and kissed my cheek.

"Hey." I snuggled deeper into his hold. "Did you stop at your mom's?"

It had been over a month since we'd gotten back from Vancouver. Luka had officially moved in with me a couple of weeks ago. His presence in this home, our home, had shaken that unknown thing, that something missing, that lonely ghost from the foundation and walls. We'd found our way back to old routines, breakfasts at The Early Bird, and counting stars in the waning blue hour. But even so, every morning was like a fresh start, and every night I'd fall asleep, dreamless, and safe in his arms, knowing more about myself, about him, and about the way our bodies had been made for each other.

"Mmm," he hummed, nuzzling his nose into my neck, sending a riot of goose bumps along my spine. "I did. Nora bought that place she's been eyeing for the last two weeks and had to tell me in person."

"The one on Elm?"

"Yeah." He squeezed me tighter. "The fixer upper."

"Oh."

I felt the warmth of his breath on my neck as he laughed. "I already know we'll be over there every weekend for the rest of our lives helping her renovate. She's already started making plans, and you know how much my sister can get carried away. If it wasn't for my mom, I would have never gotten out of there to-night. Nora would have held me hostage in the den with all those design magazines she's been hoarding her entire life. Anyway, I made it out alive." He leaned over my shoulder and inhaled. "Wow, that smells amazing. What are you making?"

"Tacos," I said and set the wooden spatula on the side of the pan. As I turned to give him a proper kiss, Maribelle barked at the lack of attention. Luka smiled, his cheeks tinged with pink, his hair damp with spring rain. "You need an umbrella," I said and melted my mouth over his. His lips were chilled, but warmed up quickly as his tongue dove into my mouth.

His hands skated under my t-shirt and skirted around my hips to rest at the small of my back. "I have an umbrella," he said and nibbled my bottom lip. "I just forgot to use it."

"You should leave one in your car."

"Meh… it's fine." He pressed quiet kisses along my jaw, below my ear. "I kind of like playing in the rain."

"You always did," I said as my hands slid along the curve of his spine. This is what I'd always wanted, this delicate intimacy, these everyday moments where we couldn't stop touching each other. And there didn't have to be an ending. I could be like this, with him, hands on skin, and *how was your day*, and lips that tasted like sweet mint, and never feel unsatisfied. We'd fallen in love sometime between then and now, between the pages of our youth and climbing trees and the touch of his hand in mine and the heartache of missing each other. We'd found a way to this, to these familiar days and nights, and I couldn't be happier.

My lips spread into a smile against his mouth. "Remember how you used to drag me outside for every storm, and I went even though I hated it?"

"Wait…" He planted his hands on my chest and stared at me in disbelief. "You hate the rain? Since when?"

"I don't hate the rain," I admitted. "I just hate being wet and cold and—"

"Our entire childhood is a lie." His gasp was all drama and I cracked up. "I'm glad you can laugh at this charade you called friendship."

He was teasing, but I loved getting him riled up. "How many times did you suffer through *The Sandlot* for me?" I asked. His eyes widened, and a full-bodied laugh broke from my chest. "Now who's the liar?"

"I didn't hate it," he said, and I pinched his hip.

"Luka… You mocked the movie every time we watched it… or fell asleep."

"It was a shit movie." He dropped his forehead to my shoulder. "So overrated."

I ran my palm down the back of his neck. "Ahh… The things we do for the people we love."

His laugh stuttered and his smile dimmed enough I noticed as he wriggled from my hold. Maribelle took that as an opportunity to push her way between us. "I better give her some attention before she chews another pair of my shoes in a jealous rage." He bent down to the dog's level and scratched her behind the ears, avoiding my eyes as he said, "I… uh… got an email from Dale."

I could hear the meat sizzling in the pan behind me, smell the slightly smoky scent of it burning, but I was powerless to move. "Dale."

He stood, and Maribelle trotted off to sleep under the table. Luka wouldn't look at me as he washed his hands in the sink. "Yeah. Nothing really… Just an email relaying how much Reese's team manager liked the article we ran in *The Herald,* and that he loved the photos we'd picked."

"That's good, right?"

He stared out the window above the sink, inhaling a tight breath. "It is."

"Then why do you sound upset?"

He wiped his hands with a dishrag I'd left on the counter and turned toward me, forcing a smile I knew better than to believe. "I'm not… I just remembered Nora volunteered us to help move her shit to the new house next weekend. She's unbelievable."

"I'm sure my dad will let us borrow his truck," I offered, ignoring his not-so-subtle change in subject. "But what else did the email say?"

"Rook, the meat is—"

"Shit." Annoyed that he was clearly diverting, and that dinner was possibly ruined, I moved the pan from the heat and dropped it against the stove with a little more force than was necessary.

"It's okay, we can get takeout or—"

"Why are you lying to me?" I asked, and Luka's face paled. I attempted to even my tone. "What else did Dale have to say? Was Zach right? Did he offer you a job or something?"

Resigned, he exhaled. "I don't want it."

"What's the job?"

"Why does it matter?"

"What's the job?" I asked again, and his eyes welled with tears.

"It doesn't fucking matter."

"It matters, Luka, because you matter. Your life matters, and I want to know what you're throwing away because of me."

"It's not because of you. I already told you I—"

"Goddamnit, Luka." I hadn't meant to shout. I never yelled, it wasn't like me to snap like that, and when Maribelle whined, I fisted my hands at my sides, frustrated with myself, and with Luka. My throat ached as I swallowed. I didn't want to lose him again, but I couldn't be the only reason for him to stay. What we had now, what roots he'd barely started to lay would end up rotting. "I'm sorry I raised my voice. I shouldn't have, I—"

"Vancouver wants to offer me a temporary position as their team photographer," he whispered, his voice as scratchy as mine. "I'd have to interview next week, but Dale said he thinks that's just a formality. The job would start next month. It's only a one-year contract, and I'd work alongside their PR team. It's a great opportunity, but I don't want it."

I will always choose you, Rook.

He was choosing me. And I couldn't let him.

My chest hurt as I reached out for his hand and tugged him into my chest. I kissed the top of his head, and when he looked

257

up at me with watery blue eyes, my heart broke. "You have to go. You're too talented. Imagine all the doors this could open for you."

"I don't want doors… We're finally happy. I told you in Vancouver… I'm happy here."

"But… what if… What if we could make it work?" I asked, and my mind started to sprint with ideas, with ways we could still be together. "We could try and—"

"What? Long distance for a year, maybe longer? That sucks, Rook. I'll be traveling with a hockey team. When will I have time to visit? We just moved in together. We've started to build something, and I want this, I want us more than I want some shitty job offer."

"You and I both know this isn't a shitty job offer."

"I don't care. It's not worth it," he said, his fingers gripping the side of my t-shirt. "You're worth more to me."

I will always choose you, Rook.

Maybe it was time I chose him.

"I can be a midwife in Canada," I said and as soon as the words flew from my mouth the knot in my stomach loosened a little. "I'd have to research how to transfer my license up there, but I could come with you."

"What? You love it here. Your literal dream was to raise a family here, I can't take that from you."

"You're right, I love Hemlock Harbor. But this is just a place, Luka… a place we can visit whenever we want. What I want more than anything… is to have a life with *you*, raise a family with you. I can do that in Vancouver."

And maybe it wasn't the total truth. Leaving here would be hard. I did it for college and told myself I never would again.

Homesickness has a way of changing you from the inside out, but love did, too, and I'd rather be homesick than heartbroken.

"You're serious?" He stared at me, and the hope blooming in his eyes was enough of an answer for me.

"Yes… relationships are about compromise."

"You realize our parents are going to hate this idea… And what about all your patients? Your practice? And I'll be on the road all the time. You'll be alone. The team is only offering me a year. Is it worth uprooting your entire life with the possibility of it being all for nothing. In Vancouver, you said you were worried about me resenting you… but what if—"

"Stop." I chuckled and framed his face between my hands. "You're spiraling."

"I think this entire situation warrants at least a mini spiral."

"I know it won't be easy, and our parents will most likely freak out. But it's not their life. It's ours." I dusted my thumbs across his cheeks as his tears spilled over. I was scared too. Hemlock Harbor, my practice, my family, leaving them indefinitely would be the hardest thing I'd ever do. This choice wasn't without sacrifice. But he was worth it. Without Luka, this place could never truly be home. "We can do this. We can make it work, as long as we do it together."

Luka crushed our mouths together, the kiss frantic at first, slowed into something soul deep. His breath was mine, and as he breathed me in, we silently agreed to new beginnings, to new roots, and to the rest of our lives.

CHAPTER TWENTY-FOUR

Luka

THE EARLY MORNING LIGHT seeped through the parted blinds as my eyes opened to the sound of my alarm. Half-asleep, I smacked my phone on the bedside table and groaned when it fell to the floor. Trying not to fall off the mattress, I bent down and switched off the alarm. Too tired to move, I dangled there, on the side of the bed, my fingers brushing the carpet, somewhere between sleep and reality. In the back of my mind, there was a responsible voice telling me to get up and get ready for the day, but then Rook's strong arm wound around my waist and pulled me back into the bed and against his chest. His morning erection in a semi-salute, buried itself between my ass cheeks, and despite the hour, I had no intention of moving a muscle. It wasn't a tough decision. Sexy naked cuddles, or be on time to work? Sexy cuddles for the win.

Rook's warm lips found the curve of my collarbone as his fingers dusted across the planes of my stomach. "What time is it?"

"Six-thirty."

He hummed something I couldn't decipher, his lips on the side of my neck as he gave my cock two lazy strokes. I rolled onto my other side, facing him, and laughed at the sleepy smile on his lips.

"Good morning," I said as he nuzzled his nose right below my ear and offered me a mumbled *good morning* of his own.

I tried not to think about the interview I had today, or the decisions we'd made over the past week. I made an effort to live in this moment with my boyfriend and his hands on my waist and his mouth on my skin. Hadn't I always wished for days like this, days where I could wake up next to Rook, and he was mine and we loved each other irrevocably? It was all surreal, moving in with him, having him like this, and sometimes I worried I'd fuck it all up again and it would all be gone.

"Hey." Rook pushed a strand of my hair from my forehead. "Where did you go just now?"

"What?" I shook my head as he stared at me, inching his hand up my stomach to my chest. "Sorry, I'm still waking up."

"Are you nervous about today?"

No.

Yes.

I didn't know how to answer him, but I gave him a half-truth anyway.

"A little."

I wasn't anxious about the interview. I was anxious about saying yes to the job offer. Anxious about telling our families, and uprooting our lives, and having it blow up in my face.

"There's no way they wouldn't hire you. Dale said it's a sure thing," he said, his optimism contagious. "This is good, Luka. It's going to be good."

He pushed me onto my back, his body blanketing mine, his heat taking away some of the vestiges of uncertainty. With the weight of his kiss on my lips, it was hard to think about what ifs, and I allowed myself a reprieve as his cock rutted against mine. How many mornings had we missed over the years, how many moments had I squandered and wasted on worry and doubt? I had what I wanted, right here, everything else could wait.

"Look at me," he whispered, knowing that I needed that anchor. I held his gaze, his rich, amber eyes had become my entire world as the friction of our bodies pulled me under, dragging me into that place between heaven and earth. "Love you."

Those two words were sure and steady, and I fell in love with him all over again.

We became a tangle of limbs and sweat, panting lips, and pre-come. We edged each other, taking it slow, and forgot about the clock, forgot about Vancouver and choices and everything waiting for us outside of this room. Hip to hip, with hearts pounding, and messy kisses, we relinquished control, the heat of our climax coating our chests and stomachs as we both trembled in each other's arms.

"I'm scared," I said, breaking the heady silence, the thought slipping from my lips before I could stop it.

"Me too." He grazed a sweet kiss across my cheek. "But I think being scared means we'll be careful. One day at a time, right? We'll make it work."

We'll make it work.

That sentence became a mantra, running through my head while we got ready for the day, and drove into town together. Our morning sexcapades had us running later than usual, but we managed to still squeeze in our daily breakfast date at The Early Bird. The familiar scent of bacon and spice greeted us as we walked in and took a seat. A sort of melancholic twist warmed my belly as I stared at the two bear statues by the front door, and the *come back soon* sign that hung crooked no matter how hard the owner tried to fix it. All the humming chatter and laughter crowded inside my chest, and I fought back the narrowing ache in my throat.

"Let me guess." Charles smiled at us as he pulled a pad and pen from his apron pocket. "Two orders of pumpkin pancakes."

"Please… and two coffees," Rook added.

"With cream and sugar," he said as he wrote down our order on the pad like he didn't have it memorized. "Coming right up."

"Thank you," I said, and the older man smiled at me through his thick white beard.

That same wistful sensation coursed through me as I smiled back at him. I'd known him since I was a kid. This place, the smells, everything down to the sticky floor and too strong coffee had become a part of me.

He leaned in and lowered his voice as he spoke. "A little birdie told me you two moved in together."

"By little birdie, do you mean Nora?" I asked.

"A good man never reveals his sources." Charles grinned. "But I gotta say… I'm happy for you two. I always wondered, but you know I don't like to stick my nose in other people's business."

"Of course not." Rook chuckled. "But thanks, we're happy too."

Charles looked us over again, his smile stretching wide. "I'll get your order in, shouldn't be too long."

When he walked away, Rook reached across the table and looped his pinky with mine. "What's with the frown?"

"I'm not frowning."

"It's definitely not a smile."

"I don't know…" I couldn't place this growing feeling of unease. It had to be anxiety about the job and moving and telling our families, but it was more than that. This narrowing of my ribs, it was hard to breathe. Maybe I was having a panic attack? I inhaled a slow, metered breath and met Rook's gaze. "I think my nerves are finally getting to me. Maybe we should have talked to our parents before the interview? Are we being impulsive? We are, right? Totally impulsive."

Rook pressed his foot against mine under the table and laced our fingers together. "Are you having second thoughts?"

"No… maybe? Shit… I don't know. I don't want to make the wrong choice."

"The video call is at eleven. See what they have to say. If it feels right, you'll know. I trust you, Luka. You'll make the choice you need to make."

I trust you.

God, why didn't that make me feel any better?

Before I had a chance to respond, Rook's phone rang. He looked at the screen and sighed as he answered. He nodded a few times, said something about membranes and leaking. He looked at me as he mouthed the words, "I'm sorry."

"How far apart?" he asked the person on the other end of the line. "Two minutes? Yeah, I would head in. I'll meet you there... It's no problem. Better safe than sorry. I'll see you soon." He started to stand and slipped his phone into his pocket. "I have to head to the hospital, one of my patients is in labor."

"Shit... okay. Um..."

He leaned down and gave me a quick kiss. "Luka... this is the dream, right? It's going to be okay."

"Right," I said and gave him another kiss, trying like hell to believe him.

Luckily, Charles hadn't started on our orders yet, and once Rook left, I was able to get my food to go. My office wasn't more than a few blocks away, and I looked forward to the walk. The crisp morning air was exactly what I needed to clear my head. It had rained earlier, and the heavy scent of the forest and the bay hovered all around me. The briny, clean smell was something I'd known for most of my life and was almost as comforting as the smell of Rook's body wash. Across the street, the gas lamps lining the walkway up to the Edge Water Inn flickered in the light breeze, catching my attention. The double-paned windows leaked a cozy buttery light, and I wondered why I'd never noticed how beautiful it was before. Everything was in Technicolor, like I was looking through the lens of my camera and seeing something I wanted to capture and keep forever. I cataloged all the shops and their quaint storefronts and smiled at the people I'd started to recognize again over the last few weeks as they walked by. Mrs. Gold and her yappy dog, and the guy with the suspenders whose name I could never remember. And the mom with her two kids bundled up in their stroller, offered me a wave.

"Nice day," Mr. Beckett said as he waited alongside me at the crosswalk, looking up at the sky. "Maybe the rain will hold off long enough to go sailing?"

"Maybe," I said, not sure if I was meant to answer.

We crossed the street, and I passed the bookstore and felt Rook's lips on mine. I raised my fingers to my mouth and smiled, allowing the nostalgia to consume me. I turned to look down the side street where we'd ride our bikes when we were kids to this massive hill behind the Village Market, remembering all the summer storms and muddy tires, and how I'd thought for sure the days would stretch on forever. I was stuck in memories as I made my way down the sidewalk, and almost missed it when Dot called my name.

"Luka," she hollered, practically chasing after me. Her cheeks were stained pink as she huffed and puffed, her hand on her hips. She was all flour and sugar in her flowing evergreen dress. "My goodness, son. Didn't you hear me?"

"I'm sorry, I was—"

"It's okay, you looked preoccupied. I wanted to tell you… I've been meaning to call your mother, but then you know how it is… And you know, ever since that lovely article you wrote about the bakery, I've had to hire some help. We've been so busy. People all the way from Seattle come around asking about my cupcakes."

"That's amazing."

"Isn't it?" She patted me on the shoulder, her smile waning with her furrowed brows. "But how's everything? With your family…"

"We're good, Dot. Thank you for asking."

"I heard you and Rook moved in together… and then Nora went and bought that place on Elm, you tell your mom if she ever needs any company, I'm just a phone call away."

A month ago, this conversation would have annoyed the fuck out of me, but after I'd interviewed Dot for the paper, I realized as snoopy as she was, she genuinely cared about the people in this town.

"I'll let her know."

"I believe you and that boyfriend of yours have a birthday coming up next month. Isn't that right?"

I laughed. "I can't believe you remember that."

"It's my job to remember everything," she said. "You just tell me what you want, and I'll make you both a cake you'll never forget."

We wouldn't be here next month.

The thought hit me harder than it should have.

"Thanks. We… uh… we'll let you know."

After an awkward hug, and a promise to call her soon, I headed to *The Herald*. I was grateful Zach and my boss weren't there yet, and closed myself off inside my office. I set the bag with my breakfast in the trash, my stomach too tied up to eat anything. It was like everything about this town had turned me upside down. I was Alice, staring through the looking glass, hoping to find a way home. Ever since I was a kid, I'd thought I wanted to live in a big city. I'd thought I'd never be able to have the life I wanted trapped in the confines of my dad's shadow. I'd thought moving away would be the key to my happiness. But I'd left, and tried to live that life, and suffocated inside my poor choices, inside the memories of this place. I didn't allow myself to see, to see how every cobblestone and tree branch and the craggy cliff sides had been written inside me and inside Rook. Hemlock Harbor was a part of us, it was a vital organ, attached to our hearts and lungs, and if we left this place, left its memories to fade, then Rook and I would fade along with it.

I was sure of it.

This wasn't a panic attack, or an overreaction.

I could feel it, slipping away, and we hadn't even left yet.

I wanted a life with Rook, in a place where we had history, more than the inflated childhood dreams I'd clung to because I'd been afraid. Afraid I'd never have what I really wanted. What I thought I'd never deserved.

Him.

I opened my laptop, and with the confidence I'd been searching for all week, I typed out an email to the Vancouver team manager regretfully declining the offer to interview. Once I pressed send, I felt the thousand-pound weight lift from my shoulders, and pulled my phone from my pocket to text Rook.

Me: Call me when you're back at the office.

Rook: It was a false alarm, heading back to the office now. I'll call you when I get there.

I shoved my phone back into my pocket, pacing around the room a few times, my need to see Rook boiling over until I couldn't take it, this itching feeling under my skin. It wasn't like I was worried Rook would be upset about my decision, but more this overpowering desire to tell him I was ready to start *this* life, this life with him, with Hemlock Harbor, and nosy neighbors, and cozy morning sex.

I didn't wait for Rook to call me, leaving Zach staring at me as I breezed by him in the hall with a quick, "I'll be right back."

It usually took me about seven minutes to get to Harborside Family Practice on foot, but running the majority of the way, I'd made it in five, and as I came rushing through the door, Charity stood abruptly behind her desk with a worried look on her face.

"Holy hell, you scared me, is everything—"

"Is Rook back yet?" I asked, trying to catch my bearings.

"Luka?" The deep and husky cadence of his voice calmed my beating heart, and as I turned around, I found him standing behind me.

His bag was slung across his chest, the button down and tie I'd chosen for him this morning without a wrinkle. I was the complete opposite with my shirt sleeves shoved up past my elbows and sweat beading on my forehead. I was sure my hair had to be wild from my anxious fingers.

"I didn't—"

"Is everything—"

We both tried to speak at the same time, and when I laughed, the crease between his brows softened. "What's going on?"

"I don't want to move," I blurted, forgetting where I was, that his receptionist was behind me. That his father was possibly here somewhere. And I didn't care. "I sent an email declining the offer to interview."

"You did?" His confusion was tinged with a smile, and fuck, my entire body relaxed.

"I'll be in the break room… making coffee." Charity pointed over her shoulder. "If you need me."

"I want Dot to make our birthday cakes next month," I said as soon as his receptionist disappeared down the hall.

"Um…*okay*," he said and took a few tentative steps toward me. "But—"

"Let me finish," I said, and he nodded, resting his hands on my hips. "I don't want to get lost in a big city and forget who we are. It doesn't feel right, leaving all this behind. And the more I open my eyes, the more I see how much I love this place as much as I love you. I want to eat breakfast at The Early Bird, and have Dot make our birthday cakes and our kids' birthday cakes. I want to build a fort in our backyard." I gripped the strap of his bag, pulling him closer. "You know that spot, between those two trees near the dock, it's the perfect place for a treehouse. I want our kids to have that, Rook. I want them to have everything we did. I don't want to have to try and make it work somewhere else. This is where we make sense. This is our home." My voice cracked as I reached up and cupped his cheek. He leaned into my hand and turned to press his lips to the center of my palm. "I want to marry you, Rook. Tell me yes… tell me you want that too. To get married here, in our spot… Meet me there, in the blue, one last time?"

"Yes," he said without hesitation and ghosted a kiss across my lips as he whispered, "I will always meet you there."

EPILOGUE

Rook

THE STRING OF LIGHTS *glittered in Luka's eyes as the sun set and the blue, gray sky turned to pitch. His fingers trembled in my hands, his nervous laugh stirring up the butterflies in my stomach. The small crowd of friends and family gathered with us under the canopy laughed, too, as he stumbled through the last few lines of his vows.*

"This ring is a symbol…" he said with a deep, stuttered breath, and I wanted to kiss him right then, not later when we were supposed to, but he took my hand and slipped a simple silver band onto my left ring finger. It was the same as the one I'd given him not more than a minute ago. "Of how we've come full circle." Luka rubbed his thumb over the metal, his stare fixed on mine. "It's always been you, Rook. Always this place…" The wind whistled through the trees as if they agreed, the wood of the old fort creaking behind us. "And I promise to love you forever, to be your partner in this life and the next."

Somewhere in the white noise, I heard the officiant speak, but his words were wasted in the rush of my pulse as Luka's mouth cov-

ered mine. We were supposed to wait, wait for that iconic moment when we were announced as partners, but Luka and I had spent too much time already waiting, hoping, wanting, and we were ready for this next chapter to begin.

Two years later

"Grab that two-by-four by the shed," I called out, and Ron gave me the middle finger as he walked toward the dock. Laughing, I added, "Please."

"I just got here and you're already bossing me around." He picked up the piece of wood, stacking a few extras in his arms. "Where's your husband?"

"Inside, refilling our water bottles." I wiped the sweat off my forehead with the back of my arm. "Thanks for coming."

"It looks really good," he said, dropping the wood onto the grass. The summer sun filtered through the branches, and he squinted as he stared up at the treehouse. "Just not sure what an infant is going to do with a two-story fort."

"When he gets older, he'll appreciate it. Why not build it now, while we have the time? Once he's here, who knows when we'll have the chance."

"I see lots of sleepless nights in your future." Ron clapped his hand on my shoulder. "I don't envy you that."

"Thanks." I laughed. "Luka's been sleeping in every morning because he thinks he can save up energy."

"Why is that kind of cute?"

"*Rook*," Luka shouted, and I turned in time to watch him burst from the back door of the house with Maribelle hot on his heels. "We have to go."

"Go where?" Ron asked. "I just got here."

"The hospital…" Luka's chest heaved as he braced his hands on his knees. "Water broke… your dad called, he said—"

"Shit." For five full seconds I didn't know what to do.

The midwife. The guy who had rushed to so many deliveries before. I stood stock still, my mind racing too fast to catch a thought.

"Babe, we gotta go." Luka grabbed my hand, the heat of his skin a jolt to my nervous system, and I woke from my stupor to see Ron and my husband grinning at me. "Come on."

"Congrats, Daddy." Ron gave me a small shove. "I'll take care of the dog. Better hurry before you miss it."

I couldn't remember if Luka had even stopped at any of the traffic lights, and I was grateful the universe had gotten us there in one piece. I hadn't ever been this nervous about anything before. I knew too much. The knowledge of everything that could go wrong choked me as we made our way through the sliding doors of the main entrance of the hospital. One of the volunteers was playing the piano in the lobby, and I didn't know the song, but the melody soothed me as we waited for the elevator. It filled my chest, and I squeezed Luka's hand.

"Are we ready?"

We had diapers and clothes and Jesus, had we gotten those colic drops my mom had mentioned to me the other day?

"It's going to be okay," he said, and I smiled because this time he was the one soothing me. "We're ready, Rook."

"We are," I said and kissed him as the elevator doors opened. "We can do this."

A labor and delivery nurse I recognized greeted us at the

front desk as we walked onto the unit. "Your dad is already here," she said. "Room seven."

We followed her to the room, my palms starting to sweat as she opened the door. It was a scene I was used to. The warmer for the baby was lit up in the corner, a nursery nurse huddled next to it waiting for her turn to shine. My dad sat on the end of the bed, his dress clothes hidden beneath the blue paper gown that never seemed to fit him correctly. He'd always bitched about being too tall for personal protective equipment.

"Just in time," he said, his excitement etched into his ear-to-ear grin. "I'm ready to meet my grandbaby. Your moms are going to be so jealous."

The adrenaline spread through my veins, and I tried to reach for that confidence inside me. The same confidence I brought with me to every delivery. But this was different. This was our child, and all my hope was held inside the rapid gallop of the baby's heartbeat thundering from the monitor. A reminder that life wouldn't wait for me to catch my breath.

"Holy shit," Luka whispered as he leaned into my side, and Leah, our surrogate, suppressed her laugh. "This is totally happening."

Luka and I had struggled for a while to decide whether or not we wanted to adopt or go the surrogate route, but then we'd found Leah through Luka's sister and everything sort of fell into place. She was one of Nora's good friends from Seattle and had already been a surrogate for a couple a few years ago. It also helped that I was close with one of the fertility doctors at the hospital, and in the end, we'd decided to do IVF with a donor. Eventually, if we were able, Luka and I wanted to have another child, but honestly, we were just happy to have a chance to raise a family at all.

"Are you okay? Do you need anything?" Luka asked Leah as he fidgeted with her cup of ice chips on the bedside table.

"I'm good," she said with the slightest cringe. "Thank God for epidurals."

Leah braced the back of her legs, and my dad fell into his clinical role. "I need you to take a deep breath, and push. Okay. Just like before."

She drew in another breath, and my instincts kicked in as I started to count to ten.

My dad nodded toward her left leg. "Come on, boys, we could use your help."

"Ready?" I asked Luka, and some of the color drained from his face.

"I think you might need to cut the cord, I'm feeling light-headed."

Everyone in the room chuckled, and as Luka took Leah's hand, I helped hold her leg as she pushed through another contraction. It was strange, being on the other side of birth, knowing that at any moment, this tiny creature would arrive and belong to us for eternity. All that anxious energy faded, and my heart found its usual, easy beat.

"You've got this," I said, and Leah pushed even harder.

It could have been one more contraction or five, and maybe in a few days I'd recount every second of this like I hadn't been in a dreamlike state, but when I heard that first garbled cry, and felt Luka's grip on my arm, and saw my son for the first time, everything I thought I understood about life had been reworded. This was love. This was everything.

Leah's eyes brimmed with tears, Luka's hand shaking as he wiped her cheek and told her *thank you for this, thank you, thank you.*

"It's a privilege," she whispered while the nurse wiped towels and blankets over the baby's pink skin, his chubby, dusky toes spread wide as he wailed his way into my arms.

Luka turned to me, his cheeks stained with tears, and we both held our child with reverence and uncertainty and pride.

My dad snapped off his gloves and stood to peek over the bundle of blankets. "Hello, little fella."

"Did you decide on a name?" One of the nurses asked, and I nodded.

"Whelan Isaac Abrams."

Our son wrapped his delicate hand around my finger as Luka whispered, "Welcome home."

THE END

AUTHOR'S NOTE

Thank you so much for reading Luka and Rook's story. This book is very personal, especially Rook's sexuality and his discovery of attraction. I realize his story might not look like everyone else's, but I also hope it is relatable as well, as it reflects my own experience through fiction. Sexuality as a spectrum is such a beautiful thing, and I am grateful I got a chance to tell a story I hope resonates with you in some way. As always, thank you so much for taking this journey with me. I hope you'll come back for Ron and Carter's story in the next installment in Hemlock Harbor. Want to know when the pre-order goes live? Or keep up with news about what's coming next from me?

Sign up here for my newsletter:
http://bit.ly/NewsLetterAMJBooks

or

Join my reader group of Facebook:
https://www.facebook.com/groups/AMJOHNSONBOOKS

Thank you again for taking the time to read this book, and for your support!

Much love, Amanda-

PLAYLIST

Spotify
http://bit.ly/3WQOVBS

ACKNOWLEDGMENTS

Thank you to everyone who supported me through the process of creating and writing this book and creating this series. To my betas, and editing team, and friends who all held my hand and cheered me on and helped me be a better writer. To Paul from your Veronica. I am in your debt. To my family, I'm sorry for these last two weeks of shitty takeout. Londonderry needs better food for people on deadlines. Ha!! To the word wrapped, don't even try me, I will kindly delete the hell out of you every time, see you next book. To my amazing readers and reader group, you are my heart. Thank you, Chip, for being my Luka. And last but not least, to my ladies behind the scenes who keep my ship afloat, Ari, Charity, Mere, and Layla... of course, my flighty ass needs four of you. Bill me the therapy hours, m'kay.

As always, if you are in my life, you are loved...

Side hugs, Amanda~

OTHER BOOKS BY A.M. JOHNSON

Forever Still Series:
Still Life
Still Water
Still Surviving

Avenues Ink Series:
Possession
Kingdom
Poet

Twin Hearts Series:
Let There Be Light
Seven Shades of You

For Him Series:
Love Always, Wild
Not So Sincerely, Yours
Dear Mr. Brody
To Whom It May Concern
Forever, con Amor

The Rulebook Collection
Breakaway

Stand Alone Novels:
The Glow Up
Sacred Hart

Erotica:
Beneath the Vine